BREAK
MY RULES

JILLIAN D. WRAY

Break My Rules

JILLIAN D WRAY

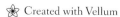 Created with Vellum

Dedication

For Chris and (My Friend) Cindy,
Thank you for answering my millions of questions about
pilots and planes
and for watching our demon cat while we gallivant across
the globe.

Chapter 1

Natalie

I've never really paid attention to how much of my present is shaped by my past. In fact, I've always prided myself on living in the moment...although I'm coming to realize maybe I'm not as good at that as I think. Recently, my past seems to be dictating the majority of my choices, but bad breakups that leave you with an awful aftertaste, will do that to you.

After my parents' divorce, I refused to be one of those women who let their life be dominated by their man. Best laid plans and all of that though because now that Luca is out of my life, the effect of him being *in* my life is still in full swing. It actually feels like he has more control now than he did when we were together.

Case in point, I've apologized about a hundred times to strangers on this train pretty much just for existing. Like, *sorry I need to take up this small amount of space, but I'd like to go home too.* Why should I apologize for riding the public train? I shouldn't, but Luca damaged my confidence more than I care to admit and some days are worse than others.

My phone rings as I set my stuff down in the empty seat beside me. Hastily , I try to swipe the screen and answer the call before I apologize, again to these strangers, for having my ringer on so loud and disturbing the peace.

"Hi, Mom," I whisper.

"What? Honey, speak up, I can barely hear you," she says into the receiver.

"I'm on the train, Mom." I say it hoping she'll say that we can talk later but of course, she doesn't. I love my mother but life is always on her timeline.

Even after they divorced, my mom never said a bad word about my father. Of course, she never said many good ones either, but I always appreciated that she never said anything terribly negative. They split when I was eleven and it wasn't that big of a sob story. He resented her for spending all of his money and she resented him for leaving her home alone all the time with three kids.

Granted, I'm not sure what she expected when she married a pilot or what his financial expectations were after having so many kids, but there you have it.

I pinch my phone between my shoulder and my ear and move my bag out of the seat next to me so someone can sit down at the next stop while my mom prattles on.

"Yes, Mom. Ty is coming here for his birthday." Pause. "No, he's not up to something. Christ, I just haven't seen my brother for a few months and we want to catch up."

Tyler and I are the closest of our siblings. People often assume I'd be closer to our sister, but Ty has always been my safe place. He got angry when he had to go to middle school and I had to stay behind in elementary school for another two years. Suffice it to say, he definitely has the protective older brother thing down. We also look exactly alike and our personalities complement each other well.

People often mistake us for twins although his hair is more yellow-blonde to my strawberry-blonde. We have the same blue, round eyes and light lashes. I stopped growing at 5'6" while Ty made it to six feet even, which he's always been thankful for.

I can sense our mother pouting on the other end of the line and it's confirmed in the tone of her voice when she speaks again. "I'm glad you guys are close, but it pains me that I won't see him for his birthday this year." I roll my eyes thankful that she can't see me.

"Mom, give the guy a break. He's turning thirty-two. Just send a card like every other parent that has grown children. Besides, he hasn't been anywhere since he and Melissa broke up. *Plus*, there was all that drama at work." There's *always* drama at work in the airline industry, and like our father, Tyler is a pilot.

I hear her guffaw on the other end of the line. "You kids and your need to be in the air. I swear you all should have been born with wings instead of feet." We say goodbye and I lean my head back against the glass.

My siblings and I got to fly a lot as kids and we all developed a deep love of traveling. There really wasn't any back-and-forth between homes because Dad was gone all the time, so we settled in with Mom for the day-to-day and did our traveling with Dad. Hell, I became a flight attendant because of it. We also all learned to speak 2-3 languages after we all fell in love with Europe, and have been fortunate enough to have seen some incredible places.

Shockingly, despite her resentment toward our dad, our mom never warned my sister or I to avoid getting involved with pilots, even though we're both flight attendants. She also never said a word when Ty became a pilot himself. I guess she's familiar with the draw to that lifestyle. However, after my own work drama eleven months ago, I'm thinking perhaps I could have used a warning.

Pilots are playboys.

Pilots need a challenge and get bored easily.

Never give your heart to a pilot because his heart already belongs to adventure.

Really, anything would have been helpful. Although, to be fair, even if the warning *had* come, I probably would have said something dumb and naïve like, *Luca is different.*

But at least the warning would have been there.

Instead, I fell hard and fast – like usual – for a pilot who fit all the stereotypes.

As it turns out, Luca was only after the challenge of winning my closely guarded heart, and once he had it, it was no longer fun.

He dumped me one morning, *by text message,* on my way to my first flight of the day. We'd been together eighteen *months* and the bastard dumps me by text.

WTF, man?

Luca wasn't even the first pilot to break my heart, and with it in pieces yet again, I've vowed to never date another pilot. In fact, I would have made a blood pact with myself if I'd had anything that would've pricked my finger.

Never again.

Sitting on the Blue Line from O'Hare back to my small, but cozy, two-bedroom apartment, I ask myself why I even bothered dating a pilot twice. But it doesn't take long for me to find my answer. As a flight attendant, pilots are who I'm around all day and if you don't fly much, or haven't seen these guys in action...*Good Lord.* I am one hundred percent a sucker for a pilot in uniform. Also, I've always loved planes and the fact that these guys have the knowledge to *control* them...God, I get warm just thinking about it.

It takes a certain type of man to be a pilot and it has always been a turn-on for me. They're usually mildly controlling - great, I hate making decisions. They're usually calm under pressure - awesome, because I'm a total basket-case if my plan starts to fall apart. They tend to like traveling - an absolute must. And they tend to be really good with their hands - also a bonus for reasons I'll leave to the imagination.

As my skin grows flushed from these thoughts, I silently reaffirm my vow. *I will never date another pilot.* The last two pilots I'll ever love are my brother and my dad.

When the train reaches my stop, I'm thankful to exit. The odor of the blue line is both hauntingly disgusting and oddly comforting. I drag my roll-on suitcase across the sidewalk and stop in front of my red brick building, looking up. It's well-kept. The neighborhood is clean and the noise comes mostly from its proximity to the rail, which is better than sirens or gun shots.

Home.

I love my job. I love the pace. I *usually* love the people. I *definitely* love my co-workers, but it's always nice to come home.

Chapter 2

Jameson

God, I hate being at home.

The boxes strewn across my condo are a not-so-subtle reminder that I had to move and start all over. The space looks appropriately like the bachelor pad it is: white walls, sparse - albeit, nice - furniture. At least have decent food, wine, and liquor stocked already. I'm not a complete monster.

I survey the view from the floor to ceiling windows, deciding it could be worse even if I am still raw from the reason I find myself here. With my laptop open and the UFC fight on the flatscreen above my fireplace, I check in with my sister and answer a couple other emails.

Chicago is new to me. Having moved in seventy-two hours ago, I've spent the majority of my time at the airport filling out HR paperwork and getting additional credentials for security and employee passes. It's a change to the Charlotte-Douglas Airport and I miss my routine in North Carolina. I can't say I'm jazzed about the Chicago winters but there was an opening for the base crew here and this airline gave me a job when my last one cut me loose. Beggars can't be choosers as they say.

I open a box and groan. *How can I possibly have more clothes to hang up?* I'm in a uniform or sweatpants ninety-nine percent of the time. In no mood to hang up more t-shirts, I move on to the next box. A framed photograph of my sister and I stares back at me and I smile, pulling it out and placing it on the mantle.

My sister has always been my cheerleader and she was almost more pissed than I was when four weeks ago, I got slapped with a harassment suit after a flight attendant felt *me* up despite the fact that I told her no. Got a decent handful of the boys before I could back out of her aggressive grasp, too.

Vanessa had been on several of my flights. She's a decent flight attendant but she started to get *overly* attentive.

I'm not an idiot. And I own a mirror. I know what I look like and I won't apologize. I have good genes and I enjoy fitness. That doesn't mean that I want women touching me all the time. In fact, I'm a huge proponent of personal space. As soon as Vanessa found out I was single again, she was on a mission. She finally went too far and her hand was on my zipper before I could stop her. The look she gave me was fire and ice all in one.

Her hurt feelings prompted her to run to HR with a complaint about something that never happened. Well, it happened, just the other way around. But who's going to believe me at 6'3" with a chest large enough to support an eight-lane highway, over a lean female with a small waist and a decently-sized chest of her own?

With just her complaint, I might have still been okay,

but the timing was terrible. I had just gotten my wrist slapped for supposedly using my size to intimidate another pilot. Total bullshit. I'm just big. The guy was pissed because I failed him after his check-out flight into Aspen, costing him a pay raise. Hell, it wasn't my fault he didn't take the crosswind between the mountain peaks into account and almost flew us into an unforgiving, granite wall.

Vanessa's drama on top of the first accusation is ultimately what sunk me. I was told she had a couple of strong character witness statements in her complaint but was never told who. I hadn't realized I'd pissed so many people off, especially considering in this line of work, I rarely see the same people often enough *to* piss them off.

The craziest thing is that after losing my favorite job in college as a bartender at an oyster bar for sleeping with a co-worker, I decided I wouldn't journey down that road ever again and I've actually *stuck* to that rule. Had I known I was going to end up getting fired over a girl I never even touched, I probably would've said "fuck it" way back when and slept with a lot of hot, willing girls over the years.

To be clear, I wasn't fired in college specifically because that girl and I slept together; we were *both* fired because we got caught fucking on the actual bar itself and OSHA tends to frown upon bodily fluids being placed where people eat and drink. Nevertheless, I felt terrible for costing her her job as well - despite the fact that she was a consenting adult - and I just decided I would keep work and pleasure separate.

Since becoming a licensed pilot and flying commercially, keeping my worlds apart has been easier than one might think. I love my job and no woman is worth jeopardizing it.

Thankfully, post-pandemic, most airlines are hiring, so

finding a new position wasn't hard, but I'm still pissed that my character was questioned and now feel like the only way to keep myself safe is to be completely cold at work, leaving no room, whatsoever, for misunderstandings.

The fire I have about my career has gone out some since the incident with Vanessa, but my resolve is in place to keep my distance and interact platonically.

I start the new job in two days, and I'm hoping the first crew is decent...and all male.

Chapter 3

Natalie

"*Ohmygod Nat,*" Stephen - a man so gay he told me his mom actually started calling him Stephanie at the age of four - gushes as he comes around the corner and into the crew lounge. Anytime Stephen starts our conversation out like that, I know something dramatic is going to come out of his gorgeous mouth. Stephen is about 5'11" and he is undeniably beautiful. I'm sure most men would not like to be described as beautiful, but there is no better description for Stephen. Clear skin, perfect thick hair, a nose to die for, and chocolate eyes you could melt in. With a lean build that is well taken care of, he catches a lot of attention from males and females alike. But it's his sense of humor that makes him my best friend and I know any flights we work together - which is most of them. - is going to be a good one.

"That sounds ominous, Stevie," I say, giving him a smile. Sherri - the third in our glorious flight-attendant trifecta - and I are the only ones he allows to get away with calling him by his nickname.

"Nat, wait until you see Captain Hunter," he says, drawing his clasped hands to his uniform-clad chest. "I'm pretty sure I heard Sherri's eggs come out of hibernation for this one."

My eyes go wide as I stifle my laugh because Sherri just walked into the lounge where we're grabbing coffee before heading to the plane.

"I heard that, you man-whore," she teases affectionately. "But also, you're not wrong," Sherri confirms, as she reaches for a lid, wagging her eyebrows at me. She's been happily married for twenty-eight years and jokingly claims the secret to their success is the fact that she's gone so much.

I've been working with Sherri for a few years now and I have *never* heard her comment on the looks of a pilot. I always thought she was immune. Even Luca didn't inspire any acknowledgement from her - and Luca's looks could inspire the blind - so her agreement with Stephen on this, has me more than a little intrigued.

I raise an eyebrow at her. "How have you guys met him already?" I wish I wasn't as curious as I am.

"We haven't," Sherri's voice cuts into my thoughts, "not officially, but he was on our bus coming in from the lot. Stevie read his name badge and then elbowed me so hard I think he bruised my ribs. I didn't have much time to think about the pain though because when I realized who the man was, I was more focused on catching my breath than the ache in my side." She pokes playfully at Stephen as she says this.

"Wow, so he's hot, huh?" I ask as I fix a wrinkle in my thigh highs trying to give off an air of nonchalance.

"*Hot* is the understatement of the century, Nat. This man is nuclear...core of the earth...*heat of a thousands suns.*"

Stephen flutters his eyelashes to demonstrate how wooed he is right now and a laugh escapes my throat.

Greeeeeaaaaat.

"Well, he's all yours, Stevie." I place a playful pat on my best friend's chest. "I've been off pilots ever since Luca and I'm not going back. All the hot ones are douches and players."

There are also a lot of attractive pilots but there are far more that succumb to the unhealthy lifestyle of being on the go so much. It's hard to maintain a top-notch physique with a lot of dining out, and after a twelve-hour shift at a mentally demanding job, most of the guys don't have the energy to hit the gym once we reach our destination. I get it. Most of the time I fall into bed myself, exhausted from the day, but on the occasion that we layover in a hotel with a pool, I can't stay away. The water helps me relax. Nonetheless, a hot, kind, single pilot is harder to find than Big Foot.

Stephen brushes a strand of hair out of my face in a brotherly fashion. "Luca was a bad apple, Nat. You work so much that if you don't meet someone on the job, you may end up alone forever, Sweetie." Stevie's aware of my hard *no* on pilots and my avoidance of anyone else in this industry for the time being but he and Sherri both have been pestering me to get back in the dating scene for the last six months.

I roll my eyes and bat his hand away. "I'm not alone. I have you two to keep me company."

I hear Sherri burst out in laughter. "Nat, we don't count toward your love life. You know I'd take a bullet for you, but there are just some things you're gonna need a man for, honey."

"Amen, sister." Stephen throws his hand in the air like he's agreeing with a pastor giving a sermon on Sunday morning.

My friends are concerned for me. I know they are. But I still don't like talking about it. Luca wasn't just a hook up; we dated seriously for eighteen months. I thought he was my future. Out of the blue, he told me that our crazy and demanding schedules were too much and he couldn't make it work anymore. I was devastated and haven't found the desire or the energy to put myself back out there.

"Not with a pilot. He could be Thor's identical twin and I would still have to pass." Sherri and Stephen share a look that I don't like one bit. "Come on you two, let's go properly introduce ourselves." I grab my coffee and steel myself for whatever I'm walking into.

Reaching our gate, the gate attendant gives us wide eyes and mouths "holy shit" as we badge in the door to the jet bridge connecting the terminal to the plane. Stephen mouths "I know" back and pretends to fan himself.

I hear the pilots talking before I actually see them. Our co-pilot today is Ricardo Alvarez. A favorite of mine. I hear his laugh and it causes a smile to spread across my face. I know it's his, because even his laugh has an accent. He speaks both English and Spanish perfectly, but his laugh definitely sounds Spanish.

The sound of my heels is muffled by the carpet on the jet bridge so the guys keep talking, unaware of our approach. When I turn the corner, Captain Jameson Hunter comes into view and I stop dead in my tracks so fast Sherri actually bumps into me.

"Oops, sorry, Nat," I barely hear her say behind me. My brain has gone all staticky.

Chapter 4

Jameson

Of course, my first flight out and I'm paired with the chattiest first officer I've ever met. I'm trying to keep my head down at work but he's jovial and I find myself laughing at his joke despite my desire to stay fairly closed off and professional. I can tell he's Hispanic but don't yet know where he's from. The lover of cultures in me is dying to find out, but it goes against the wall I'm trying to build until my reputation is solidified in this new place.

His current grin gets wider as he looks over my shoulder, and his eyes visibly relax. Our crew must have arrived. I brace myself to meet more new people whose names I'll probably forget and whose faces I'll likely not see very often. As pilots, we don't choose our crews, although I can see who is working my flights when I open my schedule. The only way I will see them more than a couple times a month is if there are flight attendants who need the same kind of schedule or routes that I do. A computer system does all the scheduling but there are some crews with seniority that have the ability to schedule the same routes for months at a time. The crew I'm about to meet is one of them. A home base crew for a "regular route".

I turn my head to meet the onboarding crew members and it takes me about sixteen *milli*seconds to realize what's in front of me: the embodiment of every flight attendant fantasy ever had by a human. Hair naturally the color of a copper sunset, dark blue eyes like a bottomless lake which are rimmed in black, and light-colored lips so full they could draw the most impure thoughts out of a monk. I must be staring because somewhere someone clears their throat and I quickly sweep my gaze on to the other two crew members.

Ricardo does introductions: Sherri, Stephen, and the bombshell's name is Natalie. As I shake her hand, I almost feel it tremble in mine ever so slightly, despite her firm grip. I'll spend the next sixteen hours wondering if I made that up. Never mind I should be using that time to figure out how to keep my distance. Natalie gives me a tight, barely-there smile, and a curt nod before dropping her gaze and breaking eye contact far sooner than I would have liked. She immediately busies herself with the tasks of settling into the cabin, turning her back to me.

The other two attendants shake my hand and don't bother hiding their appreciation of my appearance on their features. The truth is, I'm fairly used to this reaction. What I'm *not* used to is someone's gaze landing on me and growing instantly colder. Despite my looks and desire to keep work relationships strictly platonic, I really try not to come across as an arrogant asshole, and I don't know why she's already decided she doesn't like me. If I were being honest with myself, I'd admit that I'm more curious about her reaction than I should be.

Thank God I'm not interested in being honest with myself.

Before I can think on it too much, Ricardo ushers me back up to the cockpit so the rest of the crew can prepare for the passengers. Although friendly, he's returned to talking my damn ear off as if this is the first plane I've ever flown. "Um, Ricardo," I say, interrupting him mid-sentence, "would you mind if I step into the galley? I like to greet the passengers as they board."

"Sure, amigo. Whatever you want." He busies himself with the pre-flight check off as I scramble out of the cockpit.

The older flight attendant is milling about in the first-class cabin. No passengers have boarded yet and I don't see Natalie anywhere.

"Captain Hunter, welcome aboard Flight 256 with nonstop service to Dallas/Ft. Worth." She smiles at me and I hate myself for having forgotten her name already.

I give her a sheepish smile. "Call me Jameson. Also, isn't that supposed to be my line?" I ask jokingly, already having to remind myself to toe the line of nice and overly friendly.

"Well, I imagine it would be if you'd ever flown this flight before but since you haven't and I have, I thought *I* should welcome *you*."

This time I give her a genuine smile. "Touché."

I hear a fit of laughter come from the back of the plane that catches my attention and causes me to look up. When she comes into view, Natalie has one hand full of mini-Coke cans and one hand covering her mouth in laughter. Her joy is written on her face and can be heard in the sincerity of her laugh.

God, she's beautiful. I feel heat start to creep up my neck and out into other unruly appendages, and I have to fight the urge to slip out of my jacket or pop my top button to get some air to my scorched skin. She turns to set the cans down and stops when she sees me. It's too late to hide the fact that I'm openly-staring at her, so I quickly close my mouth and wave awkwardly.

She gives me a nod of acknowledgement as her smile fades and her eyes shutter before immediately going back to stocking the beverage-service cart. A moment later, the male flight attendant peeks his head around the corner and gives me a finger wave. I throw a hand up in response and head back into the cockpit.

Why am I out here acting like a fool?

Chapter 5

Natalie

"Fuck, is he gone?" I whisper to Stephen, flustered at the almost-interaction that just took place. Captain Hunter's looks are unnerving because only someone who bargained with the devil, himself, could look as good as he does.

"Yes, girl, *chill*. That rude look you just flashed him was enough to make the poor guy wet his pants." He chuckles as he passes me more soft drink cans.

"What? I wasn't rude! I smiled!" I whisper-shout indignantly, dropping a can of ginger ale because I'm distracted as hell. "Ow, shit!"

"Umm, *that* was a grimace of perfection from the ice-queen herself and serves you right, dropping that can, for being so ugly toward such a beautiful man," Stevie chastises me.

"Well, it doesn't really matter, does it? Captain Ranier will be back at the beginning of next week and Captain Hunter is only supposed to be with us for a couple of down-and-backs."

"Spoken like someone who feels that man's fire down

deep in her loins and is trying like hell to pretend like she doesn't." Stephen laughs at himself before continuing, "Well, if you're not going to be his welcoming committee, I will happily lay myself at his feet. You finish up here. I'm going to go see if the good captain needs anything before departure." He winks and walks to the front of the plane.

Okay, I'll admit it, Jameson Hunter is hands-down *the* hottest pilot I have ever seen in my life. Hell, he's the hottest *man* I've ever seen in my life. Stephen was right. *Nuclear. Core of the earth. Heat of a thousand suns.*

Masculinity radiates from his pores and he gives off a dangerous vibe just from his size...and his eyes. It'd be easy to get lost in those eyes. In his pressed uniform, he reminds me of a caged lion. Powerfully built but and restricted by the confines of the fabric that binds him.

Incredibly tall with dark hair, light brown eyes, and a build that makes me think he doesn't skip the gym even after a twelve-hour shift, the Captain's stripes on his shoulders encourage my look-but-don't-touch mentality to take a vacation so hard I'm actually concerned.

Once I've finished loading the cart and give the *all good* sign from the back, indicating that I'm ready, they'll let the passengers start the boarding process. Thankfully, Stevie has first-class on this flight so if Jameson comes out to use the restroom, I won't be the one boxed in with him.

Shortly after I give the signal, the phone in the back of the plane rings.

"Hello?" I'm fully expecting Sherri's voice on the other end of the line but it isn't. A deep, confident rumble comes from through the earpiece.

"Natalie, do you have everything you need for the flight?" His voice comes through the line sharp and with a definite edge. Almost like he's not sure why he called me.

That makes two of us.

Never in my seven years of flying has a pilot called to ask if I have everything I need for a flight. That's not his job. That job belongs to the ground crew, who already checked in with me and "Yes, I do. Thank you." There's a pause and when I realize he isn't going to say anything else, I add, "Have a good flight, Captain."

I hear him huff out what sounds like a frustrated sigh on the other end of the line. "You too," he says in a clipped tone.

Click.

I stare at the phone in my hand for a full minute before placing it in the cradle.

No one said you had to call me, douche.

When I look up, I see the first passengers starting to board the plane. I give my head a quick shake and step into the aisle to assist as needed. When I look ahead at the oncoming passengers, I see Jameson's head over those sliding into their seats. His eyes meet mine for a brief second before he turns to greet another passenger, the narrowing of his eyes so obvious, I can see it from here.

What is this guy's problem?

Thirty minutes into our flight, we have smooth skies and are starting our beverage service. Sherri helps me get the cart back up to the front of the main cabin so we can work our way backwards.

This is a lot of flight attendants' least favorite part of a flight but I don't mind it so much. I usually really enjoy engaging with the passengers, finding out if they're headed home or headed out on business or vacation. Today, however, I'm grossly distracted and my eyes keep wandering toward the front of the plane - which I can't see anyway thanks to the solid curtain separating the main cabin from the business class up front.

Sherri laughs and shakes her head when two guys give me their numbers. "You're not going to call either of them, are you?" she asks once we've served everyone.

"Of course not! They could be murderers. Or worse, have a wife and kids." I feign being horrified but it's true. Lies are easily concealed at thirty-five thousand feet when no one can use their cell phones to fact-check, perform a quick Google search, or a thorough Facebook stalk.

Stephen and Sherri both encourage me to actually call someone *after* performing the necessary background search, but they also take bets on how many numbers Stephen and I will get on any given flight. Stephen usually ends up winning because he's a shameless flirt.

I think about calling someone every once in a while, but my schedule is crazy, and I haven't had the buzz of attraction for anyone that would make me want to invest the time, energy, effort, or emotions.

Captain Hunter is making more than a few things buzz and I haven't even had a real conversation with him.

Shut that thought down, Nat, and get back to work, I admonish myself.

Things with Luca were so fast and so intense that when he abruptly ended things, he left me damaged and I haven't even started thinking about dating again. What makes it worse is that he still works for my airline so we occasionally run into each other every now and then. And it sucks.

I couldn't go through that again and I'm not willing to part with my job.

"Sherri, I want to move on," I try to convince myself as much as her while we go through a few cleaning procedures in the back of the plane. "I really do. But not with," I glance down at the scribbled-on napkins and laugh, "Brad Shoemaker or Paul Debose. Besides, the numbers they gave me are Dallas numbers. They're going home and I'm not interested in the long-distance thing."

She sighs and shakes her head knowing I'm hopeless.

"I'm going to call up front and see if Stevie got any numbers yet," Sherri sings gleefully, knowing it's highly likely he'll follow through and give her some juicy stories in the aftermath.

Chapter 6

Jameson

Ten days later, I'm running the same route, down and back to Dallas, as I did on my first day with Natalie and her crew. I've worked with them a couple of times now, managing to keep my distance and my interactions strictly professional. I'd done well over the last several days, casting Natalie's image from my mind as soon as it tried to infiltrate, but today she's back to being front and center in her pencil skirt, white shirt, and jacket. Her long red hair is in a high ponytail, begging to be pulled.

This is the longest flight of my life, which is crazy considering I flew transatlantic for my previous airline and this flight is only two and a half hours. I haven't been able to reign my thoughts in nearly as much as I could before today, and I can't stop thinking about he vixen the entire flight, which is a *major* problem.

Thankful when we start our final descent, I get antsy and am ready to be on the ground. We're turning right back around so we won't even get off the plane, but we'll have half an hour before the next passengers board. I could use a few minutes to clear my mind.

Landing is my favorite part. It's certainly the most technically challenging. A monkey could fly a plane since it's mostly automated. Take-off is pretty simple unless conditions are horrid, but still, as long as you know where the throttle is, you can probably get the bird off the ground. Landing though? That's where the training comes in. Speed of the plane, speed of the wind, direction of the wind, etc... so many things happening at once. Once we drop to ten thousand feet, it's pretty much all on the pilot to set you down gently. I pride myself on my smooth landings. I know it sounds cheesy but it's the only time in the whole flight where I feel connected to the aircraft. In sync. The "flow state", where everything else has to fade away so I can concentrate entirely on the task at hand. A lot of times I wished it lasted longer than fifteen to twenty minutes but today, I'm ready to get this machine to the gate. Like most of my others, this landing is perfect...until something gets messed up after impact and two dashboard lights are triggered.

Fucking great.

This means we'll be grounded for at least an hour while someone tracks down a mechanic who will do nothing but hit the damn reset button for a wire that got jarred loose somewhere.

Once we're at the gate and I've filled out the log and put in the request for maintenance, I have to break it to the crew that they'll have at least an hour of down time, although based on the clouds in the sky and what my radar shows, it'll likely be more than that if we don't get off the ground ASAP.

When I open the door, all three of the crew are talking in hushed tones and giggling like school kids in a small huddle in the galley.

"Am I interrupting?" I ask, stepping into their space, aware of how cold my voice sounds. My reaction to Natalie has me unsettled and the ice in my voice is a reflection of that.

The blush in her cheeks is impossible to miss. She won't look me in the eye and I wish she would speak to me but it's Stephen who explains.

"We, uh, sort of have a running bet on who gets the most phone numbers in the course of a flight. Natalie got three to my two this go round so I have to buy her a beer when we get home."

My skin prickles at the thought of passengers on my plane flirting with her or her with them. This is my chance to address her specifically, so I turn to face Natalie. "Looking for a date?" I'm pleased that my voice stays calm, playful even, but there's still an unwanted edge to it. I shove my hands in the pockets of my trousers and lean against the wall, aiming for casual but not convinced that I'm hitting the mark. My eyebrows are knitted together and I can feel the tension in my facial features.

How she's not married, already on lockdown by some lucky asshole, is a complete mystery to me.

I half expect her to cut her eyes at me and cock an attitude but she doesn't. Which is almost worse actually, because instead, she flushes a deeper crimson and stutters, "What? Oh, God no. Um. I mean, well, just, no."

Fuck, it's cute.

Meanwhile her friends are over here silently shaking with laughter. "Am I missing something?" Clearly, I am and I can't help myself. I want to know more.

She flashes a death glare at her friends. A silent warning to stop drawing attention to her. "No. You're not."

I let it go and break the news that we'll be on the ground until further notice.

Natalie speaks first but her tone remains guarded and professional, "Thanks for a great flight. We'll be in the lounge until the plane is ready." She turns her attention back to the post-flight form she's checking over. A few minutes later, everyone gathers their things and heads out of the plane. I'm startled when a conversation breaks out in Spanish.

"Ricardo, como es tu esposa?"

"Oh, muy bien, gracias! Muy embarazada!"

"Otra vez? Dale un respiro a esa pobre mujer!"

I found an early love of languages as we moved around to international military bases while I was growing up. During that time, I discovered I liked talking to the local kids in their local language. It also didn't hurt that my father was a linguistics specialist for the Navy, so languages were sort of forced on my sister and I. I can converse fluently in Italian and French which made Spanish pretty easy to pick up, so I know that Natalie is asking Ricardo about his wife, who apparently is "very pregnant". Natalie laughs as she tells him to give the poor woman a break.

I can't help but smile. Beauty *and* brains.

I've got to stop this train of thought.

Natalie and Ricardo continue their conversation the whole way to the lounge. I casually chat with Stephen and Sherri, keeping an ear out for any information they may share about Natalie. I want to talk to her and completely avoid her all at the same time but she makes the choice for me as *she* seems to be avoiding *me*. And choosing to speak in Spanish even though Ricardo knows perfect English as if she doesn't want me to know what she is talking about. Thankfully, I can make out every word.

I huff out a sigh, frustrated that I'm overthinking this.

After grabbing coffees, we find a table for the five of us and everyone pulls out their phones. It isn't long before another language makes an appearance amongst our group.

Chapter 7

Natalie

"Tu devrais arrêter d'agir comme une telle grace."

I shoot a death glare at Stephen who just told me -and I quote - that I should stop acting like such a bitch. Before I can reply, Jameson looks up from his phone with raised eyebrows and a shocked look on his face. People are often impressed with French because we don't hear it much in this country.

"Je ne suis pas une grace." *I am not being a bitch.* I let my guard down a little as I finish my sentence while unwrapping the ascot from my neck. Stephen and Sherri are honestly two of my best friends and it isn't like they can't guess what's going on. "Je ne sais pas comment inter- agir avec lui. Il ressemble à un orgasme ambulant et il me rend nerveux." *I don't know how to interact with him. He looks like a walking orgasm and he makes me nervous.*

"Ce n'est pas Luca, Nat," Stephen says as he places his hand over mine as I rest it back on the table. He's tried, unsuccessfully, to help me get over my hang up of Luca. And pilots. And men in general. He tells me everyone has bad experiences which I know is true, but my worst moments - and my best ones too, I guess - seem to involve these men in uniform...the hottest of them all, sitting across from me right this very minute. A girl's got a right to be a little on edge.

Sherri laughs and addresses Jameson, "I hate it when they do this shit. I only speak English. Well, that and sign language." She flips me the bird and I laugh and relax a little.

"Wow, I didn't realize this group was trilingual." His eyes shine like he is pleased with this discovery as my cheeks flush. I feel his astonished, *almost*-praise down in my toes and I know that for the rest of our time together, I want him to be pleased with me.

Stephen corrects him immediately while getting comfortable in his chair and placing his phone on the table to give Jameson his full attention. "Oh, not *us*. Just Nat." He says my name like I'm a brand new Ferrari he's trying to sell. "I was actually born in France to an American father and a Parisian mother, so I grew up speaking French and English simultaneously. Ricardo is Columbian so Spanish is his first language. Only Natalie is fluent in both."

My cheeks are already burning from being the subject of Stevie's advertisement as I watch while the slowest, sexiest, most devilish grin spreads across Jameson's features, darkening his eyes. To my complete horror, he responds in perfect French directly to me, his voice dropping an octave as he does so. "Tres bien, je suppose que nous sommes deux maintenant." *Well, I guess there are two of us now.*

What the fuck just happened?

He speaks French?

Why does he speak French?

Ohmygod. That means he understood when I said he looks like a walking orgasm. I feel my eyes widen in alarm.

"Oh shit," I whisper as I drop my face in my hands.

Stephen is openly laughing because he can understand everything that just transpired. *Asshole.*

Sherri, seeing the look on my face, says, "Okay, someone tell this unilingual chick what I'm missing."

Too embarrassed to speak for myself, Jameson laughs softly and says, "Natalie called me hot, assuming I couldn't understand her." It's the warmest I've heard his voice all day which sends my lady parts into massive overdrive.

"I did not!" I argue. I don't know why I say it. We both know I did. I carry on as if I'm not making a complete fool of myself. I hitch my chin high and muster as much confidence as I can. "I *said* you look like..." I pause briefly before plowing ahead, "a walking orgasm. There's a difference."

Did I really just say the word orgasm out loud in front of Jameson Hunter?

The whole table is openly laughing now. Including Jameson.

I slide off my stool. "Please excuse me while I go find a different flight assignment." I'm really just going to go to the bathroom for a little space but Jameson reaches out and catches my wrist. The contact instantly causes a buzzing in my ears and I feel the blush over my entire body. My eyes lock onto his and I am rendered immobile, except for my chest which is heaving obscenely.

"Please. Sit. Don't be embarrassed. It was a nice compliment." As soon as he finishes uttering words in a tone so low and deep they sound like velvet dipped in butter, all of our phones buzz at the same time.

We've just been notified that storms are heading toward us fast out of the northwest. It's tornado season here in Dallas, and they just grounded all flights for the next five hours which will throw us all into mandatory duty rest.

Looks like we won't be going home tonight.

Checking into the hotel is no big deal. There's a division of the company that focuses solely on reserving blocks of rooms for crew members as we travel - and get stranded. Normally, these days, pilots and flight attendants are given reservations at different hotels, with the pilots getting much swankier accommodations, but since this is last-minute and the return crew is the same as the outbound crew, they just booked us at the same hotel. Sherri and I bunk together, even though they issue separate rooms, because it can get lonely but also so we can gossip about what sordid sex-thing we think Stephen is up to down the hall.

"What a day, huh?" Sherri asks as she hangs up her uniform in the small closet and throws on a pair of pajama shorts. The hotel will launder our uniforms for us since we'll have to wear them again tomorrow.

I unbutton my jacket and hang it up as well. "I cannot *believe* he speaks French. God, I'm mortified. What are the freaking odds?"

"He didn't seem to mind your comment so much. I saw him eyeing you the whole time we were in the lounge."

"Sher, if I was still into hot hookups, I'd be on him in a heartbeat. Lord knows everyone else will be, but --"

She cuts me off. "Do not bring Luca up one more time, Natalie. He's moved on. You need to do the same. Stop punishing every man that might be interested in you because of the choices Luca made. It's time to let it go, honey."

I take a minute to think about her words. "I know you're right but it isn't just about Luca."

It's about my job. It's about feeling like I have to choose one or the other because working with your significant other doesn't seem like such a good idea anymore. It's about knowing I can keep my promises to myself...although that part doesn't seem quite as important as it once did either.

I feel a tug at the strings of my resolve trying to come undone.

"Well, I'd bet my last dollar that Captain Hunter is in to you. Consider giving him a chance if the opportunity presents itself, huh?" She holds her hands up, sensing my oncoming rebuttal. "I'm done. I'm done. Just think about it."

I grab my bathing suit - I always keep one in my flight bag. "I'm going to find the pool." And do everything in my power *not* to think about it...or him.

Chapter 8

Jameson

It's been a helluva day, so I do what I've always done to unwind... head to the hotel bar. Knowing enough to strip out of my uniform first, I slip into an old light-blue, v-neck t-shirt. Glad to finally peel off my stiff white button-down that I force my frame into every morning, I happily exchange it for the soft, worn t-shirt and grab my keycard.

"I'll be back after a bit. I'm going to go check out the bar." Ricardo just waves and turns to start a FaceTime call with his wife on the couch in the sitting area. The hotel put he and I in a suite so we each have our own rooms but there is a shared kitchenette and small living room in the middle. I guess this was all they had left with the storms taking out so many flights. We aren't the only ones that needed a place to turn in for the night.

Lucky us.

Seated at the bar, I order a bourbon on the rocks and stare up at the tv screens. Getting stranded due to weather isn't all that uncommon, but it doesn't happen regularly either. I learned a while ago that you might as well not let it make you flustered because you certainly can't change it and it comes with the job. I stare at the screen harder hoping it will occupy the space in my brain currently being taken up by Trilingual Natalie.

It's not working.

The storms are raging outside. The yellow Tornado Watch bar scrolls across the top of the tv and still I can't focus on anything other than the vexing woman I need to forget.

I'm three sips in to my drink when a couple of girls approach. I say "girls" because they can't be more than twenty. *If that.* Seeing as I turned thirty-six last month, I'm really not interested. Call me crazy, but once you're in a completely different stage of life from your sexual partner, your expectations change, and without the same expectations, there's a pretty good chance the night will end up a mess. It used to be fun. Now it's just fucking scary. These girls could drug me, take pictures, *post* pictures. I could wake up tomorrow handcuffed to a tiger, *Hangover* style. It could go viral in four hours and I'd end up out of a job. *Again.*

That may seem a little dramatic...until you've lost a harassment suit simply because your accuser had a nice physique and could cry on command, putting you out of the job at which you spent the last ten years of your life.

Obviously, it's still a sore subject and my trust in the opposite sex isn't what it once was.

The girls approach me, silently casting knowing glances to each other as they make their way over. I groan inwardly as I eye them in my peripheral vision.

"Are you here alone?" the brunette asks as she tries to discreetly check for a ring on my left hand. She's cute. And ballsy. It takes guts - or a whole helluva lot of self-confidence - to approach a stranger that looks like me.

I cut my eyes to her, trying to figure out how I want to play this.

"Technically, no," I say. Deciding that I can't help but have a little fun and besides, it's true. I'm not here alone. I'm here with Ricardo, Stephen, Sherri, and Natalie.

The girls look at each other and their young age comes out in their giggle. "Um, what does that mean?" the other girl asks. The brunette who spoke first is in black leggings and an oversized t-shirt that sits off her shoulder. The other is in high-waisted jeans and a crop top with a neckline that plunges almost the button on her pants. Her cleavage is on full display and she looks completely comfortable with it.

"I'm a pilot and I'm here with my crew, so technically not alone," I explain. I know what this information will do to these girls' hormones but I say it anyway. Maybe flirting with them for a while will help get my mind off the co-worker occupying too much space in my brain.

"Oh, but no, like girlfriend or wife or anything?" It's the brunette again.

"No. No girlfriend or wife or anything," I confirm as I shake my head and take another sip of bourbon, not offering any more information.

They sit on either side of me, each with an elbow propped on the bar. Their body language already clearly communicating what they're hoping to get out of this interaction. "Our flight got cancelled," Blondie pouts. "We were supposed to be in Vegas."

I've never seen *fuck-me* eyes quite this obvious. I won't of course, because again, these girls are way too young for my taste, but it's a fun way to pass the time nonetheless.

Until *her* name keeps popping up unbidden in my

mind. With everything I learn about the young girls in front of me, I can't seem but wonder more about Natalie. *Of course,* the first flames of attraction I would feel licking at me once I moved to Chicago are for a co-worker. The *one* type of person I swore I would never get involved with again.

I let the conversation go on for another forty-five minutes. I buy the girls each a drink and am pleased to discover they are actually twenty-three - old enough to at least drink legally.

Still a hard no for me.

When the brunette, Sara, puts her hand on my thigh suggestively, I know it's time to call the ball. Not a fan of having my personal space invaded, I always ask before I touch a woman, yet they never seem to do the same. Her touch turns me off as I'm reminded sharply about Vanessa's unwanted hand on my crotch and the chaos that ensued.

"Well, ladies, I'm afraid I have an early flight. It's been a pleasure. Goodnight." I nod politely and stand to go.

They stand as well and move to box me in against the bar. I'm sure they would be a good time, if a one-night stand and a threesome were what I was looking for. As it happens, I'm a one-woman-at-a-time kind of guy who prefers that my companions are at least thirty and have some real-world knowledge under their belt. I already have my share of regrets from parties and nights gone wrong. I've forgotten more names than I remember.

Sara reaches up to put her hand on my chest but I catch it before she can touch me. "I said goodnight," I repeat a little more forcefully. I hear her whiny voice saying something but I can't make out the words from the buzzing in my head over seeing Natalie as she enters the bar. Her eyes scan the area and land on mine and I'm suddenly aware of what my situation looks like.

Just another pilot on a lay-over booty call.

My traitorous eyes rove over her body and I notice that her hair is wet and she has a white hotel towel wrapped around her as she drips water on the floor. I can see bathing suit straps over her otherwise bare shoulders. Considering the storm raging outside, this place must have an indoor pool. Her legs are toned and her skin is smooth. I can only see from her knees down and already my dick is at attention, wanting desperately to see higher. Her lips part slightly as she sees me but gives no indication that she knows me as she walks up to the other end of the bar and orders something.

I stand, mesmerized, when I hear one of the girls in front of me say, "So, you really aren't going to invite us back to your room?"

When I look down at her, she's pouting with a duck face, lips pushed fully out. My dick goes completely limp at this look, which is probably for the better considering what I'm about to do. "No. Excuse me."

I know they were hoping to get laid, and I'm not judging them. That was me at one time. But it's not me today. I start to make my way over to Natalie's end of the bar even though I have no idea what I'm going to say when I get there but keeping my distance doesn't seem o be working for me either.

The bartender hands her a glass of red wine and she turns to leave.

"*Espere!*" *Wait!* I yell in Spanish so she knows I'm talking to her. I also use Spanish so she realizes I know that language too and she doesn't say anything she doesn't want me to hear, thinking I can't understand her again. Once was the only time it could happen without it being unforgivable.

She turns to look at me over her shoulder. I swear I see her shake her head once and then head off to the elevators.

Oh, to hell with this. I need to know why she hates me.

Chapter 9

Natalie

S hit.

He's following me. I saw those two young women coming on to him. Hell, he practically had one of them pinned up against himself, so why is he chasing me down the hallway in a race to the elevators?

I hit the button in a panic. *Come on. Come on.*

Alone in an elevator with that man is not how I saw this night going. I take a sip from my glass of wine to quell my nerves, but I'm afraid I'd have to chug this whole thing to feel any effect.

The pool was nice but it only served as a change of scenery in which to think about Captain Hunter. I finally climbed out of the pool when the thoughts turned to him in the heated water with me. Pushing me against the edge of the pool, nothing but the thin material of our swim suits between us...

God, I'm getting warm again. This towel feels like a parka in the middle of the desert.

He's almost here and still no elevator.

I blow out a breath and turn to face him taking in the

cotton n-neck of his t-shirt and the way the color and the lights in this hallway add depth to his eyes. I can make out the outline of his muscular chest through the thin cotton and I have a hard time tearing my eyes away. My skin is heating even more just from his proximity and I'm sure my pupils are dilated, trying to take him in completely. No small feat since the man is huge.

"I didn't expect you to leave your company. I just wanted a glass to-go." I hold up my glass in explanation. "What you do on a layover is your business." I'm horrified for a second time as the last sentence comes out as barely a whisper.

"It was time for me to leave. I'm not really into that anymore."

I don't have time to fully process that statement before the elevator arrives and we're joined by four more people. My room is on the ninth floor, so it will be a long ride up for me from the lobby.

Captain Hunter and I get crowded into the far back corner and I try desperately not to touch his body. I can feel the heat radiating off of him in waves and I'm not sure whose surface level is hotter right now: his or mine. The temperature is starting to melt the ice around parts of me I haven't been interested in since Luca, and it unsettles me.

"Disfrutaste de la piscina?" he whispers, his breath on the back of my neck, causing goosebumps to rise despite the aforementioned heat. *Did you enjoy the pool?*

"Oui. Ça m'aide à me vider la tête." *Yes. It helps to clear my head.*

Let's see how well he can switch between all three languages.

"Quale lingua preferisci, Natalie?"

I bow my head and smile as he switches to Italian and

asks which language I prefer as he demonstrates his proficiency in a fourth. I've never met a guy who can keep up with me linguistically. I love having Stephen as a best friend because he helps me keep my French up to par and I can use my Spanish almost daily at work these days, but there are other languages I don't get to practice very often. Italian is one of them.

"Non Italiano. Non sono fluente." *Not Italian. I'm not fluent.*

I feel him smile behind me and I hear it in his voice. "Tres bien," he says as he switches back to French. His next statement catches me off guard. "J'ai l'impression que tu m'as évité toute la journée."

We stop on the fourth floor where the other passengers get off, leaving Jameson and I alone. I step away from him to create space as I answer him in English. "I have not been avoiding you all day. I've been working."

Not true.

I have been avoiding him.

Like the plague.

Finally, I offer a bit of truth. "I'm just embarrassed about what I said earlier." And right now, I could kick myself for even bringing it up again.

"I told you there was no need to be embarrassed," he says as he takes a step toward me. I'm not even sure he knows he's done it.

I roll my eyes in an effort to seem unaffected. "Yeah, well just because you tell me to do something, or not do something, doesn't mean it will just happen." Pilots and their arrogance.

He chuckles and tries his hand at a joke. "Isn't that actually the definition of our jobs? I tell you to prepare the cabin for take-off...and you do it?" He takes another step.

It's so hot in this elevator right now I could die.

What else would he ask me to do?

Thankfully the elevator pings to alert us to our arrival on my floor. As the doors slide open, I grip my towel and my wine tighter. "Goodnight, Captain Hunter."

"Goodnight, Natalie."

I am so screwed. I saw him with those girls and I hate to admit it but I was jealous. Looks like I haven't done as great a job of getting that under control as I had thought. His face is enough to want to lay claim to him but the body beneath the shirt doesn't hurt his case either. Add in his ability to talk dirty in multiple languages *and* he can fly a plane? One glass of wine isn't going to cut it. I'm lusting after him *hard*.

When I open the door to mine and Sherri's room, Stephen is laying on my bed holding up his phone to show Sherri a picture. One look at my flushed face and the two of them are on me in a heartbeat.

"Girl, are you having a hot flash? Your face is as red as a beet!" Sherri exclaims.

"Sherri! I'm thirty, not fifty!" I throw my towel playfully at her, careful not to spill my wine.

"Well, what happened that has you blushing so hard?" Stephen narrows his eyes at me in appraisal.

"It was a heated pool and I'm drinking wine, now will you two back off?"

"Ooh, she's defensive. That means something totally happened. Ohmygod, did you run into Jameson?" Stephen pauses like he's thinking about something, "Mm, God, even his *name* feels good in my mouth." He flops onto his back on my bed dramatically.

I can't help but laugh out loud, swatting him playfully on the arm as I fill my friends in on the last ten minutes of my life.

"Then he asked me what language I preferred in *Italian*. Multilingual and a face that looks like that? Too bad he's a frigging pilot."

"Let's not forget about that ass...and don't tell me you haven't noticed. The man could crack walnuts with how tight that thing is. Also, you're the only one in this room who has an issue with banging a pilot." Stephen feigns a look of pity as he pats my knee before adding, "Well, and Sher of course, because of that whole being married thing."

Sherri surprises us both at her joke. At least I think she's joking when she says, "I'd be willing to make an exception." Wow, Jameson has done a number on her, too.

"Isn't it time for you to return to your own room?" I tease Stephen, but also it's almost 10:00 p.m. and I'm ready to climb into my bed which I can't do with him laying across it.

He kisses Sherri and I on our cheeks and heads out the door to a room down the hallway. As much as I want to think about anything else, I fall asleep to images of Jameson in his V-neck t-shirt.

Chapter 10

Jameson

My next several flights are add-ons that I picked up while I wait for my next run to Dallas with Natalie. I can't stop myself from scanning the lounge for her, the employee bus, or the terminal on my way to the gate - which is crazy of course because she could be en route to Arizona or Guatemala for all I know. But still, I look.

It's unnerving how quickly she's gripped my mind. She's everything I was hoping to avoid with this relocation but the more I try to get her out of my thoughts, the more she becomes embedded. A woman has never gotten under my skin like this. I see her face in my mind at night and I feel the disappointment roll into anger on the days I don't see her face in person.

After what seems like forever, Thursday comes around and I've got the route to DFW again with Ricardo as my co-pilot. This doesn't happen often, but he's trying to pick up quick flights since his wife is due any day. I figure since he and I have a little rapport built from our layover in Dallas, now/s my chance to see what I can find out about Natalie.

"So, how often do you work with Stephen and the girls?" I ask, hoping I sound far more casual than I feel. This girl's got me all torn up and we've barely interacted today. But when we *did* interact, I swear I could have been burned by the electricity flowing between us. Ever since the night on the elevator when I was close enough to see her flushed skin and blown out pupils and the way she stood her ground even as I came closer, I've wanted to see just how close she'll let me get. I feel like I'm trying to earn the trust of a wild animal. Slowly and surely, piece by piece.

"Not too often," Ricardo says, jarring me back to the present. "Every once in a while, they'll ride on a stand-by crew for some extra cash and they'll be on my flight, or I'll pick this one up. I always enjoy that because all three of them are great individuals, but they're definitely happier when they get to work together. They have a flow and keep things running smoothly. Very competent."

"Yeah, they're a great crew. I'm sure you've had some nightmares in the past. I think we all have." I don't know how to discreetly ask the questions I want answers to so I just try to keep him talking, selfish bastard that I am. It's a stark contrast to the day we met when all I wanted was for him to shut up.

"Oh yeah, there are some real doozies. I'd put in to be Dave Ranier's replacement just to fly with Stephen, Sherri, and Nat, but I heard they're switching Dave's current domestic route to international and I just can't do that. Not with baby number four on the way." He laughs a delighted laugh that reaches his eyes and I feel nothing but respect for this man who so obviously loves his family and loves providing for them.

As for Dave's route, this is the first time I'm hearing about this. I didn't know Ranier's route was opening or that it was being switched to international. All I knew was that Dave was out on vacation and they needed a cover for the last few weeks - a blessing that was timed with my arrival and need of a schedule.

"So, Dave's retiring?" My mind is spinning a mile a minute and I will myself to calm down.

"Yeah, I don't think they've made the official announcement yet but he's been pretty vocal about it. Got a few grandkids and a house in the Keys. He's ready for the next phase, you know?" Ricardo eyes me quizzically. "Would you want to fly international?"

"I'd love to. I flew international for my previous airline. No wife, no kids, increased pay, fewer runs overall." Sounds even better if Natalie is on my crew.

Jameson, get it together, man.

The angel and the demon are waging war on my shoulders:

Angel: *You just met her a couple weeks ago.*

Demon: *But she speaks multiple languages and loves to fly.*

Angel: *You don't date co-workers and you know nothing about her.*

Demon: *I know her face flushes and she stutters when she's embarrassed.*

Angel: *Stop thinking with your dick.* (Okay, maybe the angel wouldn't use the word dick.)

Damn. I have no response for the last one. I *am* thinking with my dick. I'm being the very part of the male species I loathe the most.

Natalie is gorgeous, but also a mystery. I know nothing about her and she doesn't seem intent on changing that. Perhaps that challenge is part of the appeal.

Finally, right as I decide to let it go, Fate throws me a

bone. Ricardo chuckles and says, "Well, on second thought, maybe don't apply for Dave's route. Nat doesn't seem to like you very much."

"Yeah, any idea why that is?" I hear the anxiety in my voice and I don't like it. *Cut it out Hunter, you weak-ass dipshit.* I turn to face Ricardo in my seat so I can read his facial expression.

He answers in a casual tone as he says, "She was hot and heavy with another pilot a few months back. Apparently, he hooked up with another flight attendant the same day he broke it off with Nat. She was heart-broken. Vowed never to date a pilot again."

We sound like two office ladies talking shit over coffee but I can't stop myself. "How do you know all that?"

"Nat is something of an enigma." *No shit.* "She has no ties to Chicago, doesn't talk about her family much except for her oldest brother, but her looks ensure that pretty much everyone who works for this airline out of Chicago knows who she is. More than one passenger has been kicked off a flight for harassing her. But also, she's just really nice, you know? She puts the passengers at ease and does her job well. She always asks about my wife which allows me to ask about her life every now and then. I don't think she's been out with anyone since Luca though. Some of the pilots have a bet on who can get her to crack first and go out with them, but I keep telling them it's hopeless."

Luca.

Ce n'est pas Luca, Nat. Stephen's earlier words come back to me. *He's not Luca.*

"That seems creepy and really fucked up." Anger is starting to rise on her behalf. Harassment so bad that passengers have been removed from flights? And a betting pool on who can "crack her" first?

"It *is* creepy and fucked up, but you know pilots. Most of us have overinflated egos and control issues. We love this job because we love a challenge and we hate being told that we can't do something." He yawns like we are simply discussing the cloud bank in front of us.

I hate that he's right. I hate that I'm just like that and I *just* confessed to myself that the challenge has kept me a player in this game. My mind is whirling as I connect the dots. Natalie doesn't *hate* me. She's *attracted* to me. And she doesn't want to be because I'm a pilot.

I laugh out loud at the realization that she and I are in the same exact boat trying to row in opposite directions.

"What's so funny?" Ricardo asks.

"Life, man. Life is a funny bitch sometimes."

"Yeah, I hear you, amigo."

Now, potentially knowing *why* she's so cold toward me, I *can't* let it go. I want to prove to her I'm different.

Even though I should keep my distance...

Distance...

And just like that, I've decided to pick up Dave Ranier's international route as far out as I can schedule and I'm going to try like hell to get the trio of perfection to do it with me.

49

Chapter 11

Natalie

I t's been a month since Jameson first started flying our "regular" route. It's as regular as a flight crew can get at least.

I still think about him far more than I should, but he's been pleasant enough to work with despite the raging attraction I feel on my side and the tension I feel on his. I've tried to lessen my bitchiness toward him realizing that Stephen and Sherri are right: Jameson *isn't* Luca and it's not Jameson's fault that he's a breathing innuendo.

I wear my hair down today and run my fingers through it as a brush - low maintenance at its finest - and I slip into my uniform, opting for the skirt and heels far more often these days than in the past, but I still refuse to acknowledge any reason for the change.

Since we alternate, I'm in first class today. Jameson stands up front and greets the passengers with me as they enter the plane and I can feel his eyes slide to me several times during the boarding process. Standing so close to him is already making my armpits sweat more than is healthy. I'm dreading having to do the oxygen mask demonstration since it requires me to lift my arms, even though I have a jacket on. I'm pretty sure I'm getting dehydrated from the fluid loss over here and I can only hope that no one smells the nerves and lust seeping out of my pores.

I guess I can tell my brain that we are *not* doing this all I want, but my body has other plans.

One woman's eyes go wide as she appraises Jameson while entering the galley from the jet bridge. Swallowing hard, she says, "Good Lord, are you a model or our pilot?" I can never decide if I admire people who say things like this or if I loathe them. Today, I think I loathe it because I do *not* like the flare of jealousy her statement causes in me. It probably needs to be examined over three bottles of cabernet sauvignon but I don't have time for that right now so I shove it back down wherever it lives.

Out of the corner of my eye, I see Jameson give her a tight smile as he replies, "I definitely make a better pilot than I ever would a model."

"I don't know about that," she huffs skeptically as she moves on toward her seat, throwing a glance back over shoulder halfway down the aisle.

"Eso te pasa mucho." A statement. Not a question. *That happens to you a lot.*

We seem to be finding a rhythm and as long as we keep our conversations neutral. Barring no more close-quarters talks while wearing towels, I think I can do this. It's still easier to talk to him in any language other than English though. English feels like my "real life" and each language lets me alternate between personas. I use them like a shield. Anything that gets said in French or Spanish immediately gets forgotten when you switch back to English...unless you call someone a walking orgasm. Unfortunately, *that* shit gets carried over.

"Probablemente con menos frecuencia de lo que te sucede a ti." *Probably less often than it happens to you.*

My heart rate kicks up at his words and I feel the first trickle of sweat between my boobs. Did Captain Hunter just call me attractive?

As if he conjured up the worst of the patrons with his statement, a man who looks drunk already - even though it's only 9:19 in the morning - boards our aircraft and eyes me appreciatively. This close, it's easy to tell when someone is checking you out. The man licks his lips and winks at me after dragging his eyes up my body so obviously I have to suppress a shudder. Mid-forties, balding, expensive suit, probably rich-as-hell, and thinks everyone wants to be with him. We've all seen the type.

I feel Jameson stiffen next to me. "Sir, you're holding up the line, please proceed to your seat."

"Just checking out the view, Cap." He has a mild slur. Yep, this man probably spent the last two hours sipping bloody Marys in the frequent fliers' club.

"She's a stewardess, not a piece of meat, now move on before I have you removed from my flight."

When Jameson Hunter defends you, it's like an entire army just enlisted to ensure your safety on the throne of the fucking world. I remind myself that he probably does that for everyone and there is no need to go into total seventh-grade-girl mode, but I'm swooning anyway, despite my half-assed efforts not to.

The passenger decides I'm not worth the fuss, thankfully, so he just grumbles and moves on. Of course he's a first class passenger which I fully expected after the bling from his Rolex damn near blinded me as he headed for his seat.

We watch as he slides into seat 3B and Jameson leans

down whispering in my ear, "If he gives you any trouble, I want you to call me."

I look at him and raise an eyebrow. "So you can kick him off mid-flight?" I ask jokingly.

"So I can blacklist him from the airline and ensure he never lays eyes on you again," Jameson says in a dark tone that somehow tells me he's dead serious and deserving of the word *dangerous* in his list of personality traits.

The absurdity of his statement, however, actually makes me laugh. Loudly. I cover my mouth with my hand and try to quiet down as the other passengers continue to board. Sherri is behind us and she's laughing too.

"What's so funny?" Jameson asks, his tone not any lighter than it was a second ago.

"Honey, if you blacklisted every passenger who hits on Nat, there would be no passengers left on our flights!"

"Jesus, it's that bad?" Jameson asks as he turns his attention from Sherri back to me, raking a hand down his gorgeous features.

I start to shake my head *no* when Sherri pipes up again, "Sometimes. Girl's got thick skin but occasionally they think they can touch as well as look."

Jameson's face reddens in anger. I know it's anger because his jaw is clenched so tightly I'm afraid he's going to break a tooth and his hands are fisting at his sides. He's casting glances at the man in 3B and I subtly shake my head no at him- *don't say a word* - and turn to greet the next passenger.

Jameson getting upset over rude passengers turns my insides into molten liquid. I shouldn't care that he cares, but I definitely do.

I fall for guys fast and hard. It was an issue even before Luca, even though he was the fastest and hardest I'd ever fallen. People like to blame everything on my parents' divorce, saying that I'm stand-offish because I have trust issues and that I fall for guys so fast because I'm afraid they'll leave, so I feel l like I have to act quickly.

Um, no.

I'm stand-offish because I'm an introvert despite my passion for my career choice and I fall so fast because I get caught up in the butterflies easily. But as thirty-one approaches, I want to have the stability that comes from a committed partner. That's part of the reason my reaction to Jameson is so scary. I haven't known him long but there's something stirring in me the way it does when you see someone that is undeniably attractive. Like, *really* attractive and you immediately imagine them shirtless. And barefoot. And then totally naked. And then naked and above you while leaning down to kiss your neck. Which spirals dangerously fast into daydreams of waking up next to them on a lazy Sunday morning while your kids snuggle with you in bed.

Whoa, slow down there.

I realize after a beat too long that I'm openly staring at Jameson with my mouth hanging open. The onboarding passengers have totally faded away. I'm staring up at his jawline when I hear him clear his throat as he cuts his eyes to me, eyebrows raised.

Ohmygod, I'm no better than the drunk man in first class.

I reluctantly drag my eyes away, inwardly groaning, and turn to greet the last few passengers as he whispers, "Tu regardes." *You're staring.*

"Je sais. Je suis désolé." *I know. I'm sorry.* No point in denying it. If I'm not mistaken, I see his eyes widen slightly at my admission of guilt and I can't help but feel like I just crossed some boundary by doing so.

Sherri and Stephen are right. It's time to let my hurt over Luca go and move on. Just because I enjoy gawking at Jameson doesn't mean I'll end up in bed with him. We have a couple more flights together this week and then he's probably expanding his routes and picking up a different schedule. New month usually means whole new schedule and then I can return to my plan of avoiding all pilots, especially ones that look like Jameson Hunter. But for now, maybe I can stare just a little.

Chapter 12

Jameson

Natalie is killing me. Her face is bright and rarely do you see women without makeup, but I prefer her this way.

I'm insanely curious about the conversations she's been having with herself and her friends over the last several days. We've been more jovial with each other and she even admitted to openly staring at me, but the timing and situation hasn't yet been right for me to ask her more about her personal life. Or beg her for her phone number.

The scarf she wore yesterday is gone and the first button is undone on her blouse. I stand about five inches taller than her, even in her heels, so I have to be careful not to let my gaze drag down her chest as we stand in the galley greeting the passengers.

Knowing I would see her at work this morning made getting up much easier and clocking in, far more enjoyable. I can't help but feel that burst of excitement when I see her.

People often judge others for being shallow or appearance-oriented, but isn't almost every relationship started by a physical attraction? I have far more friend-couples who are together because one of them said *holy shit that person's hot. I want to get to know them,* and far *fewer* friend-couples that started because they were first attracted to a personality trait other than looks. It's a fact of nature. Males in most species carry brilliant colors and exquisite calls to attract a mate. Humans are no different, except our females also play the game. So, the fact that I'm insanely attracted to Natalie after such a short period of time isn't desperate. It's normal. It's fucking annoying and causing me a fair amount of stress, but it's normal.

Or so I keep telling myself. I'm fully aware that I'm walking a dangerous line, especially knowing both my past and a little about hers.

Thankfully, there's no more trouble out of 3B and we're halfway through the flight. Unable to help myself, I call Natalie on the phone and ask her to block the galley so I can use the restroom. Of course I don't have to use the restroom, we only left an hour ago, but I would like to stretch my legs. *AKA - I am purposely trying to put myself in her space.*

When I step out of the cockpit, I see Sherri and Natalie deep in conversation over the cart that is blocking access to the cockpit from the cabin. They're both leaning over the cart with their elbows propped on top, facing the passengers, their backs to me. I step off to the opposite side of the bathroom, over behind the oven and little sink. The ladies turn to look at me, their question clear on their faces.

"Everything going okay out here?" I ask casually,

working really damn hard to keep my eyes on Natalie's face and not her bent over form.

"Fine, Captain," she answers hesitantly, "How are things on your end?"

"Smooth and fast," I reply in regards to the flight but as soon as it leaves my mouth, I realize that it sounds like a double entendre.

Sherri picks up on it as she laughs and says "Sounds like how I got pregnant."

I cringe and risk a glance at Natalie who is hiding her smile and avoiding eye contact.

"Captain Hunter, while you're out here, can I get you something to drink?" Sherri asks me. I could kiss her for allowing me to have a few more minutes.

"A coffee, black, would be great, Sherri. Thank you."

As Sherri leaves her post at the cart, I move to switch sides of the galley so that she can work around the sink, oven, and coffee maker. Unfortunately, she and I meet in the middle which forces me to squeeze behind Natalie as Sherri passes behind me, against the door to the cockpit.

I brace my hand on Natalie's back to let her know I'm here and to also ensure that I politely keep the rest of my massive frame from bumping up against her. I'm frozen for a beat as she is bent over the cart, head turned to say something to Sherri over her left shoulder, while my hand lands on her back and I'm directly behind her, looking down. My hand takes up most of her petite back.

Fuck.

I'm hard.

I can't seem to make my feet move. Or my hand. I'm drowning in an image of Natalie on her hands and knees while I brace myself behind her, showing her that I'm worth the risk. I'm stronger than her fear or failed relationship. A shudder rips through her like she got a chill but I arrogantly know it's from the contact of my hand. As I keep moving to slide over to the right of the galley, I can't stop myself from dragging my hand down her back just a little before lifting it from her completely.

I'm disgusted with myself because I didn't tell her I was going to touch her, nor did I ask if I could. I'm also so turned on that I hope Ricardo is up for landing this flight because the only thing I want to land currently has her ass dangerously close to my dick. I bristle at the realization that I want to bury myself in her and lose all sense of time.

She stands slowly and then immediately busies herself with fixing things on the cart. Sherri hands me my coffee with a knowing grin on her face, but thankfully, she stays quiet.

When I make no move to head back into the cockpit, Natalie says, "Captain, I've got a light on at 5A, are you going to spend much longer out here?" She can't move the cart and provide service to the passengers until I'm tucked back into the cockpit behind the locked door. If I'm not mistaken, her breathing is a little irregular and her voice doesn't have its full strength.

I've seen beautiful women. Hell, I've *slept with* beautiful women. More than I care to admit. But Natalie awakens something deeper than just lust. I feel a growing desire to protect her and know her and restore her faith in the male species, which is completely insane. This knockout with her love of languages and flying is getting to me. How am I going to get to know her better when my own well-thought-out rule prevents me from even asking her to dinner?

Perhaps it's time for a change in the rules.

Chapter 13

Natalie

"I've never seen a man that makes a uniform look so good," Sherri says long after Jameson is back in the cockpit. She and I are in the jump seats up front, on our final approach.

I stay quiet because I don't trust myself to speak. I still feel his massive hand splayed on my back. His touch sent heat straight between my legs and I'm shocked my knees didn't give out.

The flight was pretty easy. Once 3B found his seat, he promptly passed out and has been quiet, much to my delight. Sherri stayed in first class with me for the duration of the flight except to help Stephen with beverage service in the main cabin.

"Are you on again tomorrow?" I ask her. As a senior flight attendant, she usually gets most of the bids for the schedule she requests. As mid-level, Stephen and I get about 80% which isn't bad since we work for a legacy carrier - one of the big airlines who fly internationally and have hubs all over the world.

"I've got the next three days off. You?"

"I'm on tomorrow and then off the next. Crap. If you aren't on tomorrow's flight, I wonder who I'll be working with."

Sherri clicks away on her phone and pulls up the schedules. When she gives me a look of disdain, I know exactly who is on with me.

"Amber?" I ask even though I already know the answer.

"Amber."

Shiiiiiiiiiiiiiiiiiit. Amber is young and obnoxious. How she passed her stewarding certification is still a mystery. I don't buy into the whole "dumb blonde" stereotype, except maybe for her. Barbie could perform our job tasks better than Amber can, and Barbie doesn't even have elbows that bend. With huge boobs that she loves to stick out, bottle blonde hair, fake nails, and fake eyelashes, Amber is the whole nine yards. It's not her appearance that bothers me though, it's just *her*.

There are a lot of steps to what we do. They aren't necessarily complicated or challenging steps, there are just a lot of them. And they happen in the same order, *every* time. She somehow manages to get them *out* of order, *every* time, making my job three times as complicated as it needs to be.

"Please tell me Stevie is on with me tomorrow?"

"Yes, it's you, Stevie, Amber, and Jake."

Damn, if Jake is on our flight, that means Stephen is going to be tied up trying to flirt his ass off with Jake the whole time and I'll be on my own with over-the-top-Amber. Dread fills my stomach like a lead weight at the thought of tomorrow's flight.

I lean my head back against the seat and prepare to touch down. Jameson lands flawlessly. It's so smooth I can barely tell when our wheels have touched the pavement.

Smooth and fast. So much power at his fingertips.

God, his fingertips...

The passengers deplane and I finish filling out my paperwork and doing my log when Stephen trots up to the front just as the cockpit doors open and Jameson and Ricardo file out.

"Nat, you want to meet at Pancetta's tonight? Cash in on that beer I owe you from that flight a few days ago?" Stephen asks.

"Sure, meet you at 6?"

"6? That puts me on the hook for dinner too. You know I'm cheap. Let's do 8."

I just laugh. "Stevie, how about I buy *you* dinner and we meet at 6. I'm going to be in bed by 8."

"You have yourself a date." He smiles as Jameson looks our way with an eyebrow raised.

"I thought you said you weren't looking for a date?" Jameson casually leans back against the small sink, remembering a conversation from what feels like a lifetime ago. He's smirking and crossing his ankles, waiting on my response, while Sherri and I grab our bags out of the closet.

"I wasn't. I mean, I'm not," I stutter. "Stevie's gay so it doesn't count as a date," I say in a flustered rush.

"Hey, I take offense to that," Stephen protests and folds his arms across his chest while putting a full pout on display despite the fact that I know he is in *no way* offended by that comment.

"Okay, fine." I pause for dramatic effect and smile seductively at Stephen. "It *is* a date. Stephen is paying and afterwards he's going to take me home and ravish me on my kitchen table."

The look of absolute disgust and horror on Stephen's face makes me burst into laughter.

"Never mind," he chokes out while pretending to dry-heave, "I am so *not* offended by it not being a date. In fact, maybe we shouldn't even grab a beer if you have those nasty thoughts in your mind."

I can't help but laugh harder as I sling my bag over my shoulder, my other hand clutching my stomach. "Come on, *Stephanie*, let's catch the bus." I loop my arm through his and throw a look over my shoulder. "Adios, Ricardo. Dile a tu esposa que dije hola." *Tell your wife I said hello.* I wave, then look at Jameson and issue a goodbye in French because I can't resist. "Au revoir, Jameson, à demain." *See you tomorrow.*

Glad to be home for a bit, I shower and change into jeans and a t-shirt and slide my feet into an old pair of Vans before knocking on Stephen's door. He signed a lease on an apartment down the hall from me about four months ago.

He looks so handsome in slim-fit black pants and a sweater. When he isn't working, he wears black rimmed glasses that are absolutely delicious. Stephen is basically the perfect man and I've tried on more than one drunk occasion to convince him we should get married. Spoiler alert - it never works.

He loops his arm through mine and kisses the top of my head as we head to the train.

We have a great time getting dinner at my favorite Italian restaurant, dissecting every word spoken on our last flight and Stephen makes talking about Jameson an art as he describes all of the reactions he has to being in close proximity to the man.

"So, the multiple languages thing is hot. As if he needed anything other than that face and body he's rocking. Honestly, if I could get fifteen minutes alone with him, I would change his whole world."

With my mouth full, I laugh. "Yeah, the face and body are working for him, huh?"

"Working for him and me both. I swear he raises the temperature of a room by at least sixty-five degrees...and that's fully clothed." Stephen's eyes are almost completely rolled back in his head while he talks and for a second, I'm afraid they're going to get stuck that way. "Nat, he totally can't take his eyes off of you anytime you're near him."

Now, both Stephen *and* Sherri have made the same observation. My self-esteem is within a normal realm, but no way a man that looks like Jameson Hunter is into me, despite our mildly flirty interactions. Besides, even if he is, I'm not going there, so no need to get my hopes up.

"Mmm hmm. I get a vibe from him, I'm just not exactly sure what kind quite yet. Maybe like new-kid-on-the-playground. I'll admit, he does make showing up to work a little less painful. Amber is going to be unbearable tomorrow though." I squeeze the bridge of my nose and feel my eyes squinting shut tightly, signaling the stress that tomorrow will no doubt bring.

Stevie and I spend the next hour gently making fun of Amber's anticipated reaction to Jameson.

As our night winds down, Stephen turns serious. "Natalie, promise me you'll go out with him if he asks you."

"Stevie, I just can't. I can't have a growing list of pilots I need to avoid. I already hold my breath every time I step into the lounge waiting for Luca or Blow-Job-Betty to be right around the corner." For the record - her name is actually Lauren, but I like Blow-Job-Betty *way* better. "You know I get attached fast. Which is okay as long as I don't have to see the guy daily once it ends." I can feel Stephen starting to protest and I can already hear him - *But you don't see Luca every day* - so I up the ante and cut him off. "*But* what if I *do* promise to go out on a date in the next week?"

He narrows his eyes at me, waiting for the catch of the deal. "With who?"

Ugh. I really don't want to do this. I mean I do. I want to get back out there and find someone to get all gushy over and settle down with, but dating, itself, actually really blows. "What about Evan?"

Evan Langford. He's been after me for a date for as long as I can remember. I honestly wouldn't be surprised if he turned me down for taking so damn long. Evan and I met organically at the community pool, so I know we at least have that in common. He's a five to Jameson's twenty-five - all on a ten-point scale of course - but he's nice, active, and local. He works for an accounting firm, so he would probably have that whole stability thing down.

"Fine. Evan. But you have to actually give him a shot. Not let him buy you dinner just to satisfy this promise to me. Also, I need pictures. No pics means it didn't really happen."

"Fine." I sigh in resignation to this damned promise.

"*Also*, you have to text him no later than tomorrow. I want to make sure this doesn't get conveniently forgotten or pushed under the proverbial rug."

"God, you're pushy." I roll my eyes lovingly. I know he just wants me to be happy, but he also happens to want it on his timeline.

At the end of the night, we split the bill, but he buys my beer, and we head back to our apartment complex as even more dread pools in my stomach...I'm more full from that than I am the dinner I barely touched.

Once tucked safely inside my apartment, I pull out my phone. I might as well get this over with.

NATALIE 8:07 PM

> Hey Evan. It's Nat. Sorry it's been a while since we talked. Anyway, I was wondering if you were free this weekend? Maybe we could grab a bite to eat?

Much to my dismay, the answer comes immediately.

EVAN 8:07 PM

> Natalie! I thought you'd given up on me. Dinner sounds great.

> Saturday at 7?

> Oriole?

> I'll swing by and pick you up.

I should've known how this would go. Evan has money and he likes to flaunt it. I don't think he's rolling in billions, but he drives a Porche Cayenne and just chose a restaurant that has four dollar signs next to the Google reviews. I don't want to seem ungrateful or uppity in a different type of way, so I agree to his choice, but honestly, a pizza and a movie on my couch is the faster way to my heart. However, I promised Stevie I would try.

NATALIE 8:09 PM

Sounds great.

Chapter 14

Jameson

I spend the night tossing and turning and replaying the events of the day in my mind. I can still feel her under my hand and the sensation of loss is strong when I realize I'm alone in the new king-sized bed in my fancy condo overlooking the city.

I thought about calling Jason, my best friend since high school, or even Rachel, my sister, but I'm not ready to outwardly acknowledge this thing yet. Hell, I'm not even on board with *inwardly* acknowledging it yet, but neither my brain nor my body seem to care.

A few hours later, I begin my morning routine and I'm jittery and excited like a high school freshman. I feel ridiculous. I need to reinforce my resolve and address Natalie only when necessary. And only in English...which I can't seem to do.

How long do I plan on lying to myself?

Apparently, only another five...four...three...two...one seconds... I'm almost giddy with relief as I finally relent and admit to myself that I want this girl. *Bad.* But then reality comes crashing down. I'm only on this route for a couple more days. If I get Dave Ranier's route, I want this crew with me which certainly means I can't be dating one of them.

Right?

As I think about this, an image enters my mind of Natalie straddling my lap in her uniform skirt as my hands slide up her thighs before diving into her gorgeous hair, pulling her face down to mine while she....*Jameson, stop.*

I struggle to turn this fantasy off in my head, grab my coffee mug, and head to the airport. Having moved from my previous base in Charlotte, I'm still getting used to the new traffic patterns, lot entrances, and security checkpoints. An employee bus is waiting as soon as I park my old Toyota Land Cruiser in the parking deck and I head straight to the gate instead of stopping in the lounge.

As soon as I board my plane, I see Natalie's long copper hair. Loose curls drape over her shoulders and I silently beg my pulse to slow down. Natalie's back is to me and the flight attendant she's talking to sees me first. To my dismay, it's not Sherri.

I see the eyes go wide on a tall, lean, blonde flight attendant. My guess is twenty-six or twenty-seven years old. Judging by the tone of Natalie's voice, she's over this day already.

"Amber? Are you even listening to..." She turns around to see why Amber has stopped responding to her. "Oh, good morning, Captain Hunter." She gives me a small smile and nods like my appearance explains everything. She also sounds exhausted and not as excited to see me as I am to see her. "Amber, this is Captain Hunter. Captain Hunter, Amber." There is no tone to her voice at all.

I nod my head once to Amber, concern causing my brows to inch together. "Nice to meet you. Welcome aboard." I don't reach out my hand for her to shake. Based on the look on Amber's face, I'm getting Vanessa vibes already. She's drinking me in from head to toe and not being discreet about it. *At all.*

I usually offer for the crew to call me Jameson. Although I'm proud of my rank, shoving it in crew members' faces is hardly a good way to get the staff to enjoy flying with me but I'm desperate to put some professional boundaries in place STAT with this girl, so I don't make the offer.

"Thanks. You're quite an upgrade from Dave Ranier." She scans me again and I feel my skin crawl.

"Captain Ranier has about twenty thousand more hours of fly time than I do, so I doubt that, but thank you for the confidence," I bite. I really don't want to be a douche, especially in front of Natalie, but I've got to shut this girl down *now*.

Unfortunately, Amber isn't on board with that plan. "I meant how you look." She's playing with the open collar of her uniform and giving me an expression of pure lust.

Keeping my eyes trained on hers and my expression cold, I deadpan, "I know," and turn my attention to Natalie. "Natalie, do you have everything you need? Hopefully we'll have better luck on today's flight." I flash her a genuine smile, clearly indicating that she is my preference of the two women and also hoping that she warms up a little...to me at least.

"I do. Thank you." Another curt nod and shy smile and only very brief eye contact.

At that moment, we see Stephen turn into the plane. He kisses Natalie on both cheeks in greeting. "It's nine in the morning and I could already use another one of those beers from last night." He keeps his voice down but we can all hear him anyway.

"Well, it's your turn to have the first-class cabin, so hopefully it won't be too bad," Natalie answers him.

Damn. I forgot they trade each leg they work together and Natalie had it on the way back yesterday. It's not like I can say anything so I just excuse myself and head for the cockpit to start the flight pre-check, my clothes already feeling too tight after sixty seconds in Natalie's presence.

Two minutes later, there's a knock on the door. I didn't think we had started boarding yet, but I could have missed it. Sometimes there are kids or military guys who want to see the cockpit, or just nervous passengers who like to meet the pilot. I squeeze out of the seat - envious of the size of the first-class cabin seats as I do so - and push the door open.

"I thought you might like coffee before takeoff, Captain Hunter," Amber purrs as she stands with a coffee cup on a tray. I've got a decision to make. I can take the coffee and invite further conversation or I can decline and have her think I'm a total dick.

"No, thanks. My mug is still full from the house." Might as well tear the band-aid off now. I start to duck back inside and let the door close. She catches it before it latches.

"Well, do let me know if you need anything," she says as she bites her lower lip in a total attempt to set my blood boiling. It doesn't work and I let the door shut on her words with no response.

The cockpit is usually a place of comfort for me. As comfortable with all the buttons and dials and screens as I am the steering wheel of my car. Today, however, it feels claustrophobic. A single minute in Natalie's presence this morning and I just about exploded with the need to invite her to dinner.

Immediately, my brain hits overdrive fantasizing about what she would wear, where we would go, how incredible she would look sitting in the passenger seat of my Land Cruiser.

This is uncharted territory for me. I've never worked this hard to avoid a girl *or* get a girl. With equal desires to get to know her better and also stay away from her completely, my head is starting to throb and I'm getting concerned about this erection that's threatening to accompany me every day to work.

Chapter 15

Natalie

I knew Amber was going to be unbearable as soon as she laid eyes on Jameson, but I honestly didn't think it was going to be *this* bad. She's even worse at her tasks now than usual - and that pretty much means she isn't even bothering to do them at all.

"So, does he have a wife?" Amber asks while I go back over her poorly assembled beverage cart - pissed because it's still missing half the items it needs.

"I have no idea, Amber. It's not like we've sat down and played twenty questions." I'm hoping she'll drop it based on my attitude, but she's as clueless as ever. I push my hair out of my face, wishing I had opted to put it up today.

"Well, what route are they assigning him? I mean there aren't that many open if he wants something consistent. Unless he's just going to bid for his routes? Wait, he is based out Chicago, right?"

Some senior pilots choose a specific route they fly regularly. Like Dave Ranier. At sixty-one, he has seniority to put his name on every Monday, Tuesday, Thursday flight from Chicago to Dallas and back again. Most of the time he does it twice. And that's his schedule. Other pilots bid on their schedules. It's all computerized now so openings pop up for pilots based on airport, aircraft type, flight length, etc... and they can choose what works for them. Five days in a row, a couple of overnights, red-eyes, whatever. As flight attendants, our schedules mostly work the same with a few minor differences.

"Amber, I have no idea where he lives. Now help me finish this cart. Jake and Stephen are welcoming the passengers up front already." Sure enough, we're starting to get passengers filing into the main cabin and we don't even have the damn drink cart done yet. Ugh. I loathe working with Amber.

The phone rings, frustrating me even more. "Yes?" I say into the receiver, maybe a little sharper than I mean to.

"Nat, everything okay back there?" It's Stephen.

"Mm hmm," I bite off sarcastically so that he knows it's so *not* okay back here. "What do you need, Stevie? I'm still stocking the drink cart."

"Christ, she's getting worse," he replies in a tone so serious that a laugh escapes my throat. "I called to let you know that you have an underage kid in the exit row. Sorry, bunny."

He gets *Stevie* and I get *Bunny.* Shoot me now.

I'm not sure how the website allows people to select a seat in the exit row if they're under fifteen. How is a six-year-old going to manhandle this door open? And *why* does a six-year-old need the extra leg room that comes from getting this seat? Since I've done the whole damn beverage cart, I tell Amber to deal with the kid and his mom.

Two minutes later she comes back, "Um, they said they were okay getting the door open if needed and they don't want to move."

I narrow my eyes at her in disbelief and total judgement of her lack of intellect. *How are you allowed to be a flight attendant?*

Taking a deep breath so I don't throat punch her, I say, "Okay, well the FAA regulations *and* the regulations of this airline state that no one under the age of fifteen can sit in the emergency exit row, whether mommy says they want to or not." I brush past her, clearly frustrated and go talk to the woman myself. My anger is barely contained below the façade of my demeanor.

I basically stomp to her row with my hands on my hips. The curtain to first class hasn't been pulled yet and Stephen is watching me with wide eyes knowing this most likely isn't going to be pretty. "Ma'am," I say curtly, not even trying to hide the irritation in my voice, "I apologize for the inconvenience, but FAA regulations prohibit you from sitting in this row with a child under the age of fifteen."

She smiles at me, sweet and sour. "Oh, it's okay, I already spoke with that nice girl and I explained that I can handle the door; my son won't be any trouble."

That nice girl. There isn't enough beer in Chicago today.

"Yes, well, as I explained to *that nice girl*, we won't be able to taxi away from the gate and take off until you and your son are reassigned. Again, I apologize for the inconvenience." *Especially considering that it wasn't my damn fault you were able to choose this seat in the first place.* My jaw is starting to hurt from clenching so hard. I can actually hear my molars grinding together.

She starts to argue but a sudden hush falls over the plane. I see her look over my shoulder as she gets that mesmerized look in her eyes telling me Jameson has just come into view.

"Ma'am, I'm Captain Hunter, your pilot for today's flight and I need to inform you that Natalie, here, is correct. I can't move this plane until you and your son are safely seated somewhere other than the exit row. My kind flight attendants will be happy to take care of this for you, but it needs to happen, and it needs to happen right now."

She stutters her agreement and reaches for her bag under her seat, eyes still slightly enlarged. It takes everything in me not to roll my own eyes; the only thing stopping me is the knowledge that all the passengers around us are watching and can see my reactions. Not to mention half of them are probably videoing this whole thing to put on TikTok later. Instead, I let out a deep breath, plaster a smile on my face and direct her up the aisle to Stephen who is the senior flight attendant today and will be in charge of reassigning their seats. As she heads toward Stephen, Jameson steps in close to my side and whispers in my ear.

"Pas besoin de gagner un pari, tu es la prochaine bière est sur moi." *No need to win a bet, your next beer is on me.* He flashes a quick wink as I look up at him, making an immediate change of my undergarments necessary so I don't have to walk around saturated by my own arousal this entire flight.

Chapter 16

Jameson

I couldn't even make it one flight without purposely entering her orbit. So much for being able to find my resolve. What resolve? It could be biting me on the sensitive tip of my dick right now and I wouldn't even know it.

Hell, we haven't even pulled back from the gate, but I could tell she's having a bad day already and that was all the excuse I needed. I know I shouldn't have said it, but I just wanted her to feel better. Give her something to look forward to. Then again, that's awfully fucking arrogant, isn't it? Who says she thinks a beer with me is such a great offer anyway? *Great job, Hunter, you asshole.*

Then an idea hits me. I'll invite Stephen and Sherri too. I can tell them I'm planning to bid for the new international route and get their thoughts on it. I can turn this into a casual business beer.

I smile to myself, proud of my plan. Real genius.

Once we've returned to Chicago, I try to catch Stephen and Natalie alone but it seems Amber or Jake are always around, so I take a different approach and call Stephen over to me.

"Hey, Stephen, could I talk to you really quickly?"

"Sure thing, Captain." Stephen is always in a good mood. I don't know how he does it, but he just raises the spirits of those around him. I can see why Natalie likes him so much.

"Hey, I was just wondering if you, Natalie, and Sherri would want to grab a beer sometime? I'm putting in a bid to request Dave Ranier's route long term and I'd love your thoughts on it...and to know if you guys have any interest or ability to fly a regular transatlantic? I really appreciate how well you guys work together and I'd love to have a fairly consistent team." I know I'm rambling. These are the most words I've ever said at one time. Especially to another man.

Maybe I've said too many of them because he's looking at me like I just sprouted a second head.

"You want to grab a beer? With us?" he clarifies.

"Um, yeah, but no pressure or anything." I'm not sure what to say and I shove my hands in my pockets feeling awkward, unable to gauge his reaction.

Until he breaks into a huge grin and says, "Oh man, the pilots never want to hang out with us anymore. Grabbing a beer would be awesome." His enthusiasm puts me at ease right as that voice in the back of my head speaks up again, *Jameson, what in the actual fuck do you think you're doing?*

It takes me a second to realize Stephen is still talking. "Here, I'll give you our numbers, that way you can just text us whenever it would work for you." He holds out his hand for my phone.

"Ok, great. I'll send a text so you guys have my number too. Thanks for your help today."

"No problem, Captain."

I chuckle, feeling light and happy that I now have Natalie's phone number. "Stephen, Jameson is fine." I could swear he flushes a little.

As soon as it's out of my mouth, I hear a voice behind me. "I'll say you damn sure are. Want another number to add to that phone, *Jameson*?"

The problem here is that I outrank Amber and anything *I* say can be misconstrued to make it seem like I'm taking advantage or abusing my power. The other problem is that I'm a man. A woman can get away with saying a *lot* of things that could never come out of my testosterone-fueled mouth. Even still, I'm shocked at how bold she is.

And the answer is still no.

I choose to keep my mouth shut. I give them both a nod and head out of the plane ignoring her comments entirely. I hear her heels behind me not long after I exit. Enough is enough and I let the impatience seep through my voice, "I hate to be rude, but I'm not interested." I don't even turn around as I say it. The end of the jet bridge is near and then I can hopefully lose her.

"Well, that *was* rude and to be clear, I never thought you *were* interested."

Natalie.

I whip around. "Ohmygod, Natalie, I am so sorry. I thought Amber was following me up the jetway."

Her smirk is delicious as she comes to walk next to me

and I'm afraid a stain is about to become visible on my pants. What is this woman doing to me? Her eyes are warm as she talks. "She's a tough pill to swallow, isn't she? Anyway, I haven't gotten a chance to thank you for the help with that mom and her son from earlier yet, so, thank you. A lot of our pilots just hide in the cockpit and make us the bad guys."

"No problem. It's the uniform. Particularly, this hat is pretty amazing. I put this thing on and I'm sure I could command an army. Here, you try." Before I can register what I'm doing, I'm pulling my hat out from under my arm and placing it on her head.

I'm *flirting*. Openly. Unmistakably. We're in the middle of the terminal back at O'Hare heading for our layover lounge, Natalie is laughing and saluting me and I think I've died and gone to heaven. She keeps it on a beat and then hands it back.

"Thank you, but I think it suits you better." She's blushing. "I hope you have a smooth flight later. I'll be back on the DFW route Thursday."

She walks away from me leaving me damn near breathless and dying for Thursday.

I know I should leave it alone, but I can't. I enter the lounge - curious about where she went - and type a group text to her, Stephen, and Sherri.

JAMESON 3:42 PM

Hi all, this is Jameson Hunter. Wanted to invite you all out for a beer sometime this weekend and talk about Dave Ranier's route switching to international. I've put in for it. Just let me know.

. . .

I blow out a breath I hadn't realized I'd been holding and lean my head back against the wall behind my chair. Damn it, I want this girl. And I want her to want me. Time to up the ante.

Chapter 17

Natalie

With four hours before my next flight, I booked a massage at the airport. It's my favorite thing to do on a long layover and after my morning with Amber, I could use an hour to decompress. While I'm headed toward the terminal, my phone buzzes in my pocket.

He wants to grab a beer with us? Who *is* this guy? Doesn't he know that pilots don't really hang out with the flight attendants? Unless they're fucking us, of course. *Don't go there, Natalie.*

I don't want to be the first one to respond, so I wait for someone else to do it. Stephen is probably holed up in one of the "escape pods" - private rooms with wi-fi, individual temperature controls, mood lighting, and a table - with Jake. Maybe Sherri will answer first.

I check in for my massage and try to relax although now I feel like my entire body is on high alert.

I was really looking forward to this weekend since it is the first time I will have both Saturday and Sunday off in three months. Granted, I've done that on purpose because why sit at home when I can be making money, but I've kind of been running myself ragged lately. If I work myself to death, I have far less time to think about other aspects of my life. More specifically, my *dating* life.

Not to mention, I need to get the apartment ready for Ty's visit. Which of course mostly means that I need to blow up the air mattress, put sheets on it, and buy Modelo for the fridge, but still, shit needs to get done.

The masseuse calls me back and I try to force the tension out of my shoulders.

An hour later, I feel akin to a limp noodle. I have one more flight to go today but it shouldn't be too bad.

Dressed and headed out the door, I make the mistake of checking my phone.

STEPHEN 3:52 PM

Sounds great! I'm free Saturday.

SHERRI 4:05 PM

Me too, for once.

Shit.

NATALIE 5:08 PM

Um, I could meet for lunch but I have plans Saturday night.

JAMESON 5:10 PM

Saturday lunch it is. You guys up for grabbing a pie at Gino's on the South Loop?

> **STEPHEN 5:10 PM**
> Does a leopard have spots?

> **JAMESON 5:12 PM**
> Um, yes??

> **SHERRI 5:12 PM**
> He means, yes, of course we're good with Gino's.

> **JAMESON 5:15 PM**
> Great. Natalie, does that work for you?

I stare at my phone. There is no way he can know Gino's is my favorite, right? He doesn't have my phone bugged or anything, I'm pretty sure, but can this be just a coincidence?

> **STEPHEN 5:15 PM**
> She's totally in. Gino's is her favorite food group.

> **NATALIE 5:15 PM**
> Thanks, Stevie. Yeah, that's good for me.

I hate that I'm more excited over grabbing pizza with co-workers than I am over a $300 steak and $250 bottle of wine on a date at one of Chicago's premier steakhouses. My stomach clenches as I think about the stupid date with Evan.

Stevie calls me on my way to the gate.

"So, what's got you all tied up Saturday evening?" I can hear the lilt in the smug bastard's voice.

I blow out a sigh. "Evan."

"Oh, you naughty girl, I didn't know you were into that kind of thing," he says, barely containing his laughter. It takes me a second to catch on to his joke.

"What? Ohmygod, No! Evan is not tying me up, you asshole." It takes me a second to realize I just shouted that in the crowded airport terminal. I lower my voice and continue, "I meant I made *dinner* plans with Evan and that is why I can't do Saturday night."

Stephen gives a *very* drawn out, dramatic "Mmmmm hmmmmmm."

"Fuck, you're the worst. I only did it because of you."

"You love me and you know it." I can feel his contagious smile through the phone.

"Unfortunately, that's true. Hey, did you tell Jameson that Gino's was my favorite?" I'm sure the answer is no, but it doesn't hurt to check. There are like 837,248 pizza places in Chicago, and he picks my favorite? The odds aren't in his favor and I'm trying to *not* think about the fact that maybe he and I have a love of Gino's in common along with our knowledge of languages. There is only so much a girl can take.

"I did not. I guess the man just has good taste."

"Hmm. Well, I've got one more flight today. I'll see you later."

Thursday's flight to Dallas is relatively uneventful passenger-wise. Neither Sherri nor Stephen are with me which I hate, but because this is my regular route, it ranks me as senior flight attendant. Suits me fine. I put myself in first class and try to not be distracted with thoughts of Jameson coming out of the cockpit...until he does and it's all I can do not to melt into a puddle on the floor. He has his standard pilot uniform on, which you would think I'd be used to by now - but totally am *not*.

My mind briefly flashes back to the dark jeans and v-neck t-shirt he wore in Dallas which seems like a hundred years ago. Both outfits work for him, although I have suspicions that he could wear a banana costume and still make *all* the panties drop. His navy-blue suit and tie against his crisp white shirt really have me on edge and I can't stop staring. Unblinking, lips parted, heavy breathing...it's a little obscene but I can't quell my reaction to him.

Completely forgetting I have my phone in my hand, it falls to the floor as I continue to stare at the man in front of me. A slow smiles spreads across his face as I watch the dawning of recognition once he realizes what he does to me.

The same thing he does to every woman no doubt, but right now his gaze is zeroed in on *me*.

Despite my earlier French confession of my thoughts on his looks -i.e. the walking orgasm - it's clear he now knows that those thoughts spin out of control and end with him doing unspeakable things to me. I feel the embarrassment of being caught in the flush of my cheeks.

Jameson leans down to grab my phone; the screen still on. I was checking an unread text message when it slipped. I see his eyes as they dart to the screen, out of habit or nosiness, I'm not sure. When he hands it back to me, his eyes have gone cold and his mouth is set in a hard line.

"Um, thanks," I manage to whisper. The look on his face is now glacial and I don't know why.

"Are you ready for the passengers?" he asks without

even acknowledging my thank you.

"Yes, I'll call the gate," I nod, unsure of what has happened.

He turns on his heel to go back into the cockpit and yanks the door shut behind him.

WTF?

Only when I look down at my phone do I start to connect the dots.

> TYLER 7:48 AM
>
> Nat, I can't wait to see you next week! It's been too long. Call me when you get a second. Love you.

Ty has always been affectionate toward me. We really nailed the protective-big-brother, doting-little-sister-roles well. He's the oldest of the four of us and I'm the second in line. We were each other's entertainment before the other two came along and once they did, we banded together to help Mom while Dad was working and then even more, after the divorce.

I can't help but smile a little at my own realization: Jameson thinks I'm seeing someone. He's jealous. *Stephen is going to eat this shit up.*

It shouldn't make me as happy as it does, but I can't stop smiling as I call the gate and tell them to release the hounds - I mean let the passengers start boarding.

Jameson doesn't come out to greet them with me and I deflate just a little but carry on as usual with my duties, letting my mind wander, forgetting *completely* that I want nothing to do with pilots.

Chapter 18

Jameson

I'm trying every mental trick I can think of to calm myself down. Counting, rational self-talk, yelling at myself ... but nothing is taking the edge off of this burning desire to punch a hole right through the windshield of this plane.

Who the fuck is Tyler? And what the fuck is happening next week? I'm seething and I feel unhinged. I had thought the Jiu Jitsu classes were helping with that, but apparently, I was wrong. The anger and possessiveness are still there, like old friends I haven't caught up with in a while.

I lock myself away in the cock-pit. Too pissed to greet passengers and I need to get this under control before I interact with her again. She's allowed to date whomever she wants, but I had falsely believed that Ricardo was right when he said she hadn't dated since that douche, Luca, and that *she* was telling the truth when she said she wasn't looking for a date.

Thirty minutes later, the phone in the cockpit breaks through my rage. At some point, my co-pilot arrived, though I can't even remember if we said hello.

"Hello?" I bark into the receiver.

I hear the smile in her voice and it infuriates me. "We're ready to roll back. Feel free to give your welcome speech anytime, Captain Hunter."

I'm pretty sure something in me cracks when she says my name. And it's not even my first name. The alpha in me was shaken awake when I saw another man's name on her phone and now that wolf refuses to lie back down. Her use of my formal title has me straining against my pants and I'm thankful for the clipboard in my lap so I have some chance of keeping this to myself. I don't say anything else to her. I just flip the phone to the PA system and start the damn speech. My voice sounds strained even to my own ears and I wonder if she knows it's because of her.

Halfway through the flight, my co-pilot - a first lieutenant about twenty-eight years old - calls the galley and says he needs to use the restroom. I imagine Natalie blocking the aisle and giving him the green light. It irritates me that I'm stuck in here while *Logan* is out there chatting it up with her.

Okay, Hunter, get a grip on yourself. It's not like she's sucking his dick in the bathroom.

Before I can process what I'm doing, my hand flies out for the phone. Natalie picks up before the first ring has gone all the way through.

"You guys sure are needy today," she says instead of *hello.* I run a hand through my hair as I relax a little knowing that if she's talking to me, she isn't on her knees in that small ass bathroom - not that I really think she would be. Too much time passes while I process this and she speaks again. "Captain Hunter? Are you there? I was just kidding. Do you need anything?"

I need so many things, but when I find my voice, I simply ask for coffee.

"Absolutely! Coming right up," she chirps cheerily. I stare at the phone in my hand until Logan comes back.

Trailing behind him is Natalie carrying two cups of coffee on a serving tray. She's wearing the navy pencil skirt, patterned shirt, and jacket they give our flight attendants. Her long hair is up in a ponytail and still falls halfway down her back. Reaching for my coffee, I can't help but look up and see her gorgeous blue eyes as they bore right into mine.

"Merci beaucoup." *Thank you very much*

"Je vous en prie. Rien d'autre?" *You're welcome. Anything else?*

I decide it's now or maybe never. We have a lunch scheduled on Saturday but I need to talk to her sooner. I need to find out more about her. I need to stop obsessing over seeing her. See, Natalie? I need so many things. I inhale and jump off the proverbial cliff.

"Oui. Je veux te parler, mais pas maintenant. Pas ici." *Yes. I want to talk to you, but not now. Not here.*

She looks at me with wide eyes full of concern. I want to pull her in my arms and lick away any trace of confusion, angst, and stress I've caused. The discovery and admittance of this startles me as she starts to speak again, slowly. "Ai-je fait quelque chose de mal?"

She wants to know if she has done anything wrong.

"Non. Pas du tout." *No. Not at all.* "Parle moi quand on atterrit." *Talk to me when we land.*

She doesn't answer but nods with a solemn expression. I didn't mean to worry her. I chose French because I'm certain Logan can't understand it and this is a very sensitive matter. I can't believe I'm opening myself up to this, but it seems I won't rest until I know if I have a shot.

Before I can linger on these thoughts anymore, Logan breaks into my reverie. "Whoa. That chick is hotter than this coffee she just served." My irritation at his tone forces me to cut my eyes at him. He pays no attention to the stone-cold look on my face as he keeps talking. "Is she French? I swear I heard her speaking English earlier."

"She isn't French, but she's fluent in it." *As am I*, I want to add childishly as if to mark my claim on her because we speak the same languages. It would be unnecessary though since he just witnessed our exchange.

"Man, it was hot. Do you know her? Like personally? Think I could get her number?"

I am a hair's breadth away from punching Logan in his mouth as I grind my teeth yet again and choke out my response, "She's seeing someone."

"Damn, too bad. I'd love to hear some French roll out of that mouth while I've got..."

"Logan, if you finish that sentence, I will personally report you to human resources when we get back." I can't believe I'm resorting to threats over her. I'm just thankful I didn't threaten physical harm which is what I'm really thinking about. Reporting him to HR seemed like the least severe action while also letting him know that I am not interested in hearing his dark fantasies involving Natalie's mouth.

"Yes, sir," he replies wisely, correctly understanding that my rank and my size demand his respect. He stays quiet for the remainder of the flight.

Chapter 19

Natalie

My excitement over the fact that Jameson is jealous is short lived as I exit the cockpit after delivering coffee to him and his co-pilot. I'm insanely curious about what he wants to discuss and it's making my hands jittery. This feels like the longest flight of my life but then again, that seems to be every flight these days.

Finally, we touch down in Dallas and I brace myself for bad news or a gentle let-down of some kind. But nothing's even begun. What could there be to let down?

When the final passenger deplanes and the cleaning crew comes aboard, the non-traditional members of this route head to the back of the plane to regroup for the next flight, except for Logan. He deplanes totally, headed somewhere else and our next co-pilot has yet to arrive.

Jameson looks around to see if anyone is watching and then grabs my wrist to pull me into the cockpit. I'm startled at the contact but manage to whisper, "Wait!" He looks at me with a confused expression on his face.

"Weren't we going to talk before the next flight took

off?" he asks, totally unaware of how holing ourselves up in the cockpit will look. Even if no one notices now, they sure-as-shit will when I come walking out of it when the conversation is over.

"Yes, but we need to do it, like, out here." I point around us in the galley. "No one else is around and I can't just come waltzing out of the cockpit after out little 'talk' and then not expect all those flight attendants to jump to conclusions and do some talking of their own. Neither of us needs that, Captain."

I say a silent prayer of thanks that my rationality hasn't totally abandoned me in his presence. He seems to realize I'm right but I get the feeling this isn't how he wanted to have this conversation, whatever this conversation is. He looks at war with himself as he debates over what to say, and I can't help but fidget while I wait. I'm deep into messing with the dials on the oven and the coffee burners and busying myself with refilling the coffee maker and placing mixed nuts into little dishes when he starts talking.

"Natalie, look at me." When Jameson's deep voice says those words, you don't disobey. I still my hands and look at him. "I know this is none of my business, but are you seeing someone?"

Relief floods my entire being. He wants to discuss the text he found on my phone. I could be one of those uppity bitches, claiming "you're right, it is none of your business", but the truth is I want him to know that I am *not* dating anyone, so I don't play games; they just complicate life anyway. "No," I answer simply and shake my head. When his eyes stare into mine, they wear me down and finally I ask sweetly, innocently, "Do you have siblings, Captain Hunter?"

"Call me Jameson," he rasps, his eyes still narrowed at me. "And yes, I do. I have a sister."

I smile to myself claiming a small victory. "Well, I happen to have three siblings. One of whom is coming to visit next week. His name is Tyler." I pause while he stares at me, unblinking. I watch as it slowly makes its way to his consciousness. The name on my screen. The "love you" text.

"Oh," he starts. "Oh, fuck. Natalie, I'm..."

He's probably a lot of things right now. Embarrassed being at the top of the list. We both know how he reacted after seeing Tyler's name and message on my screen. And we both now know what it means, although, I'm not totally sure either of us is willing to admit it to the other just yet.

I could put him out of his misery but I'm more intrigued to see where this goes, so I lace my fingers together behind my back and wait for him to figure it out and continue. I only make it until he runs a hand through his hair, indicating his stress before I break first.

"Look, Jameson, it's no big deal." I try to let him off the hook, but he isn't having it.

"Natalie, it *is* a big deal. I don't do this." He waves a hand back and forth between us. "I don't pursue or date co-workers and it was totally unprofessional for me to act like such an ass over something that is none of my business."

I deflate a little at his words. "Well, he isn't my boyfriend, he's my brother. I'm not seeing anyone right now." As soon as the words leave my mouth, I think about Evan and I feel a sucker punch to my stomach. I don't know what I'm doing here, but if I can prevent another misunderstanding like this from happening, I'm all for it. I cringe and divulge the truth. "Well, except for Evan. I kind of promised Stevie I'd get back out in the dating world and agreed to a date with an old acquaintance." The relief from spilling the truth is welcome even if I'm still a little crushed from Jameson's declaration of the fact that he doesn't date co-workers. Hoping that I haven't read too much into an innocent situation, I look back up at Jameson's face. Everything I need to know I see right then in the way his eyes darken, his nostrils flare, and his jaw clenches. Whether either of us "does this" or not, and whether we say it out loud or not, it's painfully clear that we are undeniably attracted to each other. His next word confirms this unbelievable reality.

"Cancel." His voice is low and rough. More of a growl than actual English.

"What?" I ask in disbelief.

"Cancel your date." He's not joking. Not even a little bit. His eyes are intense as they find mine like he is trying to crawl into my soul.

"I...I can't. We made plans and Evan is an old friend. I can't just cancel on him because you asked me to."

"Let me take you out instead."

Six words and my whole world gets turned upside down. Jameson-fucking-Hunter wants to take me out on a date? This 6'3" mass of testosterone in a captain's uniform, getting looks of unadulterated lust from ninety percent of our passengers, wants to take *me* out on a date.

Maybe pilots aren't so bad...

Chapter 20

Jameson

It's out of my mouth before I even think about it. Finally, I asked her out. I want to take her out instead of some limp-dick named Evan. I kind of vomited the words at her and this conversation spiraled so fast that neither of us have time to process what lines we just crossed. All I know is that I want her. I want to get to know her. I want to know everything about her. The way she looks up at me with those round, inviting eyes has me wanting to rub my thumb across her bottom lip after it's swollen from kissing me. I want to watch those same eyes flutter closed while her hand is in my hair and my tongue strokes her flesh until she loses her mind.

I'm very familiar with the "give an inch, take a mile" analogy. That's exactly what my desire for her has done. I acknowledged its presence mere hours ago and already she has me practically begging. And I don't beg.

"Captain Hunter," she starts.

"Jameson," I correct her again, wanting to reach out and touch her so badly I think I might combust.

"Jameson," she whispers and I about come unglued in

the middle of this goddamn galley for everyone to see. "I can't," she says emphatically. Almost like it pains her. "I told him I would go and I need to keep my word. Evan has sort of, um..."

She pauses to finger her hair while she tries to find words to finish her thought and it drives me crazy. Everything about her drives me crazy. I try to encourage her to continue even though I'm not sure I'll like what she has to say.

"Well, he's kind of had a thing for me for a while and to cancel our date now would be really mean." Okay, so she's loyal. And who can blame Evan for falling for her? I still don't like it, but it's not my choice.

"After, then. Let me take you out after." *Let me show you that whatever he does, I can do it better.* I shove my hands in the pocket of my pants to try and discreetly adjust myself while also trying to prevent myself from touching her.

She laughs at this and it floods my nerve endings. "Okay, truth be told, he's taking me to Oriole. It's one of the nicest steakhouses in all of Chicago and it's not really a meal I can rush. Plus, it feels kind of weird leaving one date and going straight into the next. Like speed-dating or something."

Before I can back up and ask her properly to go out with me a different night - like the very next night - another flight attendant starts walking toward us from the back of the plane.

"You guys ready? The gate just called. They're ready to send them down." I.e. the passengers are getting restless and we need to board this plane now. Natalie takes a fraction of a step backward but it's enough for me to notice.

I blow out a breath. I need to hit a gym somewhere and release this tension.

The flight attendant approaching us is mid-fifties, gray, thinning hair. He has an arrogance about him that I don't like, but maybe I just don't like him because he interrupted Natalie and I.

She nods. "Give them the green light." As he turns his back to us to call the gate, Natalie puts her hand on my forearm, my hands still in my pockets. "Safe flight, Captain." I swear I see her pupils dilate and her chest rise and fall more rapidly. I can feel the heat of her hand through my jacket sleeve and suddenly I'm dying to get it off as if it just personally assaulted me by preventing her from being able to touch my skin.

Her eyes follow my other hand as I loosen my tie and undo the top button on my shirt, everything feeling too tight. Her tongue makes a slow sweep over her bottom lip before she pulls it between her teeth while she eyes my own mouth. It's the sexiest interaction I've ever had with a woman and she isn't even touching me anymore. Nor I, her.

The man hangs up the phone, the sound breaking our spell. I nod at Natalie and turn to head into the cockpit before I get caught looking disheveled with a very noticeable erection.

Back in Chicago, I can't get off this plane fast enough. I rush through the post-flight log and fill in all the boxes. At least I hope I filled in all the boxes. It feels like forever before one of the flight attendants knocks on the door to let us know all the passengers are off. I move extra slowly so I don't look like an overeager toddler on Christmas morning as I open the door. When I come out of the cockpit, Natalie looks up at me, a shy smile on her beautiful face.

She seems to be hanging back, taking her time to gather her things. Of course, in my mind, she was stalling to wait on me.

John, the return flight co-pilot nods at us once, shakes my hand, and deplanes, leaving Natalie and I alone with one other flight attendant who is cleaning leftover trash out of the seats.

"I need to go help with that," Natalie says as she tilts her head in the direction of the woman cleaning the seats.

I nod. I switch to French when I tell her that I would like to walk out with her. The employee lot isn't dangerous, but this is Chicago and it's already dark out. "Je vais attendre près du tableau des arrives pour ne pas avoir l'air visible." *I'll wait by the arrivals board so I don't look conspicuous.*

She flashes me a full smile this time. "Jameson, you stand out no matter where you are."

I've never been more appreciative of my genes than I am right in this moment. I return her smile and exit the plane.

Chapter 21

Natalie

The employee bus is old and I swear they never run the heat in this damn thing. Thankfully, it doesn't smell as bad as the blue line but I wish they would give us some kind of upgrade. It isn't terribly crowded because it's late, but there are enough other passengers to prevent Jameson and I from talking like we want. We could speak in a different language, but that would be terribly conspicuous here because the whole bus is silent. We're all tired. I take the seat across from Jameson. It's impossible to miss the eyes that keep straying to him from the other passengers. I guess they aren't too tired to ogle him.

I slip my heels off and pull my flats out of my bag. My feet are tired and I don't like to ride the train in heels in case I need to run. It's unlikely, but I like to be prepared.

Jameson leans forward and whispers, "Don't like driving in heels?"

"Oh, I don't drive. I live right off the Blue Line. I take the employee bus to the train stop right next to the employee lot."

His eyes grow dark as he processes this information. His

next whisper comes out more urgently. "Natalie, you ride the train at night? By yourself? And then *walk* to your apartment?"

I shrug a shoulder. "Of course. I live downtown. It doesn't make sense for me to own a car in this city. I don't even know where I would keep it."

His jaw is clenched and he looks ready to throw down. Honestly, the masculinity is pouring off of him and I'm pretty sure he isn't even aware. It awakens a desire to do very bad things to him right on this god-forsaken bus. But why is he pissed that I ride the train?

"Let me drive you home."

"What?" I huff out a laugh as I say it, stalling so I can process.

"You heard me," he grits out.

"There really is no need. If you're worried about my safety, that's kind of you, but I've been riding the Blue Line ever since I moved to Chicago and I've never had an issue." I'm not sure why I'm arguing with him. Spending extra time with him actually sounds quite nice, but the longer I'm in his vicinity the faster I feel myself falling. I have warning bells going off in my head: *Look what happened with you and Luca. Don't repeat the same mistakes.* Of course, this is quickly followed by Stevie's words from earlier in the week: *He's not Luca, Nat.*

He may not be Luca, but I'm still me. I know I fall fast and usually without giving much thought as to what in the hell I'm doing.

It's all so confusing. There was a reason I vowed to never get involved with a pilot again but being near Jameson, seeing his face, feeling his power and confidence being driven into my very skin, it's hard to keep him at arms' length.

101

"Natalie." Again with that demanding tone. I raise my eyes to meet his stare. "That was before you met me. Before we were on this bus together and before you knew that I have to drive downtown to get to my condo anyway. Let me drive you home."

Oh, what the hell, who am I to argue? He wants me to skip the stinky Blue Line one night? "Okay, sure," I hear myself say. Traitorous mouth.

His shoulders drop two inches when he relaxes once I agree to his request. Well, *demand*, actually. He leans back in his seat and takes his tie off. Every eye on the bus snaps to him as he does it. It's like watching real life porn despite the fact that he's still fully dressed. His dark hair is no longer neat and orderly but looks like he's been running his hands through it, which I'm sure he has. He has slightly more than a five o'clock shadow, giving him a dangerous look.

I squeeze my thighs together and shift uncomfortably in my seat. Jameson leans his head back against the wall of the bus and closes his eyes. I briefly wonder if he's regretting making the offer, considering he doesn't "pursue" or "date" co-workers.

When we get to the first stop, he stands and nods to me. I guess this is us. I grab my bag and follow him off the bus, aware of the stares that follow. This lot is for the pilots only and I'm clearly in a flight attendant's uniform. It shouldn't bother me that people will make conclusions, but it does. Luca and I were pretty open about our relationship and most of those who fly for our airline and are based here, knew about us. Stephen was right, Jameson is so *not* Luca, and I don't want people thinking I'm just making the rounds.

Another pilot gets off the bus as well. He doesn't say anything, but I can feel his eyes on me as he watches me follow Jameson. I can't shake the feeling that he's going to watch Jameson and I to see if we get in the same car. Sometimes men gossip worse than women.

The brisk night air sends a shiver through me and I tighten my grip on my bag. It doesn't escape Jameson's attention. He immediately tries to shrug out of his jacket but I stop him with a slight shake of my head and throw a small nod behind us at the pilot who seems to have parked in the same row as Jameson. Until we know what this is, I'm not ready for an excessive amount of rumors or attention.

Jameson stops and unlocks an old Toyota Land Cruiser. I don't know a lot about cars but I know this one probably wasn't cheap, despite its age. It doesn't have a key fob so he manually unlocks my door and holds it open for me.

Sliding my bag onto the floorboard, I'm hit with the scent of his space hard and fast. A small groan escapes my lips. "Oh my God, it smells so good in here. This definitely beats the Blue Line."

I hear his low chuckle as he climbs into the driver's seat. "Thank God for that. I don't think I could drive every day if my car smelled like stale vomit and B.O."

I barely hear him as I sink down into the worn leather of the front seat, not even caring that he just dissed my most used form of transportation. Tucked away in this dark car, with the rich scent of man - leather, cedar, and the faint smell of Hoppes 9 gun oil - my lady parts are in overdrive. He turns up the heat and hands me his phone.

"Put in your address," he pauses, his grip still on his phone even as I try to take it, "unless you want to grab a beer before I drop you off?"

I try to gather my thoughts, figure out if I think this is a good idea or not, and I glance down to give my brain a break from Jameson's gorgeous features that look even more dangerous in the glow of the dashboard lights. That's when I notice his car has a manual transmission. Good with his hands - check. Likes control - also check. I hear myself say "Yeah, okay," and I'm glad he can't see the blush on my cheeks in the dark. My armpits are sweating my nerves right on out and I fear I may sully his interior with my own scent.

Chapter 22

Jameson

I can't believe she's in my car. I also can't believe she rides the train at all hours of the night after a flight and then walks to her apartment alone. I'm never going to sleep again.

I know it's late and I shouldn't have asked, but the opportunity was too good to pass up. One beer and then I promise myself I'll take her home. I work tomorrow but I don't have to be at the gate until 9:30 so it shouldn't be a big deal. It isn't like I was going to sleep much anyway after this car ride. If I don't find release soon, I'm going to ruin these pants.

Her next question catches me off guard. "Could we swing by my place so I can change really fast? Even without the ascot and thin jacket, I still look like a flight attendant and these panty-hose are starting to get really uncom-fortable."

Images of her sliding her stockings down her legs and slipping one toned leg out at a time is immediately flashing in my mind. I must take too long to answer because she starts speaking again. "If it's too much trouble, we don't have to stop though."

I look at the directions on the GPS screen to discover that we only live about two miles from each other. Of course, in Chicago, two miles could be a twenty minute drive, but her apartment doesn't take us that far out of the way and at this point, I'd pretty much give her anything she asked, so I pull up to her apartment building and she hops out.

"I'll be really quick." She flashes me an excited smile and I relax a little.

I check my texts and emails while she's upstairs changing and I'm shocked when less than five minutes later she's climbing back into my SUV, completely stealing my breath.

Jeans and a maroon long-sleeved t-shirt with an emerald green coat. She looks wonderfully down to earth and also a little like a Christmas gift I'd like to unwrap. Suddenly, I don't care how late it is or how long we stay out. I'll watch the sunrise with her if she wants.

Realizing that I'm still in my pilot's uniform, I ask the same favor of her. "Mind if I change as well? The place I'd like to take you is within walking distance of my condo, so it isn't out of the way." She nods her agreement.

I want to take her to Hook and Ladder, a local watering hole I've discovered in the short time I've been here. She sits up a little straighter and stares out the window as we cross the north branch of the Chicago River, signaling that I'm back in my neck of the woods.

"Wow, east of the river, huh?" She smirks. She thinks I'm rich. I don't do so bad. I get paid well and I work a lot but I don't live in a $3,000,000 condo like the look on her face says she thinks I do.

When I pull into the garage under my building she whistles. "Damn, Captain Hunter, nice place," she says in awe. Parking garages - especially heated ones - are coveted here. I pay almost as much for my parking spot as I did for the condo itself but no way was I leaving my Land Cruiser unprotected from the elements and from thieves. It's the only remaining piece I have of my dad, wonderful man that he was, and I refuse to part with it, or subject it to staying outside in the harsh Chicago winters.

Knowing I'll most likely take more than five minutes, I turn to Natalie as I shut off the ignition. "Care to come up?"

Her eyes light up like she just won the lottery. It stirs something in me to see her so seemingly carefree and happy. "Yes, please. I've always wanted to see how the upper-crust live."

I watch while she grabs her purse and slides out of the SUV. I shake my head in disbelief that she's actually here. That I am actually about to do this.

Swiping my key card to let us into the elevator, I push the button for my floor as she stands with her back to the elevator wall with a shy, thin smile, and downcast eyes.

"What are you thinking?" I ask her. I don't want to make her uncomfortable.

For a second, I think she isn't going to answer me until she looks up and admits, "I was thinking about the last time we were in an elevator together." God help us. I remember every detail - the scent of chlorine on her skin. The way her hair was brushed back off of her face. The way she gripped her towel with white knuckles like I was going to magically make it disappear. The way her suit straps gently dug into her shoulders.

I hear her giggle softly, prompting me to ask, "What's so funny?"

"I was going to ask what *you* are thinking about but I'm not sure I have to anymore." I see her eyes slip down to my hips. Wouldn't you know it. Memory lane gave me another damn erection.

Fuck.

"I...uh...sorry about that," I say with only half the sincerity that I should. I'm not really that sorry. Let her see what she does to me.

She lifts a shoulder nonchalantly. "No need to be sorry." She never breaks eye contact while she worries her bottom lip between her teeth again, hesitating like she wants to say something else but isn't sure she should.

Once we exit the elevator, I stop in front of her before the moment passes. Knowing we both feel the heat from our proximity, I ask her, "What else were you going to say?"

"I'm glad it isn't just me."

Chapter 23

Natalie

Something about Jameson makes me remember how to be flirty. Even more shocking is the fact that he makes me *want* to be flirty. I have to admit, I'm a little surprised when he doesn't hide his current condition. I'm not a prude by any means, but even for all his good looks and playboy image, Luca didn't have a lot of self-confidence which rubbed off on me more than I realized while we were together. Around Jameson, I feel my own confidence start to rise. It's nice seeing Jameson just accept the fact that he's hotter than the sun. In fact, I'd be lying if I said it wasn't turning me on.

Our height difference is even more noticeable now that I'm in flats. I'm taking in everything I can at eye level when he says, "The hallway is nice, but the apartment is better." He reaches for my hand just as I'm starting to think I'd follow him anywhere.

Holding the door open for me, I feel him studying me as I survey his living room.

"When did you move in?" I ask, taking in his beautiful, clean, bare-walled condo.

"About two months ago." Hard to believe that much time has passed already. "Make yourself comfortable, I'm just going to get out of this suit and I'll be right back." He heads down a hallway off the kitchen. It isn't a penthouse, I'm pretty sure - because we aren't on the top floor - but it's a very comfortable size. The living room has huge windows overlooking Lincoln Park. I'm sure this wasn't cheap, and he's not that old. I draw the conclusion that he's good with money and therefore gets a check in the "stability" column as well.

God, Nat. Slow down. You haven't even had a drink with the man. You don't even know what the hell you're doing here yet; let's not go picking out baby names. I mentally reprimand myself because I feel like it's the appropriate thing to do, but also, I've already decided on Gabriella if we have a girl and Micah if it's a boy.

Kidding! I'm just kidding.

I like Nicholas better.

I sit down on the sofa - one of the few pieces of furniture in the living room - and am struck by a yawn as the day catches up with me like a solid punch to the throat.

Unfortunately for me, Jameson comes around the corner at that exact moment. "I'm sorry, this morning feels like it was six years ago," I try to explain. I really don't want him to think I'm rude - or bored.

A wicked grin spreads lazily across his perfect features. "How about we open a bottle of wine and just hang out here? Personally, I could do without the crowds, loud music, and smoke from a thousand cherry flavored vape pens."

I'm truly delighted with the change of plans and I sink back into the couch. "Sounds like heaven."

The kitchen is visible from the living room, just over the bar, and I can see the look of concentration on his face as he tries to decide which bottle to choose from the rack next to the fridge so I offer some helpful advice.

"Jameson?"

"Yeah?" His voice is naturally low and a little gravelly and I feel it much lower than my stomach.

"I usually drink the $3 wine from Trader Joe's so whatever you pull out of that rack is going to blow my mind."

"I was looking for the one with highest alcohol content." He lets out a laugh but I'm not sure he's joking.

I decide to play along because I'm tired, and he's hot, and I'd bet any amount of money his bed is soft as shit. Not that I'll be staying there of course.

Of course.

"And why do we need the one with the highest alcohol content?" I ask, tucking a leg under me on the couch and pulling the sleeves of my shirt down over the backs of my hands. It's a comfort thing.

I hear the cork pop as he starts to pour and answers, "Because I'd like to get to know you and that means you probably get to ask me a few questions of your own as well, which means I probably need to have a buzz." I start to laugh but only an exhale escapes before I see the look on his face. He's as serious as a heart attack. It gives me pause and makes me wonder what he's scared to reveal.

Three things in life totally erase my filter: 1. Alcohol 2. Sleep deprivation 3. Hot guys. Looks like I'm about to get royally fucked by the trifecta of filter removals tonight.

When he comes into the living room, I get a chance to see the rest of him and Lord help me. I'd better sip slowly and tread carefully. He's in another pair of jeans that hug his muscular thighs and a plain white t-shirt with a green plaid button-down over top. The button down is open so I can very clearly see how the t-shirt clings to the contours of his chest. *Fuck me, I didn't even know they made men that look like this.* His sleeves are pushed up to his elbows, showing off his forearms, and his hair - which is longer on the top than the sides - is behaving itself in that it-looks-like-I-just-had-sex-but-my-hair-always-looks-like-this   kind   of way that *really* hot guys are blessed with.

My eyes travel back to the inside of his left forearm where a striking tattoo of a compass rose is placed. He sees me eyeing it. "It's gorgeous, isn't it?" he asks and the awe in his voice is unmistakable.

"It is. I know it's a fairly popular design, but I've never seen one that looks quite like that. Did you design it?" The needles that point north, south, east, and west are designed to look like the propellers on a plane. It's very well done.

"My sister actually did this for me." He relaxes as he takes his first sip of wine sitting on the couch next to me, stretching his long legs out and propping them on the ottoman in front of us.

"She's extremely talented." We start to fall into a natural conversation. I tuck my other leg up under me to join the first, and turn to face him fully now. I clutch my wine glass tightly in my hand, careful not to spill on his light grey microfiber couch. "Are you two close?"

He proceeds to tell me they are. It was both really fun and really lonely growing up in a military family. Making friends easily but losing them quickly as well when it was time to move on, so he and his sister always stuck together.

From there we move onto my own siblings. I tell him about Tyler's upcoming visit. I also tell him about Melissa and how she took that bullshit job in Alaska. How close Ty and I are and how he flies out of Miami. I talk a little about my sister and my other brother - how we're all in the aviation field and about our dad, who is still a commercial pilot for a different carrier.

I have no idea what time it is but I'm just finishing my second glass of wine when Jameson turns to face me. Well, his head turns, his body sits up with his knees spread wide and his forearms propped on his knees while he asks me his next question. "So, do you normally do this kind of thing?"

I can do absolutely nothing about the giggle that escapes my throat. "Um, drink with co-workers? Sure. Stevie and I - -"

"I meant go home with the pilots," he corrects.

"Oh, that. No. No, I don't normally do that. In fact," now I laugh harshly, "I swore I'd never do this again, actually." The bitterness in my voice is directed at myself, not Jameson, but he may not realize that so I clarify by launching into the story of Luca and I.

Fifteen minutes later, I make it to the ending. "To make matters worse, as if getting dumped prior to the first flight of the day wasn't bad enough, after my *last* flight that *same* day, I passed Luca's car in the parking deck back at O'Hare and noticed it was rocking from side to side. I didn't even have to get that close to see through the window that Luca was receiving what appeared to be a truly sensational blow job from another flight attendant.

"Don't get me wrong, I'm grateful he broke up with me first, if that's even what actually happened, but seriously? Nine hours later and his dick was already down someone else's throat? That's fucked up." I sigh, remembering the hurt I felt. "Luca's playboy attitude was a façade for shitty self-esteem that I'm sure would have been greatly boosted by having attained another willing partner so fast." I take another gulp of my wine from a glass that magically refilled itself. I don't really miss Luca, especially not while I'm in

Jameson's presence, but some wounds just cut really deeply, and this was one of them. I snort a laugh as I continue. "I remember I paused and contemplated breaking his windows or kicking out his taillights for longer than was probably healthy, but ultimately decided he wasn't worth the trouble."

And just like that, I spill my guts to the next pilot who will potentially break my heart.

Chapter 24

Jameson

It's hard to stay neutral as I listen to her story. With every word she speaks, I pray that I never run into Luca. He sounds like a sad excuse for a man but unfortunately a pretty face hides a lot. The break up and parking-deck blowjob are just the straw that broke the camel's back, but even as she tells the story I'm not sure she's aware of all the red flags. He always kept his phone hidden from her but got upset if she was on her phone around him. He would get mad when she signed on for extra flights as stand-by on his days off.

The most shocking part, however, comes at the end of her third glass of wine. Her cheeks are flushed and she's on a roll. I've never known someone who can pull off adorably cute and sexy-as-hell in the same thirty second span. She pauses her story and cocks her head to the side with a puzzled look on her face.

"What is it?" I ask.

"You know...for all his cockiness and arrogance, he never even gave me a single orgasm," she says, completely serious.

I choke on my wine so hard I have to set my glass down while I cough the liquid out of my windpipe.

Natalie sits up and untucks her legs, concern on her face. "Ohmygod, I shouldn't have said that. I don't know why I said that. I'm so sorry. Are you okay?" She moves right next to me to lightly pat me on the back. It's not hard enough to actually help anything, but she's touching me, so I'm not complaining.

When I can finally inhale without my lungs burning, I clear my throat and nod my head. She's totally unaware of how stunning she is. I want to take her face in my hands and kiss her until she can't remember her name, but she needs to be sober for that.

"Okay, well, that's more than enough about me..." She pauses and, somehow, I know where her next train of thought is going even before she does. "Why'd you switch airlines?"

Yeah, I knew this was coming. Normally, I hold my cards a little closer to my chest but I seem incapable of that around Natalie. Then again, *normally*, I wouldn't have a female co-worker tipsy on my couch at God-knows-what-time-it-is in the morning. So, it looks like "normal" has flown out the window.

I rehash the story of Vanessa for what is hopefully the last time. Natalie's eyes go wide when I tell her I lost the harassment case and ultimately my job.

"That's such *bullshit!*" she says, her anger on my behalf doing dangerous things to my already overactive libido. She stands and starts pacing in the living room releasing her outrage. "What the fuck, Jameson? You don't deserve that! You gave them *ten* years! Besides, don't they *know* you? You'd never do that! Hell, I've only known you for like six weeks and even *I* know that!"

I believe her. I believe that she does know me. I've never given much thought to true love and soul mates and shit, but maybe that was just because I hadn't found mine yet. I'm pretty sure that dormant spark was brought to life the day I heard her confession in French.

I can tell she needs to vent so I sit back and let her keep going. The combination of the wine and her reaction is causing my skin to heat so I take off my plaid shirt, lace my fingers and put my hands behind my head, enjoying her outburst.

"Who even is this *Vanessa*? That's such a slutty name, too. She should never have been trusted!"

Finally, she seems to calm down a little and she stops pacing. When she brings her attention back me, her face turns the color of her shirt. "Fuuuuck," she whispers.

I raise my eyebrows in question.

"You're *really* hot," she says as if she's having an epiphany. I feel my mouth quirk up into a smile.

"So you've mentioned."

She walks back over to the ottoman where my feet were earlier and sits down, biting her lower lip again. I can tell she's waging war with herself. I'm drawn in and I want to know what she's thinking. So I ask.

"What's going on in that beautiful head of yours?" At my confession of her own beauty, she stills. My words drawing the truth from her lips.

"I want to kiss you." She pauses and narrows her eyes like she is waiting for my response. I need to tread carefully here. She mistakes my hesitation as a lack of desire and keeps talking. I'm not sure if she's trying to justify her desire to me or herself. "It goes against everything I said I wouldn't do and you wouldn't do, which means it's a terrible idea.

But then I thought maybe you like terrible ideas?" She shrugs only her right shoulder.

"I like them more when they come from you," I concede. I reach my hand up to finally touch her skin and stroke the side of her face. She unashamedly leans into my touch and closes her eyes, a small moan escaping her lips. I want her more than I've wanted anything in my life, save maybe my wings, but right now it's a close call.

She covers my hand with her own and starts dragging it down her neck. I can feel my own body heat activating like a force field around us.

"Natalie."

"Mmm?" she hums but doesn't open her eyes or stop her movements.

"Natalie, look at me." I try to keep my voice soft, despite the painful urgency she's creating in me. I still my hand at the base of her throat even though I can tell she's trying to move it lower.

When she opens her eyes, they aren't glassy. I know she isn't drunk, she's had three glasses, but it's been over the course of a few hours. However, her eyes aren't clear either, taking just a second too long to focus on mine. Although I know her a little better after tonight, I don't yet know her well enough to be able to reconcile the quiet, kind, almost-shy girl I know at work, with this sexual, open, honest woman in front of me. If the wine has anything to do with the change, that leaves room for her to regret this in the light of day and I don't want to be someone's regret. Ever. Especially hers.

"What's wrong?" she asks. "Please don't tell me I misread this," she pleads and my reservations go out the window as I draw her onto my lap.

"You definitely did not misread this." I swallow hard

and I place my hands on her thighs as she straddles my lap, willing her to stay still. "We're both about to cross a line we drew for a reason. If we decide to do this, we need to be sober." She starts to argue and I hold up my hand. "We've been drinking for three hours and we're both exhausted. I don't do one-night-stands. I'm not interested in friends-with-benefits. And I don't want to fuck this up by sharing a hormone-driven, alcohol induced kiss at one o'clock in the morning and then parting ways."

Talk about some of the hardest shit I've ever said. This, right here, is all I've thought about since laying eyes on her and now that she's here, I'm telling her no.

She looks briefly crestfallen and then rallies, her eyes darkening with reinforced desire. *Oh, shit.*

"And here I thought you were the kind to take what you wanted, Captain Hunter." She flexes her hips farther onto my lap while she keeps me in place with her eyes. So much for the innocent girl I thought she was...but I'm pretty sure I just fell for this part of her as well.

She's making me lose the ability to think coherently. My fingers dig into her thighs, which only encourages her to keep sliding back forth, rolling her hips across my erection. What kind of an asshole would I be if I didn't let her finish? It's not like I'm going to throw her off. I tried to stop this before it started but even I know it's hopeless now. Her moans come faster and she fists my hair with one hand and grips the back of my couch with her other one for leverage as she rides my lap. I can tell the seam of her jeans and the zipper from mine are hitting her right where she needs it. My heart rate is a thousand beats per minute watching her get herself off. I keep my hands firmly on her thighs, letting her drive this train, but after thirty seconds, she uses her hands to move mine to her ass.

Okay then.

I use my hands to push and pull her back and forth across my lap, helping to increase her friction and matching her speed. Her eyes are closed and her lips are parted and honestly, I'm about to come just from watching her. I know she can feel my arousal pushing up against her and she's bearing down as hard as she can.

It only takes a couple of minutes before several short whimpers tear through her and her grip in my hair tightens.

When she finishes, she leans forward and buries her face in the crook of my neck and I'm not sure if she's passed out or hiding from me.

Chapter 25

Natalie

Nothing to sober you completely up like an earth-shattering orgasm from dry-humping someone you've never even kissed.

Jameson pushes me away from him just enough so that he can see my face. I can't meet his gaze so he uses his left hand to gently grab my chin and forces me to look at him.

"You're so fucking beautiful and that was so fucking hot. Don't ever hide from me. There's no need to be embarrassed." I guess my emotions are clearly written on my face.

I'm trying to process a thousand things at once. I should probably get off his lap but I can't seem to move. His hands are at my waist now, holding me in place. I swallow hard realizing that despite what just happened, I'm not even remotely sated. This man is under my skin. He's in my head, and he's at my fingertips.

"You're really good at that," I say shyly.

"That was all you, baby." His voice has a rasp to it and his jaw is set. I wince when I realize his erection is probably getting painful and I immediately want to relieve his discomfort. I shift back onto his knees so I can access the button on his jeans. He stops me before I get there. I think of Vanessa and cringe.

"Shit, Jameson, I'm sorry. I didn't mean..."

Correctly guessing my thoughts - yet again - he says, "Natalie, it's not the same at all. Your advances are wanted. Hers weren't. I'm still not sure this is a great idea, but I can't seem to help myself when you're around."

"Looks like we have the same problem, then. Please don't think this is my normal m.o." I slide gently off his lap and sit next to him. He pulls my legs across his lap and the contact feels oh so good. I feel the panic rising in my voice as I try to explain myself. Jameson is openly smirking at me.

"What?"

"At least I can get you off," he says arrogantly, remembering the information I shared earlier.

I'm loving the familiarity and ease of conversation that has erupted between us tonight. I guess playing cowgirl on a man's lap will do that. I smile and tease back. "If I'm not mistaken, you said that was all me. So technically, the jury is still out on whether you can or not."

Lies. Pure lies. Every word. We both know he can. Easily and repeatedly.

"Challenge accepted."

Oh boy. I glance at the clock, needing a quick respite from his intensity and the butterflies that are beginning to swarm down low again. This man will be my undoing.

"Oh shit! Jameson, it's one-thirty!"

"What time do you have to work tomorrow?" he asks calmly.

"Stevie and I are flying with Ricardo down to Panama City at eleven and then I go to Salt Lake City from there before getting back home tomorrow night around ten. You?"

"I have a flight at nine-thirty but it's no big deal. I'm

headed to San Diego, someone else got the bid for the route to Dallas tomorrow. It makes me feel a little better knowing you won't be on it without me. That's crazy and selfish, isn't it?" He doesn't look apologetic. He just seems to be making an observation.

"As it turns out, I'm kind of into crazy and selfish." I smile knowing it was completely crazy and selfish to ride one out and leave him hanging. "When we have more time, I want to hear about your thoughts for the international route."

"That's what Saturday's for." Once he says it, it's like someone closes the shutters. Saturday. My date with Evan. Shit.

"Jameson, I don't know what this is yet," I gesture back and forth between us, "but I would never lead you on. I'm going to meet Evan, because I said I would, but I will also make it clear that it just won't work out between he and I. I know how much Luca hurt me and I don't ever want to do that to someone else. I feel like shit for even getting Evan's hopes up, but I've known him a while and never once has he made me feel like...this."

"And how exactly do you feel?" He is massaging the arches of my right foot while he asks. As I think about my answer, he moves up my calf.

"Like if you don't either stop right now, or keep going until we're both spent and panting, I might explode into a thousand tiny balls of fire."

"I'm glad it isn't just me." He winks as he quotes me from the hallway when we got off the elevator. His removes his hands and I have to stop myself from crying out. He must see the look of disappointment on my face. "As we just discovered, it's now after one a.m. I'll take you home and we can pick up where we left off later."

I begrudgingly gather my purse and jacket and follow him to the door and back to the elevator.

It takes us six minutes to get between our places at this hour. When he pulls up outside my building, he raises and eyebrow and says, "I want to walk you in, but I'm fairly confident we both know how that would end."

Heat floods my core at the prospect but I nod my head in agreement. "Do you think I'm sober enough to kiss yet?" I ask because I can't help myself. I feel like a cat in heat doing everything I can to get him to touch me again.

He drapes an arm around the back of my seat and leans in close to whisper, "Natalie, if my lips touch anything on you tonight, I'm locking us both in your apartment and we aren't coming out until I've done everything I've imagined doing to you...and it's an extensive list." My palms start sweating as my mind races to wonder what is on the list. Suddenly his list consumes me. "Now, go inside before my last, barely-there thread of self-control snaps."

I'm pushing him. I know I am. But I can't walk away. My whole life, I have built these incredible people - pilots - up in my mind. Sexy, powerful, confident, controlling, masculine...but Luca fell short. It made my promise to myself easy to keep because if Luca wasn't those things, there was no hope for anyone else.

Until now.

"What happens when it snaps?" I whisper in challenge only an inch from his face.

"Natalie." Jameson actually snarls this time, his fingers digging into the back of my seat in warning.

I study his gorgeous face for another beat. Finally, reluctantly, I nod and smile. "Bonne nuit, Jameson. On se voit Samedi." *Goodnight, Jameson. See you Saturday.*

"Goodnight, Natalie."

On Saturday, Stevie comes down to my apartment so we can walk over to Gino's together. The part of Chicago we live in is pretty safe, but Stevie always likes when I walk with him anyway, but don't misunderstand, it's *not* so that he can defend me from an attacker. Stephen's best defense mechanism is tossing out a limp wrist and hoping to distract with his amazing cuticles. And no, that's not a comment about how gay he is, it's a comment about how gigantic of a pussy he is. He's hoping *I'll* defend *him*.

"Are you excited about your date tonight?" Stephen asks, fishing for excessive excitement that I just don't have. I haven't had a chance to fill him in on my evening with Jameson.

"Not really," I admit, totally disappointing him.

"That's because your woman parts are holding out for the one and only Captain Hunter." Stephen is striding confidently down the road swinging his arms with a smile on his face. Like he doesn't have a care in the world and also like he knows he's totally right. He is, of course, he just doesn't know it. I decide to dish a few details. I could use some perspective here.

"So, I was at Jameson's until one-thirty yesterday morning." I throw it out there like we are discussing groceries.

Stephen grabs my arm and yanks me to a halt. "Excusez-moi?" he asks in an overly dramatic tone. Okay, maybe the tone is warranted. That's a pretty big bomb to drop. When I just smile at him, he launches into full-on drama queen talking about how could I keep this from him and why didn't I call to tell him yesterday and what a bitch I am. He then switches gears and wants to know if we had sex, details about his dick - that I don't have - and what he actually looks like under his uniform. Oh, and he's shrieking all of this on the sidewalk in French while waving his arms around like a maniac. Stevie only speaks French when he is flustered.

I'm laughing so hard I have stitches in my sides by the time he's done and he looks totally put out as he waits on my answers.

When I make it through the story, he asks what I'm going to do about Evan.

"I'm going to meet him for dinner, like I said I would."

"Oh, you bad, bad girl, you." He playfully swats me on the shoulder and then loops his arm through mine.

I roll my eyes. "It's not like that, you slut. I feel bad because *I* called *him* and asked for the date...thanks to *you*. Who the fuck would have thought that Jameson Hunter would show up and be so damn delicious...and be into *me*?"

Stephen responds with a look that says he thinks I'm really dense. "We all knew he would be into you, honey. Everyone knew but you."

"*Anyway,*" I continue, rolling my eyes, "I'm going to go out on that date and gently let Evan down and tell him that there's just nothing there, romantically, for me. But at least I'll be able to say I gave it a shot."

"Sounds like a plan, girlfriend, now let's get back to the part where you were grinding on his lap."

I laugh. "I thought for sure that's the part you would want to skip over."

"Well, I don't want you grinding on *my* lap, but if you're chasing that O on someone *else's* lap, I'm here for it.

Besides, it gives me good Jameson visuals for the fantasies I'm going to be having during this lunch."

God, I love Stevie.

When we get to Gino's, Sherri and Jameson already have a table.

"It's about time you two got here. I was getting tired of feeling like everyone thinks I'm his mother sitting here with him," Sherri says to Stephen and I.

Stephen pats Sherri's hand. "Sher, you don't look any *less* old or matronly just because we're here."

We all crack up. "Be careful Stevie, or I'll send Nat after your next boyfriend," Sherri retaliates.

Stephen feigns horror as he puts a hand over his heart. "You *wouldn't.*"

Chapter 26

Jameson

I'm pretty sure she's kidding, but as far as I know, Sherri doesn't know I've laid a claim on Natalie. Her comment makes my teeth hurt. I'm already on edge because of Natalie's stupid date tonight. In this case, I wish her heart were a little less golden than it is. I don't care if that guy's feelings get hurt. Fuck his feelings.

I hear Natalie clear her throat. She's staring at me as she speaks and I'm sure she can feel my tension at the comment of her and another guy. "Okay guys, that's enough," she says which makes me want to squeeze her hand under the table. Since we didn't have a chance to decide what this is yet, let alone whether or not we are telling other people about it, I keep my hands to myself.

We peruse the menu and place an order. This meeting was really just a way to get to know Natalie better. My decision to bid for permanence on Dave's route isn't changing whether or not they do it with me, but it would be nice to know.

As I hear them tease each other and laugh, it's a bold reminder of the fact that I'm still new to Chicago and don't have many friends. It's nice to be out with other people. Especially ones that I have something in common with, and if they *do* sign on for this route with me, I think I'd enjoy it very much.

"So, I asked you guys here because I'm planning to bid on Dave's international route. It goes live pretty soon and I'd like to be the primary captain for the route. Ideally, I'd love if you guys were able to join as the home base crew for it as well."

Stephen is practically drooling on the table. Sherri is listening attentively but even she looks a little star struck while I speak, and I'd give my next paycheck to know what Natalie is grinning about right now. Stephen recovers first. "Do you know if they're even running a regular home base crew for that flight since it's so new?"

"There's always a spot for requested crew. They give us more say on the international routes since the flights are longer as are the layovers and the potential to get stuck somewhere is a little higher. I imagine you three would be given priority since you ran his regular domestic route with him."

"Well, I'm in," Stephen says. "Just tell me where to sign."

I nod my appreciation. If he's on board, then it's more likely Natalie will do it as well.

Sherri says, "I'd love to. I need to discuss it with my husband first because that will take me away for a lot of overnights. I'm just not sure how he'll feel about that."

"Sure, I understand." Although, I would feel badly about breaking up the trio of perfection.

Natalie looks at me like she is working through something. "¿Es una buena idea firmar para eso antes de ver cómo va a ire so entre nosotros?" *Is it a good idea to sign on for that before we see how this thing between us is going to go?*

"Oh, she's using Spanish. Must be something spicy she doesn't want us to know," Stephen says to Sherri, planting his elbows on the table and his chin on his laced fingers. I give them a brief laugh before answering her.

"Si ese orgasmo fue una indicación, creo que las cosas van a ir bien." *If that orgasm was any indication, I think things are going to go well.*

Natalie's cheeks flame just as Stephen whispers to the table, "I'm not fluent, but the word for orgasm in Spanish is close to the French word, and is pretty easy to pick out." He sends a wink at me and Natalie erupts in laughter and covers her mouth. Then Stephen turns to her directly when she hesitates to answer my question about the route, a serious expression on his pretty features. "Come on, Nat. Take a chance."

I have the distinct impression that he's talking about me and not the international route. I've said it before, but I really like Stephen.

Once Natalie agrees to sign on, we all settle back and relax. The only unknown is Sherri, but I feel confident the other two will help her decide. For now, we all just enjoy lunch together. Stephen and I share stories of our experiences living in Europe. He makes me miss it and I realize I'm looking forward to taking this route. It'll be a lot easier to get over there if I take on an outbound flight to London, schedule a three-day layover on purpose and then pick up the return flight. Lunch passes in enjoyable conversation after that and all too soon, Natalie says, "Well guys, I need to get going."

"Nat, it's two. Where do you need to be?" Stephen asks. I could literally kiss him because I was wondering the same thing. "I just have a couple of errands I need to run before tonight." She avoids my gaze as she says this and I feel my jaw start to clench again.

Her departure makes everyone else start to pack up as well so I pick up the tab and head to pay. My lunch companions are kind enough to object but allow me to do it anyway.

We say our goodbyes and before I can prevent it from slipping out of my mouth, I ask Natalie, "Llámame después de tu cita." *Call me after your date.* A command, not a request.

She flashes me a devious look over her shoulder on her way out the door.

I'm in over my head and I don't care one bit.

Chapter 27

Natalie

When Evan comes to pick me up, I'm glad I made the stops that I did. Something about having new things: nail polish, underwear, etc., helps boost my confidence and I find that I'm looking forward to the evening even though I know I'll have to let Evan down at some point.

He picks me up at a quarter to seven, looking very handsome in a gray suit. He also looks very polished, a little too clean, and after spending so much time in Jameson's massive presence, I notice a lack of bulk. Jameson is a big guy but beyond that, his presence permeates all the corners in his vicinity. It's like his aura has tentacles that reach around him alerting everyone to his presence and you know immediately that he's the alpha in any room.

"Natalie, you look great. It's so good to see you again." I have to hand it to him, Evan manages to keep his eyes on my face – which, truth be told, is a little disappointing considering the time and attention I put into my outfit, hair, and makeup. I know that's a selfish thought considering I'm lusting after another man right this second, but sometimes a girl wants to be noticed.

He escorts me to the car and opens my door. Very gentlemanly. The thought that Jameson would most likely have slammed me up against the side of the car and left me wet and panting before even touching the handle enters unbidden into my mind and I feel the heat on the back of my neck.

The thought is crazy because I don't even know if Jameson is in to rough sex, but something about his movements tells me he is. His size makes it seem unlikely that he prefers to be a gentle lover. Beyond that, he's all testosterone-driven male. When he walks, he resembles a panther stalking its prey. When he talks, every word serves a purpose. I doubt he would waste time on pillow-talk, candles, and massages before tearing into his lover.

It takes me a beat too long to realize that Evan is talking to me and I shift in my seat trying to relieve the pressure caused by my mental image.

"Natalie?" he asks again.

"Oh, sorry Evan, I was, um, just thinking about work. What did you say?"

I should be impressed with his Porsche. The thing is immaculate. He flips on the heated seats and uses the touch screen to adjust the air flow to my feet. It's fancy and way out of my price range, but I find myself pining for Jameson's old Land Cruiser. No heated seats, but softer leather. No new car smell, but instead, it smells like man. Like Jameson. No fancy dial to put it in drive, but nothing is hotter than watching Jameson's quadriceps contract as he pushes in the clutch.

Gosh, it's getting hot in here.

"I guess that kind of answers my question. I asked if you've been working a lot recently. I haven't seen you at the pool for a while." I met Evan at the community pool just before Luca and I started dating. Luca didn't like that I went there without him and so I just stopped going. By that time though, Evan and I had talked enough to start reserving lanes at the same time and exchange phone numbers. However, there were never any fires low in my belly like there are now.

We launch into conversation about work. To be honest I kind of mentally check out again when it's my turn to listen. I hate myself a little for being so rude but it appears that Jameson's reach extends deep inside me and it doesn't matter if he's physically present or not; he's now always on my mind.

We pull up to Oriole and Evan checks his Porsche with the valet. Placing a hand at the small of my back, he guides me toward the double doors and gives his name to the hostess.

The stares Evan *didn't* give me are given in full force from patrons of the restaurant. I share an inward smile with myself hoping the effect is the same from Jameson. He told me to call him after my date...I thought I'd see how he feels about a visit.

My new dress is tan and black leopard print with a corset kind of top and spaghetti straps. The top of the corset is black lace and matching black knee-high boots are on my feet. I donned a black suit jacket over the straps since it's cold outside and I'm pleased with how it dressed up the whole outfit. Of course, my new bra and panties are in place and my hair is in loose waves around my shoulders, my bangs falling across one eye, behaving themselves for once. Overall, I feel pretty good about the effect. I went dark with my lipstick tonight, which I rarely do because I don't like standing out even more than usual, but this is what happens when I think about Jameson while getting dressed.

Evan and I are shown to a small table for two. The lights are low and the ambiance is great. Large modern light fixtures hang high and are dimmed to perfection. The tables aren't so close that we can hear everyone's conversation and each table has a candle in the center. The chairs are made out of real wood and are wrapped in leather, giving the place the feel of money it deserves. Soft piano music plays in speakers overhead to give a low murmur to the place and it feels alive, bringing energy to the room despite the low lights and candles. Evan and I have shifted from talking about work to other platonic topics when our waiter approaches to take our drink order - a Grey Goose martini for me tonight. As I close my menu and look over Evan's shoulder, I see him sitting at the bar.

Jameson.

He looks absolutely lethal in a black button down with a dark grey crew-neck sweater over the top and black jeans with brown leather boots. One arm casually draped around the empty chair next to him and the other holding his drink.

He winks at me and holds up his small glass of amber liquid in a mock salute.

I swallow hard and drag my eyes back to Evan with no doubt in my mind that Jameson is here just to fuck with me.

It's working.

Thankfully, Evan's back to is to Jameson; however, this means that I'm facing him and have to work very hard to keep my eyes from constantly straying to him. Evan's too engrossed in telling me about his mom's total knee replacement surgery to notice that my gaze keeps slipping.

God, Jameson is gorgeous.

To my dismay, Jameson slides off his seat at the bar and

makes his way toward our table. My eyes flash wide and I try to give an imperceptible shake of my head. Evan catches on this time and turns to look over his shoulder just as Jameson steps up beside him.

Jameson reaches his hand out to shake Evan's. *What is he doing?*

"Jameson Hunter."

"Oh, uh, hi. Evan Langford. Can I help you?" Evan narrows his eyes in confusion while I hold my breath.

Jameson's size is grossly accentuated when he stands next to a seated Evan.

"I actually just wanted to come say hello to Natalie and tell her how radiant she looks tonight." I feel my cheeks flame and I have to look away to hide my smile.

"Nat?" Evan asks, uncertain. "Do you know this guy?" *Not as well as I'd like to.*

"Um, yeah, we...uh... work together." *Oh, and I'm wearing a new thong that I bought for him to hopefully see later tonight.*

"Oh, okay. Well, um, Jameson, thanks for stopping by. Natalie does indeed look beautiful tonight. Nice meeting you." I can see the tension in his posture but Evan doesn't say anything rude or challenge Jameson in any way when Jameson continues to stand there openly undressing me with his eyes. Now *this* is the reaction I'd hoped for after carefully constructing this outfit, hair, and makeup. And if I'm honest, it's also the person I'd hoped I'd get it from.

"Jameson," I say a little too breathy, with a nod to both acknowledge and dismiss him.

"Natalie," he growls back. "Si quelqu'un essayait de s'insérer dans notre rendez-vous, je m'assurerais qu'il mangeait ses dents." *If someone tried to insert themselves into our date, I'd make sure they ate their teeth.* I'm pretty sure he's not-so-subtly telling me that he thinks Evan is a chump.

"Charmant, Jameson. Vous avez fait valoir votre point de vue. Vas y. Je t'appellerai plus tard." *Charming, Jameson. You've made your point. Now go. I'll call you later.*

Jameson quirks a half smile at me before nodding to Evan. He knows he's gotten to me as he claps Evan on the shoulder in a patronizing way before heading back to his seat at the bar.

I know his display of utter machismo should probably turn me off, or at the very least, make me pissed. But it doesn't. All it makes me want to do is climb him like a tree. It's the stuff girls dream of. Well, it's the stuff *I* dream of. Damn the whole bad-boy thing. It works for me.

Evan and I have barely gotten our conversation back on track when I feel my phone buzz in my purse. I discreetly pull it out and check it while the waiter refills Evan's wine glass.

JAMESON 6:22 PM

Take your panties off.

My eyes fly to his at the bar. How in the hell does he want me to do *that* discreetly? At the table? Wait, he never said I had to do it at the table, just to take them off. I excuse myself to the restroom in total disbelief that believe I'm doing this. I also can't believe how much fun it is to feel a little naughty. I slip my thong off and share a smile with myself. The joke is on Jameson because the lingerie I'm wearing I bought in case we ended up together tonight. I knew he was uncomfortable with this date and I had hoped to appease him later.

When I open the bathroom door to step back into the restaurant, Jameson is leaning against the opposite wall in the shadows, his arms folded across his massive chest. When he sees me, he holds out his hand.

I happily lay the new purchase across his palm and give him a very satisfied smile when he sees them. In his hand is the most expensive pair of underwear I now own. A black silk thong with "Please?" written across the front in Swarovski crystals.

I hear his breath hitch as his fingers curl around the fabric. "Tell me you didn't wear these for him." He looks ready to break something and the look on his face makes me drenched. Which is a problem because I now have no underwear to catch the moisture.

I lean in to whisper in his ear. His exhale harsh when my cheek brushes his. "Je t'appellerai plus tard." *I'll call you later.*

I head back to the table and apologize to Evan for being so distracted and for the interruption. I settle in to the rest of the date. Jameson never returns to the bar.

Chapter 28

Jameson

I knew it was risky going to Oriole tonight. My plan could have totally backfired but I had a feeling she would play along. Seeing her with another guy was not good for my blood pressure and I'm still working on bringing it down to a level that doesn't put me at risk for a stroke. Considering she and I aren't technically anything more than co-workers at the moment, perhaps my reaction is a little much.

I don't actually believe that.

Against my better judgement, and as I've already admitted, I want Natalie. And as most people correctly guess, I'm used to getting what I want. Natalie's willingness to play along with my request - along with her desire to dry hump me the first time we were alone - confirms these feelings aren't one sided.

Driving back to my apartment, I think the whole time that I hope Evan enjoys Natalie's company tonight because it will be the last time he takes her on a date.

The night drags by slowly and I replay how her cheek felt against mine at least a hundred more times. Having no plans and being too wound up to relax, I change and hit the gym in my building. By the time I finish my last set of dumbbell thrusters, she still hasn't called, so I shower and pour a little more bourbon in an effort to chill the fuck out. I haven't been this on edge since I was awaiting the outcome the harassment claim.

Finally, at nine o'clock, my phone rings and my relief is palpable.

"Natalie," I say by way of greeting.

"Jameson." I can hear the smile in her voice.

"Where are you?" It comes out more demanding than I mean for it to. I certainly don't want her to feel like she *has* to come over. But if she *wants* to come over, then I want her here right now.

"Evan just dropped me off at my apartment."

"I'm on my way." I can't help the snarl that comes out with the words.

Her giggle over the phone makes me twitch in my sweats.

"Jameson, relax, I can hop on the Brown Line to the Fullerton stop and I'm basically at your front door."

"Are you still in the dress you had on at dinner?"

"Well, he didn't take me out of it if that's what you're wondering," she replies.

Smartass.

"He'd better be damn glad of it, too." It's getting harder and harder to reign in my desire for her. "No way in hell are you getting on the train and walking three blocks by your-self in that outfit." My jaw and stomach are both clenched at the thought.

"Jameson --" she starts, but I cut her off.

"Natalie, I'm coming to get you. I'll be there in five minutes. Way faster than you could get here by train." I'm grabbing my keys even as I say it, not bothering to change out of my sweatpants even though I know Natalie is dressed to the nines.

She laughs seductively in my ear. "Someone sounds impatient."

"Someone *is* impatient." No need to hide the truth. She can probably hear my erection over the phone.

When I pull up to her building, it's murder trying to find a place to park. No wonder she doesn't own a car. Finally, after my third loop around the building, someone pulls out opening up a spot along the sidewalk. She's downstairs waiting for me in the small lobby and the minute she flashes a smile, it's all over for me.

I throw the car in park, race up the stairs to her building and cage her in against the wall of mailboxes. "I'm about five seconds away from kissing you. If you don't want that to happen, you need to tell me right fucking now." I'm leaning down for her even as the words leave my mouth. I've waited long enough for this.

Her lips part and her arms snake around my waist. It's all the permission I need. I tangle my hands in her hair and pull her face to mine. Her lips put up no fight as I try to gain entry. They're pliant as they part and her tongue is the most delicious welcoming party. She tastes sweet. No hint of dinner on her breath and I realize I don't taste any alcohol in her kiss either which reminds me that I need to check one more time she wants to do this. As much as it pains me to break away from her, I pull back.

Her chest is heaving and her eyes are wide. "What's wrong?" Concern laces her voice and I smooth her cheek with my thumb.

"You're sure about this? You don't feel like you're making this decision while tipsy? You don't feel coerced?" I hate that I feel the need to clarify. I also hate that I feel like I need it in writing to protect myself. Thankfully, Natalie is understanding and patient when she realizes what's going on. Not every woman would be.

"Jameson, I went shopping today to buy everything you see here," she waves a hand down her body, "for *you*. This," she points to her hair and the makeup on her face, "was premeditated in anticipation for seeing you tonight. I ordered *one* martini at the restaurant so Evan didn't drink alone and I didn't even finish that because I remembered what happened the last time." She never takes her eyes off of mine and she doesn't stumble over any of her words. "I'm sure about trying this if you are." At her last words, I see her natural blush shine through a little darker.

I nod on my way back to her face. "I'm sure." She stops me with a hand to my chest before I reach her and I arch an eyebrow in question.

She won't look me in the eye this time as she whispers, "Now that we're both on the same page, once we start this, I may not be able to stop, so perhaps we shouldn't start in the foyer of the building?"

Oh. *Oh.*

"Come on." I grab her hand and pull a little too aggressively toward my Land Cruiser parked at the curb.

She's laughing and the sound runs straight through me. "Jameson!" she nearly shrieks. "My apartment is right upstairs! Why are we driving to yours?" She doesn't argue as I push her up against the car door and slide my hand up her thigh on the inside of her dress. Her skin burns my hand.

"Because I'm willing to bet your shower doesn't have dual shower heads and floor to ceiling windows so you can look down at the park while I'm fuc--"

"Nope! You're right, let's go to your place."

I open the door and she hops in, her dress so short it flashes me the sweetest glimpse of her ass. Her thong is in my pocket like a good-luck charm. When I groan out loud, she turns to look at me innocently, "Tout va bien?" *Everything okay?*

"Pas même un peu." *Not even a little.* I see her wicked grin as I close her door and drive as fast as is safe through the streets of downtown Chicago to get this woman back to my condo.

Chapter 29

Natalie

I'm almost certain I'm going to leave behind a small puddle when I get out of this SUV. Thankfully, I'm so turned on right now I don't even care. It's like Jameson did some lingerie shopping of his own. He's in gray sweatpants and a white t-shirt. Honestly, of all the things I've seen him in over the last week, I'm pretty sure this is my favorite. I can't wait to trail my fingers along the waistband of those pants and watch them slide down his thighs as he springs free.

I know it's thirty-eight degrees outside, but I reach forward to turn on the AC. Jameson chuckles next to me. "Something got you all worked up, Natalie?"

"Mmm hmm." It's all I can get out.

"Care to share what that might be?"

"I think you know." I reach across his center console and place my palm over his very obvious arousal. He hisses through his teeth.

"Be careful Nat, I'm likely to blow before we get there." His words aren't even that dirty but, oh, do they fan the flames. I try my best to get into his sweatpants from the passenger seat but he clamps down on my hand with a vice grip. "Patience. We're almost there. I want to watch. I want to see you. And right now, I have to concentrate on driving."

I sit back in my seat, pouting. "This is the longest car ride ever." He laughs because we have literally been driving for four minutes and his building is up ahead. Three lights later and we're pulling into his underground garage.

I jump out of the car at warp speed eager to have my hands on him again. In the elevator, he bends down to place his hands under my ass and he lifts me up. My legs automatically wrap around his waist and his body keeps me in place against the mirrored wall of the elevator. His mouth finally lands on mine again, then on my neck. I'm lost in the sensation of him all around me when I distantly hear the ping of the elevator announcing our arrival on his floor. *Thank fuck.*

Like a hotel, Jameson has a key card to access his place. There is also a keypad just outside his unit so he can enter a code which is what he does now. As we stumble through the door, I'm trying to yank his t-shirt up over his head. *God*, this stomach. I get completely distracted by the lines disappearing into his sweatpants and pause to trace them with my fingertips. He rewards me with a sharp exhale and I like the way his muscles contract under my touch.

He pulls me along with him but doesn't stop my exploration as he moves to turn on the kitchen light.

"What the hell?" His voice startles me and I look up to see what's wrong.

A young woman is sitting on his couch wearing a sheepish grin and giving him a finger wave. "Hi Jamie. Uh, surprise?"

I feel all the blood drain from my face and clutch the counter to stop myself from falling. Jameson is quick and, seeing my reaction to our visitor, wraps an arm around me to steady me. I want to push him away, but I can't find the strength.

"Rach? What are you doing here?" His face breaks into a wide grin and I think I'm going to be sick. *Playboys, all of them.*

"Well, I thought maybe you could use some company since you've been out here such a short time and when we last spoke, you were pretty hellbent on keeping your head down and not making friends. I see that's changed." She flashes me a tight smile.

Jameson continues his line of questioning rather than give me any explanation. They keep talking as if I'm not here. I'd try to make a run for the door, but Jameson still has his arm around me. "How'd you get in?"

"You gave me the code, dummy. In the same text when you said 'visit anytime'." The way she calls him "dummy" doesn't sound like a lover's quarrel. Nor does she seem upset at my presence. She seems more like...

"Natalie, this is my sister, Rachel." He finally releases me as he walks over to embrace her while the blood slowly returns to my head and the ringing in my ears fades away. "Rach, this is Natalie, my, uh, well, we haven't quite figured that part out yet," he stammers while watching for my reaction.

I give an embarrassed wave. She basically just saw me clawing at her brother like some sex-starved addict.

"Jamie, we can catch up tomorrow. I'm sorry to have interrupted your evening. I didn't think you would have branched out quite yet," she explains. "We just got in literally five minutes ago. We put our stuff in the guest room so I'll just head on to bed. It's been a long day anyway."

"We?" Jameson asks.

His sister turns an almost pained look to her brother.

"Oh, um, I brought Nikki." At that moment we hear a toilet flush, followed by a quick run of the sink, and a door opens down the hallway. A woman who looks to be in her late thirties practically runs into Jameson's arms. I feel my jealousy kick in to high gear. I know he had a life before me, but wouldn't social politeness dictate that maybe she at least acknowledge me before a greeting like that?

He looks uncomfortable as he sets her down. She continues to claw at him. Odd behavior for someone who is greeting a friend's younger brother.

He looks at me with indecision on his face. I can tell he wants to catch up with his sister and *Nikki,* so I let him off the hook. "I can take the train back to my place. You guys catch up. Jameson, I'll talk to you later."

Get me out of here.

"Natalie." His voice stops me in my tracks. "I already told you, you aren't riding the train in that outfit especially now that it's close to ten. Come with me." He holds out his hand for me and then looks at his sister, "We'll be right back."

Initially, I think he means he's going to take me home, but he said *"we"* would be right back. I follow him as he pulls me along down the hallway and into his bedroom. The same floor-to-ceiling windows that are in the living room are here as well...overlooking the park. His bed is huge and looks so inviting with a fluffy navy-blue comforter and matching pillows against stark white walls. Recessed lighting gives a calm, sexy vibe to this room. There's a wing-back chair in one corner, his dresser matches his nightstands and above his bed is a beautiful painting of a prop plane.

"It was my dad's," he says as he catches me staring.

"The plane or the painting?" I ask.

"Both. He was the best man I knew."

Knew. Past tense. "Oh, Jameson, I'm so sorry. I didn't know." I squeeze his hand.

"That's a story for another time. For now, I'd like if you stayed and hung out. I'm not ready for you to go yet. I'm really sorry about this." He looks unsure as to whether or not he should say the next part but eventually decides to plow ahead. "Nikki, can be, uh, rather aggressive, and I'd rather not be left alone with the two of them." He opens the middle drawer in his dresser and starts rooting around, finally coming up with a pair of flannel pajama bottoms and a black t-shirt. "I'm sure they'll be huge on you, but maybe if you roll them up about fifty times they could work?"

"If you're sure?" I reach out and hesitantly take the offering.

"Oh, I'm sure." He stands behind me and brushes my hair over one shoulder and then slides the zipper down the back of my dress agonizingly slowly. I still don't have underwear on because I gave them to him earlier and I figured this night was going to look much different.

"Jameson, I, um, still don't..." I trail off because he's pulling the spaghetti straps off my shoulders and I know the dress is about to pool around my feet.

"Oh, holy shit," he says on an exhale that whispers across the back of my neck. I'm in my heeled boots, bare ass and black lace bra. I feel his hands on the backs of my thighs as he starts to run them up over my ass and I arch into him. "You know, I love my sister a whole lot, but right now I hate her just as much," he rasps.

I want him to slide his hands around to the front and relieve this pressure. Instead, he runs his hand down my arm - sending goosebumps sprawling across my skin - and grabs my hand. I feel his sweatpants, and for a second, I think he's going to let me have what I wanted in the car, but no. He slides my hand into his pocket and I feel the familiar silk of the thong I gave him earlier tonight.

"This is far from over," he leans down and whispers in my ear, "But when I lay my eyes on the rest of you, I want to worship you. Not get a passing glance that then gets hidden from me."

He can't see how red my face is because he's still standing directly behind me. I take the thong from his pocket and slip it on, carefully standing on one booted foot at a time. I feel him kneel behind me.

"Put your hands behind you, on my shoulders." I do as he asks. I'm dangerously close to doing *anything* he asks. He unzips my boots and slides them off my feet. Being flat again feels heavenly. I pull the flannel pajama bottoms on and he finally turns me to look at him. His eyes go wide and his nostrils flare - I'm still in just a bra on top. "You are the most beautiful woman I have ever laid eyes on."

"Thank you." I find that kind of hard to believe because I'm sure he's seen a *lot* of beautiful women, but I'll take his compliment. "Will you still feel the same way when I spontaneously combust all over your living room?" I ask, only half joking.

Chapter 30

Jameson

It's the most erotic outfit I've ever seen. My flannel pajama pants that swallow her up, paired with her black lace bra. Thankfully, there's an opaque lining under the lace, because otherwise I'd buy a hotel room for my sister and send her ass out of here so I could do everything to Natalie that my brain has conjured up. Like trail my tongue over her hidden nipple and watch as it beads in response to my touch.

This line of thinking is not helping my current erection and these sweatpants aren't doing a damn thing to conceal it. It looks like I've got a steel rod jutting out of my thigh.

Funny, that's what it feels like too.

"Soon," I tell her. "When you combust, I want it to be all over me. Not my living room. I promise I'll get you there soon." She groans her disappoint that "soon" isn't *now*.

I completely understand.

This thing between us has a pulse all of its own and screw our rules or even taking it slow. The past six weeks have almost killed me and I'm growing tired of being interrupted.

I hold the shirt open for her and she puts her arms over her head, looking up at me the whole time. I mentally calculate if I have enough time to get her off, but the answer is no. I don't want to rush no matter how badly we both want it right now.

"Ready?" she asks with more breath than actual voice.

"Not at all. Let's go." I grab her hand, craving the contact, and lead her back down the hall.

After my sister and I spend a few minutes on the pertinent catch-up topics - namely, our mother - she turns her attention to Natalie. "So, Natalie, what do you do?" Rachel asks casually as she swirls her red wine before taking a sip. She's sitting in the leather chair next to the fireplace facing us. Nikki is between the couch and Rach's seat on a chair from the kitchen.

I can feel her eyes on me in an instant when Natalie answers. Natalie's eyes light up when she talks about her job. Like any job, it has its highs and lows but it's clear that she loves almost everything about what she does. As I listen to her talk about it, I feel the love of my own career ratcheting up, restoring some of the fire that was lost.

"Is that how you met Jameson?" my sister asks even though she knows the answer is obviously yes.

"Okay, Rach, enough with the third degree." I place my hand protectively on Natalie's thigh. She sat on the end of the couch farthest from where she rode me the other night, with her legs tucked under her. She looks so small in my clothes. I guess she assumed my "spot" on the couch was where I had sat that night and she was trying to leave a respectful distance between us in the presence of our current company. To hell with that. I basically sat down right on top of her. I feel her muscle tense under my hand when I start to trace small circles.

We all have our faults and Rachel's, for better or worse, is being a bit overprotective. I think she still harbors some guilt for going off to college back in the States when our dad was stationed in Japan, leaving me to fend for myself. I did okay, of course. I was fourteen and already 6'1" with a healthy obsession for weightlifting. I wasn't one to get picked on.

Although recent events would suggest that some level of protection is not necessarily a crazy notion, I'm not going to let my sister's rude interrogation turn Natalie off before we even have a chance to give this thing a try.

My sister looks deceptively sweet in a cream-colored sweater and dark jeans. Hair in a slicked back brunette ponytail. Tall for a woman at 5'11" and slender like our mom, my sister, much like me, commands a room. That trait comes in handy for her job doing God-knows-what for the FBI, but she can be a bit much.

"What third degree, Jameson? I'm just trying to get to know your girlfriend." She tosses the word out there so casually and for a second, I think Natalie is going to bolt, or freak out, or both. It was a test from my sister and the smirk on Nikki's face has me seeing red. I come to Natalie's defense because this is ridiculous.

"Rach, we need to talk. *Now.*"

Rachel glares at me as she unfolds herself from the chair and follows me down the hall toward the room where she and Nikki will be staying.

"Jamie..." she starts, but I cut her off before she can say more.

"Rach, I know what you're going to say. But it's different. *Vanessa* pursued me and it got ugly when I said 'no'. *I* am pursuing Natalie and if she tells me no, then that's the end of it. There won't be any need for it to get ugly. She didn't start this. *I* did."

"Jamie, you've only been here a few weeks. After everything you *just* went through, how can you be hooking up with another flight attendant?" I hear our mother's disapproval and skepticism in her voice.

"First of all, I didn't 'hook up' with Vanessa. Second of all, in those few weeks, I happened to meet an incredible woman that I would like to get to know better. And third of all, I'm trying to pursue an actual relationship with Natalie, not just 'hook up' with her." I pause and make sure my sister is paying full attention. "Look, Rach, it was always just the two of us growing up. I know you want good things for me, and I know when the harassment claim came in, you were just as pissed as I was. But I really don't think Natalie wants trouble, so go easy on her, would ya?" I choose not to mention how unhappy I am at the fact Roachel bombarded me with Nikki as well.

"Yeah, okay. But at the first hint that she isn't as sweet and innocent as you say, I'm going full FBI on her ass."

The look in my sister's eyes tells me that she's serious. I'm glad she's in my corner because honestly, she scares me a little.

Having come to an agreement, we head back out into the living room where Nikki is in full blown I-know-him-better-than-you mode as I overhear part of her story that took place fifteen years ago. I hate this game and I'll never understand why women play it. Nikki may have known me longer but Natalie already knows me better.

Natalie sits up a little straighter and tightens her grip on her wine glass as she ignores Nikki and addresses my sister. "Rachel, I just want you to know, I've had drama of my own in the past with dating a co-worker and I swear, I would never cause that kind of trouble for Jameson."

Despite our heart to heart, Rachel still appears cold and unyielding. "I appreciate that, but I've watched what happens when a woman gets attached to Jamie and can't handle it when he's ready to walk away."

Natalie's eyebrows raise about three inches in question as she looks at me. I'm sure she's wondering what I'm hiding. Which is nothing on purpose, I just didn't realize I would have to present my sexual history dossier on our first date.

"Okay, Rach, seriously, tone it down or get the fuck out." Anger draws my eyebrows together and narrows my eyes. Siblings or not, I'm a grown ass man and I will pursue whatever relationship I want. I resent Rachel a little right now for thinking she gets a say in the matter and I grab Natalie's hand and pull her on to my lap wanting her to be close. Thankfully, she lets me. "I have no skeletons other than the ones you know about," I tell Natalie, placing a kiss on her cheek. "Sure, there were some crazy chicks in college, but no stalkers or women claiming they had my baby."

"Uhh, have you forgotten Kristen Blankenship so soon?" My sister barks out a laugh so hard I'm afraid she might spill her wine.

"Oh. Yeah. Okay, there was *one* stalker." Natalie grips my shirt in her hand as my sister launches into the story of the one girl who did actually stalk me shortly after I got my pilot's license. The beauty of having a sister in the FBI means she was able to find out all about her and "kindly" ask her to stop. With my arms around Natalie, she sinks back into me, finally relaxing. Everyone seems to relax a little, except for Nikki. Natalie and my sister enjoy a shared laugh at my expense, which I don't mind, before diving into other conversations.

Nikki's eyes keep boring into me. Every time I feel her look at me, I make sure to focus my attention on Natalie.

Nikki and I hooked up once, seventeen years ago, when I had come back to the States for college. It's a night I barely remember and have regretted ever since because she is, unfortunately, my sister's best friend. I'm not into that, nor am I into her.

Based on the stories my sister has told me and the few times I've run into Nikki over the last decade and a half, it's clear Nikki *hasn't* forgotten that night. I can only guess she's still single because she gets bored easily and never wants to be bothered to have to think about anyone other than herself, but maybe I'm being harsh.

Finally around midnight, Rachel yawns and uncurls her legs from the chair. "Well, sorry to have busted up your party. I'm going to go crash. Natalie, I feel certain we'll see each other again." Nikki's eyes cut to Rachel. I guess she came along on this trip under the assumption that she would have me all to herself. Maybe some things never change.

My sister isn't a hugger so she nods at Natalie to say goodbye, oblivious to Nikki's reaction. I kind of feel bad for Nikki. My sister didn't really think this one out. Then again why would she? Rachel has no idea her best friend seduced me that night.

Rach kisses me on the top of my head like I'm a child.

"Goodnight, Jamie. We can figure out details and plans in the morning. We're in until Tuesday. Mom told me you weren't working this weekend so I figured a quick trip would be okay."

"Sounds good, Rach. I'd tell you to help yourself, but I know you already have," I tell her lovingly. Afterall, she is forty-years-old. She can find what she needs.

"Come on, Nat, I'll drive you home." I'd rather she stayed, but even I know that's asking a bit much.

"Jameson, can I talk to you when you get back?" Nikki purrs. I'm sure it's said in a verbal attempt to remind Natalie that while *she* has to go home, Nikki will be staying in my apartment tonight, and I hate her a little more for it.

I feel Natalie's tension rise beside me and I'm desperate to put her mind at ease. I know how she was treated in her previous relationship. I go out on a limb here, telling a bald-faced lie and hoping like hell that Natalie picks up on it. "Let's talk in the morning, Nikki. I'm meeting Nat for breakfast at nine, so we can talk before I head out." During daylight hours...not cozied up on the couch in the dark, just the two of us.

Natalie gives my hand a light squeeze. *Thank you.*

Nikki looks put-out. Fine by me. I don't mean to be rude, but also, I didn't invite her here in the first place.

Not only do I not want to take Natalie home. Just dropping her curbside is even worse. I want to go in with her. I want to show her that she doesn't have to be afraid to let go with me. I'm not promising I'll never let her down, but I'll never do it on purpose. I'll never lie to her and I'll always let her know that I value her. I want to tell her all those things, but I don't. I keep my mouth shut because actions speak louder than words and words have a tendency to fall short anyway.

Chapter 31

Natalie

By the time we get to my apartment, Jameson seems to have cooled off a bit. His silence is proof that he's as lost in his own head as I am in mine. His current mood is unreadable but the light kiss on my lips is enough to stop me from asking him to come inside. I know he has company to get back to, but I don't like it. He's denying me what I've been craving. What I've been primed for the last six hours. He hesitates when we get to my building and I feel the tension radiating off of him in waves. Catching his hand, I tug gently to cause his eyes to meet mine.

"Jameson?" The inflection in my voice leaves no doubt that I'm asking a question, a hundred questions, with just his name. Maybe I don't have any right to pry, but we've agreed to giving this thing a try, we just haven't had a chance to talk about what that actually means. So I let the question hang in the air.

He turns to look at me, stress causing lines to appear on his gorgeous face.

"Sorry, Natalie. My sister's visit caught me off guard."

He abruptly gets out of the SUV and comes around to my side, opening the door.

He's not getting off the hook that easily so I plow ahead, "But I can tell something about them being here is bothering you. I'm not asking you to divulge all your family secrets to me, Jameson, I just want to know that whatever this is," I point between us, "isn't over all of a sudden just because family is in town?" I don't mean to sound needy - however a tiny bud-sized piece of me is extremely needy at the moment. I'm also not interested in being yanked around or left in the dark.

Instead of answering me, he walks me backwards into the brick column next to the stairs of the building. He leans down to catch my eyes but instead of kissing me, he runs his tongue from the base of my throat, up the side of my neck. "Nothing is over. In fact, we're just getting started." It's so cold out that my exhale hangs in the air around us. He captures my mouth with his own after that, kissing me slowly, intentionally. My brain is going fuzzy when I hear a familiar voice.

"Now *this* is one smoking hot couple, if I do say so myself."

I giggle as I open my eyes. Jameson pulls back, breaking our kiss, clearly annoyed to have been interrupted yet again.

"Stevie, what the hell are you doing out here at twelve thirty in the morning?" I ask, grabbing the front of Jameson's shirt so he doesn't duck and run.

"Nat, you say that like the eighty-year-old you truly are. Twelve-thirty is usually when the party is just getting started, but you wouldn't know that because normally, you've already been asleep for," he makes a show of looking at his watch to drive the point home, "four hours by now."

I laugh and look at Jameson. "He's not wrong, you

know." Then I turn my attention back to Stephen. "And you didn't answer my question."

"And I'm not going to." He gives me a cheeky grin. "But Captain Hunter, *this*," Stephen rakes his finger up and down at Jameson's sweatpants and t-shirt which now has a jacket over top, "this is working for you. Nat," he takes in my attire - Jameson's too big pajamas, "you not so much, Bunny." He blows us a kiss and starts to head inside, pausing only to add, "I expect full details tomorrow."

Jameson looks back down at me. "Bunny?"

"It's a long story." It isn't really. Stevie is playing off a stereotype of redheads - that we like to fuck like rabbits - so he's called me Bunny since the day we met, but now is probably not the time to share that piece of history.

Jameson's anxiety is written all over his face. "I didn't realize you guys live in the same building. I guess the cat's out of the bag." He doesn't sound angry, just resigned to the gossip and the drama that tends to follow workplace romances.

"Jameson," I breathe, starting to shiver as his massive hand rests at the base of my throat like he isn't sure if he wants to pull me to him or push me away. "Stevie is one of my best friends. He has a heart of gold and he won't tell a soul if we don't want him too. He's been after me for months to start dating again. He wouldn't make it hard or awkward for me now that I have. I mean, if that's what this is," I add quickly. I don't want to make assumptions.

"I just hoped we could have some time to figure this out before everyone starts prying." A violent shiver runs through me and Jameson walks me up the steps to the door, through which, Stevie just disappeared. "We'll figure it out tomorrow. Go inside and get some sleep."

I'm still not terribly comfortable with how we're leaving

things. Progressing quickly through the normal stages of a new fling, the butterflies were short-lived with the appearance of his sister and Nikki.

I hold his gaze a couple more seconds searching for answers but I feel him pulling away already. I tell him the only thing that I can think about when staring at him like this. "Damn, you're gorgeous."

He brushes my hair back from my face. "I'm completely average compared to you."

Okay, well, that's not true but I'm back to swooning anyway.

"So, breakfast at nine then?" I ask tentatively, unsure if he was serious or just wanted Nikki off his back.

"Why don't I bring breakfast to you and we can finish what we tried to start tonight?"

I swallow hard and nod furiously, "Yes, please. That sounds like a good plan."

All my hopes of sleeping just went out the window.

Fifteen minutes later, as I finish my nighttime routine and slip under my covers my phone dings, twice.

STEPHEN 12:44 AM

> When in the actual fuck did you start banging Jameson Hunter?

JAMESON 12:49 AM

> Just got home. The vultures are in bed. Are you still in my clothes?

I answer Stevie first because he's relentless if you try to

ghost him and I don't need him down here pounding on my door, causing a scene.

NATALIE 12:50 AM

I'm not banging him.

Yet.

Lord knows we tried but his sis is in town for a surprise visit. And some flirty bitch she brought with her.

I feel a little bad because I absolutely hate when women tear other women down over jealousy. But being stabbed in the back is a sensation I'm still raw from, so Nikki had better watch out.

My next text goes to Jameson.

NATALIE 12:51 AM

Glad you were able to get to your room in peace. And yes, I am. In fact, I may never take them off. They smell like you.

Too clingy? Maybe a little. But it's the truth.

STEPHEN 12:51 AM

Oooo Bitch better watch out. Dinner tomorrow?

NATALIE 12:52 AM

Ty is coming in Monday morning. Take out at my place for dinner? I'll catch you up while I clean.

Stephen sends back a thumbs up emoji.

> **JAMESON 12:54 AM**
> You can keep them on until 9:00 tomorrow morning. And then I plan to relieve you of them.
>
> Also, I promise you'll be close enough to get the scent straight from the source.

> **NATALIE 12:55 AM**
> I'm not sure I can wait.

I'm already panting hard just from his text. My nipples beading against his shirt. As if reading my mind, or perhaps his knowledge comes from having the same issue, Jameson texts back:

> **JAMESON 12:55 AM**
> Don't touch yourself. Your next orgasm belongs to me. It's had my name on it for six weeks.

> **NATALIE 12:56 AM**
> I'm pretty sure it's had your name on it since 1992.

This man and my hormones...

> **JAMESON 12:56 AM**
> Good. Now go to sleep. You're going to need to be well rested and well hydrated.

> **NATALIE 12:56 AM**
> I think maybe I'm not as experienced as you're used to...

This conversation has me so turned on I'm in pain, but also, nervous. What if I don't stack up? During the day it was way less scary to travel this road. I was all ready for the events of the evening and I had planned my martini accordingly. Now, I have all night - by myself - to imagine the ways a man like Jameson Hunter likes to have sex. Luca was hot, but his lack of self-esteem made him non-adventurous. He didn't like to try new things, so we didn't. Very vanilla. Easy to predict.

> JAMESON 1:00 AM
>
> Do you trust me?

I take a second before I start typing. Do I trust him? I don't really trust any guys these days. I *especially* don't trust pilots. Or at least I didn't. The rule I have clung to so dearly for the last several months has begun to fade away like a distant memory instead of the blood pact I was ready to make with myself.

NATALIE 1:00 AM

Oddly enough, I do.

> JAMESON 1:01 AM
>
> We'll circle back to the first part of that comment in the future, but for now, know that it's going to be incredible. I can't wait to put my mouth on you.

NATALIE 1:01 AM

SO not helping the sleep thing...

> JAMESON 1:01 AM
>
> Goodnight Bunny ;)

NATALIE: 1:01 AM

Goodnight Jameson.

Chapter 32

Jameson

My alarm goes off at seven so I have time to fully wake up before having this talk - whatever it is, with Nikki - and then grabbing breakfast and heading over to Natalie's where I plan to lock myself inside and devour her. After my shower, I grab a towel and wrap it around my waist as I head to the kitchen to start the coffee maker. It's only 7:20 and I hear no sound coming from the other side of my bedroom door, so I figure I'm in the clear.

Wouldn't you know, I figured wrong.

"Damn, is that how you come to the kitchen every morning?" Nikki asks, openly tracing her too-plump lips with her painted nails.

No, usually I come out naked since I live alone.

I flash her a warning glare but she's too busy staring at my waist to notice. "Let me get changed and then we can talk before I head out." I reach for a coffee mug and grip my towel with my other hand. The look on her face tells me I'm in danger of losing it.

"No need to change, Jamie."

"Cut the shit, Nikki. Natalie was just over here last night and if you think for one second I'm going to go behind her back to get some from my sister's best friend, think again. Make no mistake, it wasn't my invitation that brought you here." I hate being cold but I also don't like her insinuations at all. Nor do I appreciate how her presence royally fucked up my night last night.

She looks wounded but not shocked at my words. She pushes out her bottom lip a little more and takes a step closer to me. All of my spidey-senses are tingling and I grab my mug and turn to head back into my bedroom.

"I know how you like it, Jamie, and I can deliver," she whispers to me as I walk down the hallway. It's enough to make me pause and turn around.

"If you'll remember correctly, Nikki," I whisper in a tone so low my words should register that she's in danger of being thrown out of this apartment onto her ass, "it was *one* time. Seventeen years ago. Suffice it to say my tastes have changed...and besides, I don't make the same mistake twice." This time I know I've hurt her. Seventeen years was a long time ago. I was nineteen, she was twenty-three. We were both drunk as hell but I looked then like I do still.

She and Rach came to visit me at the frat house and Nikki lost her damn mind when she saw some girl grinding on me at the party we were having. Nikki yanked me by my wrist, sending the girl in my lap to the floor, and pulled me toward the stairs to "talk" in my room. I stupidly thought she was going to lecture me like a big sister would.

She had my pants off before the door was even shut. I was wasted and she was four years older than me. It was hot at the time. It wasn't until a day or two later when my sister told me that Nikki -and I quote- "had a great time at the party. She said she met someone and is finally excited but she wouldn't tell me any details so this guy must be some-thing special."

I knew then how badly I'd screwed up. I'd definitely sent the wrong message. I was not, nor have I ever been, in love with Nikki. Hell, I'm not even attracted to her. It unset-tles me that she's not only still in my life through my sister, but currently in my apartment.

Unfortunately, my words do nothing to prevent her from continuing her mission. "I think we've both grown up a lot since that night, Jamie, but I haven't stopped thinking about you since you were nineteen years old. It's unlikely I'll stop now. Where's the harm in seeing if we're still as compatible in the bedroom as we once were?"

"The *harm*? Nikki, you just met my fucking girlfriend last night." I'm aware that I've just referred to Natalie as my girlfriend and I'm not even sure it's true, but for now, it's what I'm going with. "I may be a lot of things, but a player isn't one of them. Is this the conversation you wanted to have when I got home last night? You wanted to try to seduce your way into my bed?" My voice is rising in anger.

"Whoa, who's seducing who?" My sister's sleepy voice comes around the corner into the kitchen where Nikki and I are still arguing. My sister rubs her eyes as she sees my towel. "Jesus, Jamie." She holds a hand up in front of her face, blocking her view of me. "You could seduce all of Chicago with those abs. They shouldn't be allowed out before 10a.m." She isn't being weird, just stating it like a newly discovered fact in a cold-case.

I run a hand down my face and kiss my sister on the cheek. "Morning Rach. No one is seducing anyone." I give Nikki a pointed glare. "I'm going to change and pick up breakfast for Natalie. I'll catch up with you guys for lunch."

I buzz Natalie's door at nine o'clock on the dot. I don't exactly know what she eats for breakfast so I got a shit-ton of options and will take note of what she picks, pancakes or biscuits, sausage or bacon, scrambled eggs or egg sandwich, etc...

"Door's open," her voice crackles through the speaker. "Take the elevator to the fifth floor."

It's a chic apartment building. Definitely older. Smaller units, but well maintained. I'm a little shocked that the elevator doesn't have a musty smell that so many of the old buildings do, but it's slower than molasses in wintertime, and I'm chomping at the bit to get to floor five. I'll never talk shit about my own elevator again.

When I exit, I look to my right and see Natalie hanging halfway out of her door, waving.

My face lights up like an idiot when I see her. Can't help it.

"Hi." She looks up at me with pink cheeks and a meek smile; embarrassed?

"Hi." I follow her into her apartment. She's in lounge shorts and a long-sleeved shirt. Her face is bright and her hair is in loose curls down her back, still slightly damp from her own shower. I love that she didn't feel the need to dress up, that she's comfortable in her own space and her own skin.

"Okay, so it's not fancy like yours, but it's home."

She shows me around and I love it because it's hers. She has worked so hard for it and like her job, I can hear the undercurrent of pride despite the warning of it not "being fancy".

The apartment opens into a tiny foyer that then gives way into the kitchen first. It's been updated to granite countertops and stainless-steel appliances with a sleek silver backsplash. It's very nice without being fussy. The molding is dark wood despite the beige walls and there is an original built-in bookshelf in the corner of her small living room. The navy-blue couch sits in the center of the room facing the wall with the bookshelf. I notice there isn't a tv. It's a very cozy place and I can't wait to have her on every surface in here.

She's shy now that the moment is here, but I don't mind taking the reins. My mind has been running wild with all the things I want to do to her, with her, so I've got plenty of options to guide her through.

Back in the kitchen, she's unpacking the bags of food, not meeting my eyes, like we're high schoolers who aren't supposed to be doing this.

"Natalie."

"Mmm hmm?" she hums nonchalantly as she busies her hands.

"Natalie, look at me." Finally, her hands stop and she raises her chin to look me in the eye. "I'll stop whenever you want me to but if I don't touch you right now, it's going to be my turn to combust in *your* living room. Got it?"

Eyes wide, she gives an almost imperceptible nod of her head, but it's there. My green light.

"Good." I pull her to me and brush her hair away from her neck, inhaling her and placing my first kiss at the base of her ear. She shivers in my arms telling me everything I need to know about the spot I picked. "Send Stephen a text and tell him you're unavailable for at least the next two hours and if he comes down here and knocks on this door, I will personally make sure he never sets foot on the flight to London. And then turn your phone off." She does as I ask while still in my arms, realizing that I'm not joking.

No one is going to interrupt us this time.

"This doesn't feel too planned for you?" she asks.

"No. Besides, we're in the aviation industry. Delays, schedule changes, quick turn arounds, sometimes it will *have* to be planned. And sometimes those plans will go to shit. I don't know about you, but I fly again tomorrow and I'll be damned if I'm going to waste this opportunity."

I start to pull the hem of her shirt up and I feel her squirm. "What's wrong?" No way am I pushing this if she isn't ready.

"It's just, I wasn't sure what to wear, so I don't have anything sexy on underneath."

"Nat, relax, *you* are the sexy thing underneath. I wasn't planning to leave anything on you anyway." Standing behind her, I love how she fits right inside my arms as I brush my fingertips along her stomach. "What happened to that adventurous girl who gave me her panties in the restaurant...while she was on a date with someone else, I might add?" She turns her head to look back at me and I see something flash in her eyes as she lifts one shoulder in a shrug and gives me wicked grin.

As I continue to pull her shirt up, I realize she isn't wearing anything underneath her clothes. Something between a hiss and a tortured exhales escapes through my lips.

I feel her smile and arch back into me. "Thought you might appreciate that," she whispers in a confident tone, right as I lose my fucking mind.

Chapter 33

Natalie

His hands are huge and they feel so good on my skin. He turns me to face him and captures my mouth with his. He has my shirt off before I can let out the breath I've been holding and his hands are working feverishly at my shorts. He's too tall to push them down without breaking our kiss which he seems to desperately not want to do.

"Nat, get them off," he says while still kissing my lips. As soon as I kick them off my feet, I'm totally naked while he's still fully dressed.

"Jameson, your turn."

"Yeah, yeah, we'll get there."

"I want to get --" a squeal escapes my lips as he wraps his hands under my ass and lifts me off the ground just like he did in the elevator. My legs automatically wrap around his waist. The button on his jeans hits me right in the center and the metal is cold, causing me to arch my back. He groans as I throw my chest into him. He sits me on the counter after taking a broad forearm and sending all of my mail, my kitchen towel, a roll of paper towels, and a spatula to the floor. Our breathing is heavy and I'm clawing at him like a rabid animal out for blood. I yank on the buttons of his button-down a little too hard, causing the first two to pop off his shirt.

"Sorry about that," I mutter in a frenzy against his lips.

His hands are in my hair and he's slowed his pace so that he's sucking my bottom lip gently between his teeth. Is it possible to come like this? I'm pretty sure I'm about to find out. My hands are searching blindly for that cold button keeping me from everything I want in this moment.

He stills my hands. "In a second." I whine my protest and he smiles. "Someone sounds impatient." He mocks my words from last night so I answer him with his own.

"Someone *is* impatient."

He takes a step back from me and undoes the rest of his buttons. I thought the hottest thing in the world would be for me to undress him. I was wrong. The hottest thing in the world is to watch him undress himself, in front of me with desire in his eyes and watching my very visceral reaction to him.

He has a white t-shirt on under his button-down and Lord help me, when he crosses his arms and grabs the bottom to lift it over his head slowly, I think I black out for a second.

"Oh my God." I know my greedy, unblinking eyes are wide and I might be actively drooling. "Jameson…" I let his name hang in the air. I've never seen a body like this. Not a real one and definitely not one that wants to touch *me*. His pecs are perfectly outlined with ridges of muscle. He is hard and beautiful, thick but not bulky. His chest runs down into sculpted abs and the lines that dip below the waistband of his jeans are causing a wet spot to form on the counter beneath me.

I'm paralyzed until he reaches forward to guide my hand onto his warm skin. He shudders as my fingertips trace the outline of his chest and stomach. Thirty seconds into my exploration he pulls me off the counter. "If you keep touching me like that, I'm afraid we won't make it to the grand finale. And I have big things planned for the finale."

I figure he's going to lead me to my room, but instead, he pushes my ottoman against the couch and places a couple of pillows on the cushion. "Come here," he growls. He lays me down with my ass just at the edge of the ottoman, angled up slightly due to the pillows. He gets on his knees and uses his massive hands to push my knees wide and places my feet on his bare shoulders. I'm so exposed that, for a second, I start to shut down. I may be thirty, but my sexual experience is still pretty limited.

"Jameson!" I try to sit up, suddenly embarrassed and out of my league with a shirtless Jameson between my thighs.

"Nat," he says calmly, placing a massive hand across my stomach pushing me back into the pillows, "take a deep breath. I've pictured you like this a thousand times and even my imagination couldn't do you justice. If you trust me, relax. There's no need to be self-conscious. You're beautiful."

"But what if I..." I can't even bring myself to say the word. I've always thought my self-confidence was pretty decent, but next to Jameson, I'm not so sure anymore. He's like the sun.

"Come?" he finishes for me with a wicked grin, now only an inch my pussy.

I nod, frantically.

"That's kind of the point, baby. Don't let me down."

When Jameson Hunter calls me baby, it's all over. My knees fall apart and I swear I hear trumpets sound to welcome him home as his tongue connects with my flesh.

I last a whopping three minutes before my orgasm fills the air around us. I whimper-scream as the climax hits me, digging my nails into the couch behind me. As I float back to earth, he growls in my ear, "Next time, I want my name on your lips when that wave hits. I want to make sure you know who that orgasm belongs to."

It's hard not to look away from him, the intensity in his eyes is so demanding. I nod my understanding as my breathing continues to slow. I've never screamed a lover's name during sex. It always seemed so intimate - which I guess it is - but it just always felt like if I said their name, they'd be brought back to reality too quickly, regretting the decision to make love in the first place.

Wow, Nat, maybe your self-esteem isn't as great as you thought. I make a quick note to evaluate that at some other time and refocus on the man in front of me.

Snapping back to the present, I reach for the button on Jameson's jeans. He catches my hands with a gleam in his eye. "We'll get there, but I think you've got another one to give me before we let the beast out of the cage."

I can't stop the chuckle from escaping through my lips. "You named your dick 'the beast'?"

"When my jeans come off and there aren't any layers between us, I'll let you decide if there's a better name for it." His face and tone are completely serious when he says this causing my heart rate to kick right back up where it was a few minutes ago.

He stays on the floor in front of me and proceeds to replace his mouth with his fingers, drawing lazy circles around my clit before plunging inside, causing my back to arch off the ottoman. He lets out a guttural groan that is almost enough to shatter me. I've never heard a man make a sound like that, feral and almost like he's in pain. Then again, I've always needed some kind of background noise to save myself from feeling awkward about the sounds of making love. But in this moment, as my body coats Jameson's fingers and I hear his ragged breathing, I'm sure I can't imagine wanting to mask any of these sounds.

I feel myself start to clench around his fingers as he places his thumb on my clit. He groans again and his words barely register before I feel his mouth on me a second time. "I thought I'd get you there with my fingers this time, but forgive me, baby, I can't keep my mouth away from you now that I've had a taste."

I had no idea guys actually said this shit.

My hands reach the back of Jameson's head and I thread my fingers loosely through his hair as he increases his pressure and swipes his tongue back and forth across me. As I get closer to the edge, I raise my hips off the pillows slightly. It's enough for Jameson to notice. He clamps his hands around my thighs, holding me firmly in place, and literally buries his face in my pussy.

There is no hesitancy on my part when the release comes.

I scream Jameson's name like it's the only word I know.

I feel him smile against the inside of my thigh as he climbs back up my body.

"That's better." His arrogant smirk doesn't hold a candle to the flame of desire in his eyes.

"Jameson," I breathe, barely recognizing my own voice, "I think it's my turn now." My limbs feel heavy but I'll be damned if I'm not going to return the favor.

As if he can read my mind, he chuckles darkly. "This

isn't tit-for-tat, Natalie. I'm not getting you off with the expectation that we'll be even by the time we're done because we won't. You'll be far ahead." I feel my cheeks blush and when I break eye contact, he gently grabs my chin and angles my face back toward him. "Tell me what you want."

"You." Even as I say it, I know it's a safe answer and he most likely isn't going to let me get away with it. I think back to the night I basically rode his lap in his apartment. God, I must have been more drunk than I thought.

"Your pussy already told me that." He licks a trail up the side of my neck while rubbing his thumb across my bottom lip. "What do you want to *do*, Nat? Say the words."

Ohmygod. For a second, I think I'm going to stay silent until he pinches my left nipple between his fingers. The sensation of pain followed by pleasure. "I want you to fuck me."

Once I made the request, there was no stopping Jameson. His jeans vanished into thin air along with his boxers - if he was even wearing any. He yanks me off the ottoman and into his arms as he carries me to my bedroom and lays me across the bed, climbing on after me. Sitting back on his heels, I notice his quads first. I've never really thought about a man's legs before, focusing more on his chest and arms, but damn if Jameson doesn't have sexy thighs. Powerful and defined, they're hard to miss in this position.

After lusting after his thighs for an appropriate amount of time, I'm drawn to what lies between them.

I'm face to face with The Beast and I have to admit, there is no better name for the massive appendage standing at attention. He takes himself in his fist as if to soothe the thing that clearly wants to rip me apart. When I hear the telltale rip of foil, my body responds with a rush of liquid.

Jameson pauses at my entrance, one hand still on his shaft. "I know a lot of guys *think* they're big. I also know that I *am* big, Nat. I'll go slow but let me know if I hurt you."

If my insides weren't already on fire for him, they definitely would be now.

He takes himself in his hand and begins to slowly nudge his way inside. I feel myself stretching to accommodate him and where I expected pain or discomfort, I only feel bliss.

My hips buck forward, trying to seat him further inside but since he's above me, on his knees, he's controlling the speed.

"Fuck, Natalie." He places the heels of his hands on my hipbones and slowly begins to thrust as deep as he can get. My hands fly to his thighs so I can feel them working. He's watching where we're connected, and I'm watching him.

Immediately, I know I could watch him forever. How does one ever get over being worshiped like this by this man?

"You okay, baby?" He asks while still thrusting slowly.

I nod, and he places his left hand on my lower stomach and pushes down lightly while using his right thumb to make circles on my clit.

"Oh shit, that feels so good," I blurt while trying to keep my eyes open. I don't want to miss a single second of the way his jaw's clenched from tying to keep himself under control, or the way his pecs are flexing.

"Faster. Please." I whimper with a sudden need to feel him slam into me. Honoring my request, he grabs hold of my ankles and spreads my legs wide. His biceps now flexing with the position as his cock hits a spot no one has ever been able to reach before.

"Oh God. Oh fuck. Yes. Jameson, I'm..."

His speed picks up and his grunts match my own as he

finds his release at the same time.

An hour and a half later, I'm drifting in and out of consciousness after my fourth - or was it the fifth - orgasms. I honestly had no idea one person could get off so many times. In so many ways. I'm reveling in how good it feels, curled up skin-to-skin next to Jameson. He's intermittently peppering light kisses on the top of my head and my shoulders. He wasn't kidding about the finale. There were fireworks and everything and the ringing in my ears is only just now subsiding.

He also wasn't kidding about his dick being an insatiable beast wanting to tear me apart.

I feel my eyes flutter open as he reaches behind me and pulls me in even tighter as if he can't quite get close enough. "Can we do this every day?" I ask, my voice full of sleep and lust as I lightly thrust my hips forward into him.

I feel his laugh more than hear it. "Baby, we can do this whenever you want."

"Well, except when you're flying a plane."

He arches an eyebrow at me like I just issued a challenge and I can't help but laugh. "No way. There are too many buttons, I'd hit something by accident and kill us all."

"I never said we would do it in the cockpit. There's always someone else up there, remember?" He gives me a grin that would make the devil envious. "But I can be discreet when I want to be."

"Jameson, with a face and body like this, discreet is not a word you know. Eyes follow you everywhere and your presence is known the second you walk into a room." I'm mesmerized by his chest and biceps even as I speak. They're perfect and I'm in awe as I lay on my side running my fingers over his skin.

"It sounds like maybe *you* watch me whenever I enter a room."

"Oh, I definitely do." I giggle. There's silence for a beat after this and it prompts the question on my mind. I wish I could just leave it be, but I can't. Not when I've been hurt twice before and just broke my own rule. Jameson could crush me, I'm sure of it. Not to mention the ill effects on my job, what his sister was saying last night completely makes sense now. I'm not sure how I'd handle it if he walks away. Jameson is the whole package and once you've been on the receiving end of his attention and affection, I'm just not sure how someone survives without it. "Can I ask you something?"

"Anything you want."

"What is this that we're doing?"

He smiles as he rolls to his back and pulls me into his side, my head on his chest. "Is this the define-the-relation-ship conversation?"

I bristle a little at his words and launch into an explana-tion. "It's just that we both had rules against this very thing for a reason and I know myself. I don't really do casual sex and I have a tendency to get attached fairly quickly, so I just need to know --"

"Hey," he interrupts me with a calm whisper despite my rising hysteria. He rolls me all the way on top of himself so that we're chest to chest and he can see my face. I lace my fingers together and rest my chin on them against his chest, meeting his gaze. "This wasn't casual for me. I also happen to not mind the DTR conversation. I appreciate clear expectations. I don't do 'hook ups' anymore. I'm almost thirty-seven years old. I was in a committed relationship for three years - a lifetime ago - and I miss the stability and the connection. I want a friend, a partner, and someone hot as hell that responds to my touch so easily." He trails his finger over my spine causing a shudder to rip through me, proving his point. "I should have stayed away from you, but I couldn't, and after this morning, I *definitely* won't be able to. So, if you feel similarly, I'd like to date exclusively and see where this goes."

A lump the size of a jet engine is sitting in my throat. I try to push back the tears stinging my eyes. I'm not sure why my body wants to cry. Happiness? Relief?

Jameson narrows his eyes at me, trying to assess my reaction. My tears abate and I smile. "Yes, please. I'd like that. Although, I have to warn you. I have a jealous streak a mile wide. It's going to take some practice and a helluva lot of effort to reign it in while other people eye fuck you in front of me all day. Are you *even aware of* how often it *happens*?"

"I could ask you the same thing."

I roll my eyes at him. "Not a contest." I grin widely.

"Why don't we grab a shower? As much as I hate to do it, I should probably spend a small amount of time with my sister before she heads out of town on Tuesday."

I can't hide the look of disappointment on my face even though I know that's not fair. I'm just not yet ready to give him up yet. He smiles down at me, seeing my emotions and interpreting them clearly. "Come on, I'll give you number six while we're in there."

I can think of absolutely nothing more motivating. I roll my ass out of bed and follow him to the bathroom...my boyfriend.

Chapter 34

Jameson

Truth be told, I couldn't be more glad that she brought it up first. All I've thought about is how to make her mine. Every movement, every touch, every time my name is on her lips, solidifies the fact that she was made for me. Yeah, this could go sideways and yes, our jobs would be significantly more awkward - especially if she gets the route to London - but supposedly "with great risk, comes great reward" - or so Thomas Jefferson says. I'm sure the guys that lost the battle probably feel that *with great risk, also comes great loss*, but we won't focus on that.

As I watch her towel off after the shower, I realize I'm not ready to leave her yet. "Come with me." It's out before I've fully processed the request.

"What? Where?" She looks genuinely confused as she wraps the towel on her head and starts rubbing lotion up her long legs.

"Come with me to hang out with my sister today." I'm talking to her but my eyes are tracking the movements of her hands. "I think it's totally appropriate for my girlfriend to hang out with my family and to be honest, Nikki could use a fresh reminder that I'm not into her and never will be."

I see Natalie's jaw tighten and can almost hear her teeth grinding when I mention Nikki. I don't blame her. Not wanting to tolerate the distance any longer, I take her towel off her head and pull her naked back against me. "I like it that you want me all to yourself," I murmur against her skin as I trail kisses down her neck. She leans into me, forgetting her tension. When she groans, I start to get hard again and she pushes her ass into me causing all the blood to rush south.

"Oops," she says, feigning innocence. "I don't think you're going to be able to tuck that back in your jeans so I should probably take care of that." I'm pretty sure this was her ploy all along. I kept her orgasms rolling in waves and it isn't until now I realize she hasn't gotten a chance to put her hands on me.

A sharp inhale hisses through my lips as she drops to her knees and wraps her hand around me. It takes every ounce of my self-control to not thrust into her mouth. I'm not a small guy. Hell, I'm not even a medium-sized guy. It can take a minute to adjust and I don't want to hurt her. When I have to grip the counter for support, she hums her satisfaction at my undoing and finally I thread my fingers in her hair.

Only a couple minutes later, I try to pull out of her mouth and say her name in warning. "Nat, baby, I'm close."

Instead of letting me pull out of her mouth, she wraps her hands around me to grip my ass and draws me deeper. *Ohmygod, she's going to swallow this.* The thought makes me come violently in her mouth, my dick jerking so hard I'm concerned I may actually fall on top of her. As she sucks the last drop from me, I'm lightheaded and the room is spinning. I reinforce my grip on the counter to steady myself.

"Jameson, you okay?" she asks, her voiced laced with concern.

"Christ, woman." It's not romantic at all, but it's all I can get out.

She trails a finger across her bottom lip and looks up at me from her knees. "So, it was okay, then?"

"I'll answer that when the room stops spinning and some of my blood gets back to my brain."

She laughs a genuine laugh and flashes me a gorgeous smile. I know she said *she* falls fast, but I'm afraid I may beat her this time.

It's one-thirty by the time we meet up with my sister and Nikki at The Purple Pig. A classier restaurant than the greasy spoons she's used to while working ninety hours a week.

I hold Natalie's hand the whole way there, reveling in the sound of her voice as she talks about how excited she is for Tyler's upcoming visit.

"I guess we're getting the meet-the-family stage out of the way early," I joke, then quickly grow serious as I think about the fact that tomorrow is Monday, one of my scheduled days to fly the DFW route. "Does this mean you aren't on my flight tomorrow?" I can't hide the disappointment in my voice.

She wraps both of her arms around my right one and smiles up at me. "Absolutely not, Captain Hunter. I will report for duty at six thirty like always on Monday. Ty's flight gets in after lunch so I'll meet him at his gate when we get back. I'm doing the early DFW run, but you'll have Sherri and Stevie for both the morning and afternoon."

I'm shocked at how much I want to ask if I can come over tomorrow night. I'd rather meet her brother and hang out in her cramped apartment than go home and entertain Nikki and my own sister. As if my thoughts flowed straight into her, Natalie's eyes light up. "I know! Why don't Ty and I come over to your place and we can all have dinner together or something? That way our company is entertained and you and I can still see each other."

"Damn, my girlfriend is beautiful *and* brilliant. Soy un bastardo afortunado." *I'm one lucky bastard.*

"I don't think I'll ever get tired of hearing you call me your girlfriend," she admits and it feels like she just drove an icepick into the remaining cubes surrounding my heart, releasing it once and for all.

When we arrive at the restaurant, I pull the heavy wooden door open for Natalie and pinch her ass as she walks through. That's what she gets for exaggerating the sway of her hips as she walks by me. She whips her head back at the contact and I briefly expect to see a chastising look on her face - *Jameson, not here!* - but to my delight, she has mischief in her eyes and a smile on her lips. I reach for her hand again, just wanting to confirm that her presence is real.

"There you are! It's about damn time, Jamie!" Rachel's voice rings out through the restaurant as she stands to greet us.

"Sorry we're late." Natalie speaks to my sister first - who shockingly pulls her in for a quick hug - then turns her attention to my sister's best friend. "Hey Nikki."

Nikki is focused on Natalie's hand, which is still in mine, and takes so long to respond that even my sister picks up on it. "Hello? Earth to Niks!"

She jerks her head up and looks right at me. "Oh, hi."

I order a round of beer for everyone. Nikki stays unusually quiet during lunch. I keep my arm around Natalie and listen contentedly as she asks my sister about her job - which truly is interesting but it makes me nervous to think of her with criminals, so I usually choose other topics.

When the conversation turns to our childhood, I chime in, finally having a chance to tell her about our father. "He passed away ten years ago. Fuck, it's hard to believe that much time has gone by already." My sister covers my hand as it holds my beer. My dad and I were close. As good of a father as a guy can ask for. Supportive without being pushy, strict without being mean, and set the best character example I can think of to follow: honest, trustworthy, hard working. Cancer claims a lot of people and I'm not sure there's anyone left in the world who hasn't been touched by it, but damn I still get mad and choked up that he's gone.

"I miss him too, Jamie," Rachel says before she casts a side glance at Natalie. "Mom is going to love the hell out of her though, don't you think, Niks?"

Nikki shoots daggers at my sister before recovering and answering, "Oh, yeah, sure, if she gets a chance to meet her."

Immediately I'm defensive. "What the hell does that mean?"

My sister is listening intently, a puzzled look on her face as if she is waiting for the explanation as well. When she doesn't immediately rush to Nikki's aid, Nikki backtracks. "Oh, gosh, I just meant with you guys' crazy schedules, it might be hard to coordinate a trip back home."

I narrow my eyes at her. That is *not* what she meant.

Natalie, sensing my anger, places her hand on my thigh under the table. Nikki follows the movement with disdain in her eyes while Natalie plows ahead, "Well, speaking of meeting family, my brother is coming into town tomorrow. He just went through a bad breakup and his birthday is this week so I was thinking we could all get together tomorrow night for dinner at Jameson's? Maybe play cards or something?"

Rachel seems to like the idea, her eyes lighting up as she answers, "Sounds fun!" Nikki on the other hand is becoming very open about her desire to have me alone.

She turns to Rachel, wrinkling her nose. "I thought we'd get more time to reminisce and hang out like the old days, to be honest."

Rachel eyes her friend like she can tell something is up. "Don't be so rude," she whispers even though Nat and I can hear. "I thought Jamie would be lonely and working himself to death so the company would be welcome. Turns out, I was wrong, but while we're here, I'd like to get to know Natalie better."

"Yeah, of course," Nikki replies with a tight smile.

After lunch we walk around Navy Pier, hit a couple of museums, and try to knock some major tourist sites off the list. Places are a little less crowded in the colder months so there isn't too much foot traffic or many lines.

Finally, after the Field Museum, Natalie breaks up the party. "Guys, this has been *so* much fun," she gushes. She leans in to hug my sister again, who shockingly, grips her back tightly this time. Two hugs in one day has to be a record for my sister. Natalie doesn't attempt to hug Nikki who has remained aloof all afternoon. Instead Nat turns back to me and says, "I'm going to catch the train home.

Stephen's bringing dinner over while I clean the apartment."

My sister snaps her head up. "Who's Stephen?" she says in an accusatory tone, making me laugh.

"Down, Rach. Stephen is Natalie's gay best friend. He's also one of the stewards on my current flight route. Nice guy. And I'm pretty sure he's more into me than he is Nat." I swallow Natalie up in my arms. "Tell Stevie I said hi since I know you girls are going to be talking about me anyway."

She laughs as I bring my mouth to hers. I deepen the kiss until she can't hold back her moan.

"Um, guys? You're about to make a baby on this very public sidewalk," my sister says half disgusted and half adoringly. She just wants me to be happy.

I swat Natalie's ass as she heads to the rail station. "Text me when you get home."

"Yes, sir," she says and does a mock salute.

My sister takes the vacancy on my arm and loops hers through it. "I like her. But still be careful."

I take a page out of Nat's book and salute my sister, "Yes, ma'am."

Chapter 35

Natalie

onday rolls in like hell on wheels. I'm excited to see Ty this afternoon but even more excited to go to work. I should probably feel worse about that than I do. Giddy, like I'm going on my first date, I dance around my apartment getting ready for work. Heat is already infiltrating my limbs at the thought of Jameson in his pilot's uniform. Especially now that I know what's underneath it.

Half an hour before I leave the house, my phone goes off, alerting me that I have a new text message. It's got to be either Stevie or Jameson because it's only five in the morning.

I feel the smile light up my face when I see the screen.

JAMESON 5:02 AM

Want to ride to work together this morning?

More than anything, I do. The problem is that I always ride the train with Stevie when we share the same first leg of the day. If this thing between Jameson and I doesn't work out, Stevie will still be here for me and I don't want to toss our routine aside quite yet.

NATALIE 5:02 AM

I really do, but Stevie and I always ride the train together. I don't feel right abandoning him.

Jameson's response is immediate. Almost like he already had it typed out.

JAMESON 5:03 AM

Bring him along. I'll have coffee and bagels. Tell him I'll be there in twenty minutes.

NATALIE 5:03 AM

<3

As soon as I send the heart, I start overthinking it. Was it too much? I mostly meant it as a thank you and like in a *we love food and coffee* kind of way, but now I'm starting to panic.

I call Stevie and ask if he wants to ride with Jameson but also let him know that I will ride the rail with him if he'd rather.

"Let me get this straight," he says through the receiver, "your hot-as-fuck boyfriend wants to chauffeur our asses to the airport *and* is serving coffee and bagels on the way, and you think there's a chance I'd opt for the rail? Girl, that cock did a number on you, huh? I'll be ready in five."

Okay...so I guess we're riding with Jameson and his bagels.

When Jameson pulls up, Stevie and I lunge for the door handles like our lives depend on it. I look at Jameson and my breath catches in my throat. "Fuck." It's becoming a catchall mantra when I'm around him. "I'd somehow forgotten how good you look in that uniform." He doesn't even have the jacket on but the white shirt and tie are making me squirm. He's a work of freaking art.

Actually, now that I'm *really* looking at him, he looks like a hired stripper that is posing as a pilot for a bachelorette party. His crisp white shirt is tight across his chest. He has the heat blasting which is why he doesn't have his jacket on and his shirtsleeves are rolled up, showcasing his muscular forearms. I give a quick glance behind me and I think Stevie is smelling his jacket where it's hanging in the back seat. He rolls his eyes back in his head and makes an obscene gesture which causes me to have to swallow my laughter.

My eyes land on the top two buttons on Jameson's shirt and the fact that his tie is still loose. Mentally, I've moved on to picturing ways to use the tie as a restraint.

Jameson's eyes darken when he catches me. "I'll tighten everything up once we get there."

Stevie decides to put Jameson's jacket down and join the conversation. "I'd really rather you didn't," he says with a laugh. "Although, Nat will probably go straight-up homicidal maniac on some of our female passengers with you dressed like that."

Jameson reaches over and squeezes my thigh as we roll down the highway. "That bad, huh?"

He rewards me with a low chuckle when all I can manage to do is squeak out an "Mm hmm." I clear my throat and finish my thought, "It's going to be a long day."

"I'll do my best to give you relief if we get the opportunity." Jameson winks at me and I hear Stevie whimper in the back seat.

"Fuck! You're going to do her on the plane? Why can't I find a boyfriend like that? Jameson, have you ever considered that maybe you aren't actually straight after all? You know, experimenting is quite normal and I'd be happy to show you the ropes."

I'm laughing so hard I'm afraid I'm going to spit bagel all over Jameson's floorboard. Stephen's outburst even has Jameson laughing and the sound is delicious. He trails his right hand up my thigh toying with the hem of my skirt - wouldn't you know, I wore the short one today - as he answers.

"Stephen, I can promise you if I thought for one second that I'd like to play for the other team, you'd be my first call, but I can say with complete certainty that I am, in fact, straight as an arrow."

"Well, I'm disappointed but also not entirely convinced. You have my number."

"Stephen!" I shriek. "Stop hitting on my boyfriend! You're supposed to be helping me keep all the other vultures at bay, not making me worried about you too!"

We pull into the pilot parking lot and a bus is waiting to take us to the terminal. This VIP treatment is awesome.

The bus has racks for our go-bags so we stash them and find seats. Jameson wraps his arm around me and tucks me into his side. I cock an eyebrow at him. "What?" he asks. "Is this too much?" The uncertainty in his voice makes me want to reassure him by kissing every square inch of him. But perhaps *that* would be too much.

"I just wasn't sure you would want people to realize we're together yet," he leans over and whispers in my ear, his breath hot on my already burning skin.

"We are together, right?"

"Yes."

Still whispering, except this time his teeth graze my neck just under my ear before he speaks, "And we are exclusive, right?"

"Yes," I manage to get out which is followed by another shudder.

"Then I want *everyone* to know so they're aware of who they'll answer to if they stare too long, try to touch, or try too hard to earn your attention."

"Oh, okay," I breathe, barely coherent. "Does this mean I get to claim you too?"

"Baby, you can do anything you want to me."

Stephen groans obscenely in the seat across from us reminding me of his presence. When my eyes flash to his, I'm pretty sure I see beads of actual sweat on his forehead. He will definitely be talking about this interaction on the flight if we get any alone time together.

Jameson's proximity is causing my own temperature to rise. "Okay, we gotta talk about something else before I make you call in sick with me and we spend all day back in bed." I swear Jameson's pupils dilate at the thought.

As the bus stops at the last covered awning, a familiar figure gets on the bus and spies me immediately. I instinctively tense up and lean ever so slightly into Jameson. He doesn't miss a beat and I feel him increase his pressure on my arm. He doesn't know what's wrong, but he can tell something is up. *I'm here* his arm tells me. As Jameson turns to look at me, Luca catches my eye and walks toward us at the back of the bus. It's too early for this shit.

Still as objectively handsome as ever, but in a refined - my family has money and I grew up vacationing in Italy at our second home - kind of way. I can see the differences between he and Jameson so clearly now beyond the pretty faces. Luca is a self-absorbed, controlling, asshat. He uses his looks and power to intimidate and coerce. However, today, he looks small and weasel-y and I'm not sure why I never noticed. The lines around his eyes, a little more prominent. His suit, a little baggy despite being pressed to perfection.

"Natalie," he says instead of hello. Like I'm supposed to melt just at his use of my name. When I'd thought he was my future and had been blind to all the red flags glaring at me, perhaps I would have.

I feel Jameson sit up a little straighter and pull me almost onto his lap. My right leg smashed against his and his right hand reaching across to my right thigh with his left arm still pulling me into his side in a territorial pose. I don't say Luca's name in hopes of getting off this bus without Jameson's fist in Luca's face. Instead, I give a tight smile and small nod.

"Are you in first today, or am I?" I ask Stevie in an effort to move on and ignore Luca.

Before Stephen can answer, Luca reaches across me and extends his hand to Jameson while eyeing the arm he has around me and the hand on my thigh. "Luca Barbieri."

Jameson looks at right at him, ignoring his outstretched hand. "Jameson Hunter."

Stevie's eyes are wide as he sits back and watches the drama unfold. Unfortunately for Luca, he only *plays* the role of an alpha. His confidence is a sham. A mask that he wears thinking it makes him invincible like Batman's suit. Jameson, on the other hand, is all genuine predator when his territory is being invaded. If I didn't know it before, I do now, as I feel his anger thickening the air, making him physically vibrate in his seat at the effort of keeping that energy pent up and under control.

Mentally willing Luca to drop it and check his email or something, I look back at Stevie. "So, like I was saying. Are you in first today? Or is it me?"

Stevie grins like the Cheshire cat and my stomach roils. He was *furious* on my behalf when I found Luca and Lauren in the car and Stevie loves nothing more than good payback.

He glances at Luca to make sure he is listening and then leans in and pats me on the knee. "Oh, honey, you definitely get first class today, down *and* back. I doubt Captain Hunter could stand it if you were all the way in the back of the plane. As much as I would love to," he pauses and looks directly at Jameson, "and I *would* love to," he looks back at me still smiling, "I'm sure he would rather have you servicing him on this flight."

"*Stephen!*" I hiss. I risk a quick glance at Jameson. I know he said he didn't care if our relationship was out in the open, but like *this* was not how I planned on people finding out.

Jameson leans over and whispers in my ear, "He's right. I won't make it all morning without hearing you come again."

I feel my face turn red at his words.

"So, Nat," Luca's use of my nickname infuriates me because he doesn't know me like that anymore, "another pilot, huh? Just can't get us out of your system?" He's openly smirking at Jameson. Clearly trying to provoke him by alluding to the fact that he had sex with me a lifetime ago.

This has got to be the slowest bus ride in all of transportation history.

I wish I could keep my mouth shut, but it opens of its own free will. "How's Lauren, Luca?"

He actually has the decency to cringe. "We aren't together anymore."

"Shocking," I bite off my reply.

Finally, the bus arrives at the terminal and we all stand to exit. Jameson lets me go in front of him so he's between Luca and I. As Jameson, Stevie, and I turn to head toward our gate, Luca grabs my wrist so hard it yanks my shoulder and I drop my bag as he pulls me too close to his face.

"I miss you," he whispers.

What?

It takes less than two seconds for Jameson to physically make Luca let go of me and people are starting to stare as Jameson stands over Luca, nostrils flaring. "If you touch her ever again, I will bury you so deep an oil rig wouldn't be able to find you. Do I make myself clear?"

I can hear Luca's reply as he looks at me around Jameson's massive frame.

"But what if she wants me to?"

I grab Jameson's arm before he can cock it back and punch Luca in the throat.

"Jameson. *Jameson*! Look at me." He blows out a breath and runs a hand through his hair. God, he's beautiful. Even when he's lethal as hell, he's beautiful. "I don't want anyone to touch me but you." God help me, it was the absolute truth and I was falling faster than I ever had before. In fact, I'm pretty sure I've already fallen.

He mutters something under his breath that sounds an awful lot like, "This is why I don't date co-workers," as he yanks his arm out of my grip and stalks off toward our gate.

I watch him go for a second before whipping back around to see Luca straightening his tie. "What is *wrong* with you? *You* dumped *me*! Now you find out I'm finally seeing someone again and all of a sudden you want me back?"

He shrugs his shoulders. "I've been thinking about you a lot recently. It's why I showed up early this morning actually. I checked the system and knew you had a flight. I don't fly out until eleven but I was hoping to catch you in the lounge. Seeing you with another man, especially another pilot, made something snap. I'm sorry I was an ass, but you'd better watch out. It looks like your new boyfriend has some anger management issues."

All lies. He isn't sorry. And he didn't show up just for me this morning. He twists the truth so it appears like he made more of an effort than he actually did. He just doesn't like when another kid on the playground has a toy and he doesn't.

"Fuck you, Luca."

Chapter 36

Jameson

What the hell am I thinking? It's not even eight o'clock in the morning and the level of drama has already exceeded my limits. I was an absolute fool to think I could do this. I almost punched his lights out right in front of the terminal. That's not the best way to keep my current job and if I lose this one due to assault, I'll most likely be out of options.

Thankfully, my plane has arrived and the gate attendant waves me on through to the jet bridge letting me know I can start the pre-flight check. I picked this flight up at the end of last week when Dave Ranier's "vacation" got extended. I have a feeling it's going to keep getting "extended" until his retirement kicks in. Lord knows the man probably has enough hours to be on "vacation" for a solid year.

Stephen and Natalie are supposed to be putting in for the London route today and now I'm not so sure it's a good idea.

No shit, Jameson.

Sherri is on board already when I arrive. Her kind face

lights up in a smile and I feel a twinge of guilt at what I'm about to do. "Good morning, Captain Hunter," she sings cheerily.

"Good morning, Sherri. Did you have a chance to think about the London route?"

"I talked with my husband and at this stage of our lives, he would be okay if I picked the route up every once in a while, but we don't think I should be part of the route's home base crew. I'm really sorry. I'd love to do it, but I have one grandbaby already, and another on the way. The overnights are hard on us old folks," she jokes.

"I understand. I'm disappointed, but I do understand. Hey, would you mind working first class for me today?" I try to throw the request out there nonchalantly and also quickly because I'm not sure how far behind me Natalie and Stephen are.

Since Sherri has missed the updates about Natalie and I and the drama from the morning, she doesn't question me, just nods. "Sure, Captain. Whatever you want. Coffee?"

"I'm good, thanks." I head into the cockpit and close the door just as I hear high heels coming down the jet bridge.

I know this isn't Natalie's fault. I know her ex is an asshole who goaded me this morning. The problem is that I gave him a reaction. I can't bring this shit to work. I have to be able to focus on flying two hundred people safely to Dallas and back. I can't sit up here stressed and distracted because my girlfriend's ex-boyfriend is a douchebag. What happens the next time Natalie gets a few phone numbers? Because apparently that shit happens all the time? What about when some drunk passenger cops a feel? My heart rate is dangerously high and I hate this.

Then another thought occurs to me: I'm certainly not going to be able to concentrate if she's on someone *else's* flight and it looks like it'll be even worse for my concentration if she's on my own. I hear Sherri outside the cockpit telling Natalie and Stephen that I asked her to be in first. I hear the disappointment in Natalie's voice when she answers with "Oh, okay. No problem, Stevie and I got the back," and my lungs lose the ability to expand.

A minute later my cell phone dings.

NATALIE 6:11 AM

Jameson, don't pull away from me. Luca is the past. One I regret deeply.

I know I should respond but I'm not sure what to say. I shove my phone back in my pocket as the door to the cock pit opens and my first lieutenant comes in.

Fuck my life. It's a woman. An attractive blonde woman. She extends her hand, no nonsense. "Landry Sullivan."

I give her a firm shake and a tight smile. "Jameson Hunter." I have to give her credit. She tries really hard to hide her reaction, but some things a person just can't help. Like the audible inhale you make when something surprises you, the way nostrils flare, pupils dilate, and lips part. Some days I wish I could change my face.

Although, it seems like maybe that wouldn't help me anyway as she tries - and very obviously fails - not to drag her eyes down my body.

I clear my throat and ask how long she's been flying. I hate small talk but this woman needs a distraction, fast. The phone rings a minute later and I excuse myself from the awkward conversation and gawking-fest to answer.

"Go," I bark into the receiver. I'm not being intentionally rude; it's the fastest way to let whoever is on the end of the line know I am listening.

"Jameson," Natalie breaths quietly and I about come unglued. "We need to talk."

I know she's right but this isn't the time or the place.

"We will. Just not now," I try to reassure her, but I'm not even reassured myself. Damn, this escalated quickly.

"Are we okay?" she whispers into the phone.

Shit. I don't know how to answer that, but I don't want to lie either. It's truly me, and not her, but thanks to every nineties' sitcom and romance movie, you can't actually say that anymore. What I'm feeling *isn't* her fault and it is *my* fear of being distracted or doing something stupid and losing my job again - only this time I would deserve it. "Let's talk later."

I know my response is going to make her worried but I don't want to get her hopes up. I need time and space from the events of the morning to process.

She chooses to hang up as a way of acknowledging my statement. It feels like I'm punishing her for Luca's stupid words this morning and I know that's not fair. My heart rate hasn't come down a single beat since the bus ride though, and I'm starting to get heartburn.

This is why I don't mix business and pleasure.

When we land in Dallas, we have a turn-around time of an hour. Thirty minutes to clean the plane, thirty minutes to reboard. The company doesn't make money when the plane is on the ground so they want her back in the air as soon as possible. Sherri, as the senior flight attendant, has done all the announcements so I haven't heard Natalie's voice since she called before we left.

Finishing the flight log, I head out of the cockpit to find her now, hoping for a minute alone.

As I suspected, she's in the back of the plane with Stephen, going through the motions of her daily tasks. Stephen sees me first and puts a hand on Natalie's shoulder and says, "I'm going to check on Sherri, I'll be back in a few minutes."

He glares at me as he walks by. "Do *not* break her heart. She just got all the pieces back together again."

Fuck.

"Natalie." It's already instinct to reach for her waist. I'm drawn to her like a planet that orbits around the sun. Alone in the back of the plane with everyone else occupied, we have eight, maybe ten, minutes before the cleaning crew is close enough to overhear us.

She pulls back from my hand like my touch burned her and she won't face me. "I can't do this, Jameson. I can't be yanked around again at the whims of another pilot I have to see every day. If you can't handle Luca's comments, then you won't be able to handle the rest of the shit I hear in a day and I don't want your reaction and ultimate loss of another job on my conscience." She leans forward to pick something up off the floor to try and hide a tear that is falling down her face and my control snaps.

I grab her hips and walk her back into the side wall of the plane, out of view of everyone, and I lean into her so she gets the full message. "My reaction isn't your problem, or your fault."

She looks down where my erection is stabbing her in the stomach. "Are you sure about that?" she asks, her voice low.

"Damn it, Nat. This is why *I* don't do this. I want to pound Luca's head into the wall. I want to cut off the hand of every passenger who even *thinks* about groping you. And if you aren't on my flights, I'm going to be worried about what the other pilots are saying or planning. Ricardo told me they have a bet going to see who you will go out with first."

The shock on her face lets me know this is news to her. When she recovers, she pushes her hips forward and says against my mouth, "Well, it looks like you won, Captain. Make sure they pay up." She palms me through my slacks and her voice grows urgent. "Tell me we're okay. It'll be hard but it would be worse to give up so soon."

All I can do is groan and push into her hand. With one arm braced on the plane wall behind her, my free hand finds the hem of her skirt and slides it up her leg. Pantyhose are going to be a prob...

"You're wearing thigh highs." A statement. Not a question.

"Yep."

This woman is going to kill me. The phone rings next to her head. She cusses as I grab the phone. "What?"

I hear Stephen laughing. "Just a heads up, you two have about three more minutes max to resolve your issues before the cleaning crew closes in."

"Thanks." I slam the receiver down a little harder than necessary. "Three minutes," I tell her as I slip my finger inside her panties. "Fuck, Natalie." She's soaked.

"Three minutes? I can't get off that fast," she says

panicked even as she starts rocking her hips against my palm with my finger moving inside her.

"I beg to differ." I rotate my wrist so I can get my thumb on her as well, clamping my free hand over her mouth when she starts to come about forty-five seconds later. She bites my palm to stop from crying out as she spasms around my fingers. Her head is resting against my chest just as I hear one of the cleaners get to the last row of seats. Natalie rights her skirt as her eyes move to my cock, which is now completely hard and completely noticeable.

"Jameson," she breathes, causing my dick to twitch at the sound of her sultry voice. "I can't send you back up there like that." Normally, I wouldn't care, except today, Landry Sullivan is flying the return flight with me as well and I would hate for her to think this condition has anything to do with her. "I have an idea," Natalie says as she moves to talk to one of the cleaning crew.

"Buenos días. Te importa si cierro la cortina? Los vapores del limpiador de asientos me estan hacienda doler la cabeza." *Good morning. Would you mind if I close the curtain? The fumes from the seat cleaner are making my head hurt.*

The woman is brilliant.

"Oy no, no! Avanzar! Estamos a punto de regresar al frente de todos modos." *Oh no, no! Go ahead! We're just about to head back to the front anyway.*

"Muchas gracias." *Thank you very much.*

Natalie pulls the curtain closed and gives me a devilish grin. There isn't much space back here so we fumble around for a second with hands and mouths everywhere before Natalie pulls back. "Okay, we don't have much time and I can't get on my knees because the curtain doesn't reach the floor and they'll either see my shoes or yours."

"What do you propose?"

She undoes my belt and pants with a motivated deftness I've never seen. I brace my hand on the small counter to my left when she takes me in her palm. She brings the fingers of my right hand to her mouth and sucks my fingers...the ones that were in her only a moment ago. Between the strokes of her hand and her tongue, I'm close. "Nat," I breathe, barely getting the warning out. She pushes my back against the counter and drops into a squat in her heels to finish me off making it look like she's only squatting down long enough to get something out of one of the lower cabinets.

She swallows my doubts...along with everything else.

Chapter 37

Natalie

All too soon, our wheels touch back down in Chicago. It feels good to be on the flight with Stephen and Sherri again, and after getting Jameson back on the same page, my mood has lifted significantly. The weekend seems to have both taken forever and dragged by slowly. Stephen and I both placed our bids for the Chicago-to-London route this morning. I clicked the *send* button slowly as I was still processing Jameson's reaction to Luca.

After getting the passengers deplaned, I knock on the cockpit door to say goodbye to Jameson. As soon as he steps into the galley, he has one hand in my hair and one hand on my low back pulling me into him.

Both Sherri and Stephen whistle. The co-pilot comes around the corner and my God, she's stunning. She gives me a polite smile and shakes Jameson's hand. "Nice to have flown with you today, Captain Hunter."

The hungry look in her eyes makes my kitty claws come out and I wrap my arms around Jameson possessively, four-year-old me pouting. *Mine.*

"Likewise," he answers her while staring at me. Once she's gone, he starts speaking, "Me vuelves loco. No podia esperar a poner este maldito avión en tierra para poder tocarte de nuevo." *You make me crazy. I couldn't wait to get this damn plane on the ground so I could touch you again.* I appreciate that Stephen and Sherri are both pretending to be busy getting the cabin prepared for the next trip to DFW even though we all know they're listening intently. I respect them and genuinely enjoy their company, but I don't need them aware of my level of desperation for this woman quite yet. Hence, the Spanish.

"Entonces nos volveremos locos juntos," *Then we'll go crazy together,* I murmur against his lips. "Ty's flight arrives in forty-five minutes."

"This flight leaves again in fifty, but they can't take off without a pilot, so I guess they'll wait a minute or two if something holds me up." He catches me by the waist as I melt into him.

"Jameson, those people have connections to make," I chastise him while rubbing myself obscenely against his crotch, on fire all of a sudden.

"I have a connection of my own I'd like to make."

I swat his arm playfully at his terrible joke.

"Go. Ty and I will be over around seven. Text me when you land. And when you get back."

"Yes ma'am."

It's been far too long since I've seen my brother, especially considering he was my best friend growing up. With a little space from Jameson, my brain and my energy have to find something else to latch onto and I'm so excited to see Ty that I'm buzzing by his gate.

As I see him walking down the jet bridge toward me, I can't contain my excitement. "Ty!" I offer a squealed warning just before launching myself at him.

His smile lights up his face and he drops his bag so he can catch me with an "oomph" as the air is forced out of his lungs.

I kiss his cheek as he sets my feet back on the ground laughing. "You give better welcomes than my ex-girlfriend."

I'm glad he can joke about it, but also, "Gross, Ty. I just haven't seen you in ages! Come on, let's get your bags, we have a lot to catch up on."

We do the small talk first while waiting for the carousel to start and then I drop the bomb.

"I started seeing someone," I say as casually as I can, not looking up at him.

"Nat! That's great!" I can hear the sincerity in my brother's voice and it hits me how much I've missed him. "I'm really happy for you. Where'd you meet him?" Ty asks the last part suspiciously. I know meeting online is a normal thing to do these days, and lots of couples have found matches like that, but my brother is so old fashioned and thinks you should meet someone from "real life".

"We, uh, actually met at work." I still don't look at Ty as I say this, in fact I purposely turn my head the other direction. When Luca broke up with me the way he did, Tyler went ballistic. He was totally on board with the no-more-pilots rule because he had now witnessed my heartbreak over two of them.

As expected, he lightly grabs my shoulder and whirls

me to face him. "Nat," he starts, "Please tell me you're dating Stephen."

That statement makes me laugh out loud because Tyler knows damn well that Stevie's into men.

"No, Ty. It's not Stephen. There's a new pilot flying my route right now because our regular captain is retiring. We clicked and well, we're seeing where it goes."

His groan of worry and disappointment is audible. "Have you told Mom?"

"I haven't told anyone because it's still really new. Stevie and Sherri know, and you." Ty knows Stephen and Sherri because we've been running flights together for years. He knows they're my support network up here so he's not shocked. "But we did run into Luca this morning on the employee bus. It wasn't great. Luca is such an asshole."

"Aren't we all? This is why you don't date pilots, remember?"

"You weren't a dick to Melissa and she left anyway. What's the moral there? One person in every relationship turns out to be a jerk?" I say it to ask a legitimate question but I can tell by the look on Ty's face, maybe he isn't over Melissa just yet. He was planning to propose, after all. "Sorry, Ty. I just meant that no matter who I date, there's a chance he'll be a total dick, but the same goes for you. Doesn't mean we should stay single our whole lives." I inwardly smile as I realize Stephen and Sherri's words have finally penetrated.

Ty grabs his bag and follows me to the employee bus so we can catch the train back to my place. "Jameson's sister and a friend of hers popped in for a surprise visit so we're going to meet them for dinner at seven if that's okay with you? Maybe if you meet him, you'll feel better about it?"

"Who's Jameson?" Ty asks as he fiddles with something in his carry-on.

It dawns on me that I never told Ty his name. "Oh, Jameson Hunter. My boyfriend." Ty goes a shade of pale green to red so fast I think it's possible that I'm having a stroke and hallucinating colors of the rainbow. He grabs my hand, hard. "Ow, Ty. What's wrong with you?"

"You're dating Jameson Hunter? Huge guy that looks like he should've picked either Navy SEAL or underwear model?" That's an interesting way for my brother to describe my boyfriend but it's also pretty accurate.

"Um, yeah, that's him. How do you know Jameson?"

"I don't," he says a little too quickly. "I just know *of* him. How do *you* know Jameson? He flies out of Charlotte...and he's got a reputation, Nat."

I'm pretty sure I'm missing four hundred and ninety-nine pieces of this five hundred piece puzzle. I want to ask Ty a million things at once, but the reaction that comes out first is defensiveness. "Of course he does, because he was *wrongly* accused of sexual harassment and lost both the case and his job!" I say heatedly. "And he doesn't fly out of Charlotte anymore. Now he flies out of Chicago." I'm starting to yell and we're still on the bus...with other people I work with. Not good. I lower my voice and try again. "Ty, Jameson didn't do that. He is the nicest, most considerate man I know," - as long as you aren't trying to hit on me or take me on a date...for instance, I doubt Evan and Luca feel the same way about Jameson.

"You're a grown-ass woman, Nat. I can't tell you who to date. I just wish maybe you'd date a banker or something."

I laugh. "I tried." And I launch into the story of my evening with Evan and everything since then. Ty doesn't bring Jameson up again and although I'm itching to delve more into how he even heard about Jameson in the first place, I let it go...for now. It's been too long since Ty and I have seen each other and I don't want our visit starting out with tension over my boyfriend.

By the time we get to my place, I'm starving. It's two o'clock in the afternoon and I haven't had lunch. "Let's grab some showers and change and I'll show you around Chicago. We don't have to be at Jameson's until seven."

Ty's response is short and it puts me on edge. "Sure."

Chapter 38

Jameson

There isn't anything I love more than the feel of take-off. That acceleration of speed and the power of the wind and the engines as they lift this massive, metal bird into the sky. It always feeds me that adrenaline rush to know I'm controlling it. Except today, all I can think about is getting home so I can see Natalie.

My sister and Nikki have both texted me today. My sister is sending selfies of them at various spots around Chicago and Nikki is sending me memories that I wish I could forget, one of which she wasn't wearing a shirt in. After that last one, I block her number. Enough is enough. After the day I've had, I wish I wasn't on the hook for entertaining Nat and I's siblings and extras tonight. I just want to curl up on the couch and watch a movie with Natalie pressed against me and block out the world.

When I get back to Chicago after my second flight, I'm exhausted. It doesn't get any better when I hit the lounge to grab a quick bite before heading to my car.

A couple of guys are by the coffee machine as I make my way to the grab-and-go snacks. One word catches my attention. *Natalie.* I slow my pace to try and catch what the guys are saying which turns out to be a huge mistake.

"Barbieri's running his mouth again. Sounds like his ex-girlfriend is hooking up with another pilot and Luca's gone ape shit." Pause. I can't hear what the other guy says but when I hear the response, I about lose my fucking mind. "No, the super hot one. The redhead with the nice ass and those fuckable lips. I'm not sure why he ever traded her in in the first place."

In that moment I feel every ounce of Bruce Banner's pain when the transformation comes and he's unable to stop it. It's moments like these I am entirely grateful for my size and my interest in hobbies like weightlifting, wresting, and jiu jitsu. I will take all of these assholes to the ground right now and *maybe* stop when they tap out.

The guys turn to look at me with raised brows as I step right in their personal space. "Can we help you?" the shorter one says.

"Natalie is now with me. Luca can go fuck himself and you two need to stop acting like gossiping church wives talking about other people's business." I drop my voice to a dangerous level to make sure they understand the severity of my threat. "And if you *ever* refer to my girl-friend's ass or lips again, I will make sure that every meal you eat for the rest of your life has to be fed to you through a straw. Feel free to let Barbieri know the same goes for him."

Great, I'm making more threats. Of course, I mean them, but if I get reported - which is likely since Luca now knows who to report - the only job I'll be able to get is "flying rubber dog shit out of Hong Kong" to quote Top Gun, my favorite movie.

I no longer feel like eating anything on my ride home so

I grab my bag and storm out of the lounge to the employee lot.

The drive home is mercifully quick and I can't wait to strip this damn uniform off. I start undoing my tie as soon as I hit the elevator to my building. It's six already so I don't have much time before Natalie and her brother show up. Just who I *don't* want to be around tonight...more pilots. *Relax, Jameson. This is Nat's family.* Yeah, well, look at what my own family dragged in.

When the elevator doors open, Nikki is waiting for me. Honestly, can this day just be over already? She's in a slinky cocktail dress, holding a glass of bourbon. Now *the bourbon*, I'll take.

"Hey, Jamie. I thought you could use a drink," she purrs. I realize now my mistake was texting my sister and telling her I was headed home and that my day was shitty - except for the ten minutes in the back of the plane with Nat this morning, which I conveniently left out.

"Thanks." I'm too tired to keep my filter in place and I was pretty sure I already made myself clear that I wasn't interested in Nikki and that I *am* interested in Natalie, so I keep my answer short. I knock back the bourbon in one gulp and hand the empty cup back to her so I can enter the code to my door.

I hear the shower running when I get inside. Thankfully, I pay enough for this apartment that my hot water never runs out and the pressure stays strong even if both showers run at the same time. My tie is draped around my neck and I set my bag down inside the door so I can undo the top two buttons on my shirt. Nikki follows my movements with her eyes - her pupils blown out. *Christ, woman.*

"Nikki, pop the lasagna in the oven, will you? It needs

an hour and a half and Natalie and her brother will be here in less than an hour."

She flashes me a death glare at the mention of Natalie. *Good. Get it through your head.*

"I'm not your maid, Jameson."

"Then go put some fucking clothes on and stop pouring my drinks."

We hear the shower stop running and Nikki stomps back to the guest bedroom while I preheat the oven and pull the lasagna out of the freezer.

"Hey, Jamie. Long day, huh?" Rachel is behind me in jeans and a lavender sweater as she towel-dries her hair.

"Yeah. Look, Rach, we gotta talk about Nikki." Before we can actually have that talk though, Nikki comes sauntering back into the living room where she can overhear us. At least she has pants on this time. "Later."

Rachel nods her head but there is confusion on her features. I guess she really doesn't know about Nikki and I's past and she's also unaware of the passes Nikki has made at me since they got here.

I head down the hallway and shut my bedroom door, finally stripping out of my shirt and pants. As I turn on the shower, there is an urgent knock on my door. "Jamie?" It's Rachel. I'm only in my boxers so I grab a towel and crack the door. "What is it, Rach?"

"I may have accidentally just knocked over a bottle of red wine on your couch and I can't find the cleaner."

Shit. I don't have couch cleaner. I'm running out of time and I don't want Nat's brother to think I'm a slob. Before I think about what I'm doing, I head down the hallway toward the living room to survey the damage.

"Jesus Christ, Jameson. How do you shove that frame in your uniform?" Nikki is gawking. She's also trying to play it off in front of my sister as nonchalance, but she's staring with her mouth hanging open and my sister notices.

"Nik, close your mouth. That's my little brother you're eye-fucking."

Nikki's comeback is too quick. "There's nothing little about him."

"Um, ew. And also, how would you know?"

Shit, I need to steer this conversation somewhere else.

"Fuck, Rach. It looks like I axe-murdered someone on my couch." I try to Google what to do and it says something about mixing baking soda and vinegar. I toss my phone to her and tell her to follow the steps while I grab a shower.

As soon as I get out, I hear Natalie, followed by the bass of a man's voice. I pull on my stone-washed jeans and white t-shirt with another flannel over the top. It's my go-to on these cold evenings. When I open the door, my heart stops. Natalie is also in jeans but on top, she's in an army-green, long-sleeved Henley with the top two buttons open. It's cut for a woman and hugs her waist, which looks so small I could probably wrap my hands around her there and my fingers would touch. Her breasts are pushed up and I can see her cleavage where the buttons are undone and I feel my never-ending erection double its efforts to join the party. Her hair is piled in a messy bun on her head and she's smiling at me, brightly. The shitstorm of a day I had melts away in her presence.

I can't stop myself. I walk toward her and scoop her in my arms, lifting her off the ground as I kiss her like my life depends on it. I'm not sure if she wants such a display of affection in front of her brother but fuck it, this is my apartment.

When I set her down, she makes introductions. Tyler shakes my hand but looks wary. I guess he knows about

Nat's past with pilots. I find myself wanting to reassure him and put him at ease. I know what it's like to be protective over a sister...even if she is older...and a pain in the ass.

I pour drinks for everyone and Nikki has gone into full RBF mode with the addition of our company. The two times Rachel and I try to pull her into the conversation, she's a total bitch.

The other four of us, however, have a pretty decent time. Tyler admits that he heard of me through the grapevine because my harassment case was with his airline and shit spreads like wildfire in our industry. I do my best to set him straight on the facts and he seems to believe me, which is good, since I'm telling the truth. He never holds eye contact for long though, making me wonder if he isn't a little squirrelly himself.

I'm taken aback at how much he looks like Natalie. Light hair, striking blue eyes, and a lean frame like her as well. They could pass for twins.

"I'm telling you, women don't handle Jamie's rejection well, *at all*," Rachel says again and Tyler looks uncomfortable as my gaze passes over him on its way to Nikki who looks like an ice queen ready to spit fire. "They've done some crazy shit over the years in retaliation."

"And on that lovely note, I think dinner is finally ready." I stand and head to the kitchen to pull the lasagna out of the oven and refill drinks while everyone files around the dinner table.

Natalie is to my left, Tyler is on her other side at the head of the table, Rachel is across from Nat and Nikki is across the table from me. It doesn't take long before I feel her heel skirting up my leg.

Anger rips through me. I slide my chair back and throw my napkin on my plate. "Nikki, can I speak to you for a minute, please?" I bite off the words, ready to be sick when she looks at me with a hopeful expression on her face.

Because of the open floor plan, I know we'll be over-heard anywhere in the apartment except my room or the guest room, so I motion for her to walk down the hall. I quietly close the door to my room, knowing this doesn't look good at all. As soon as the door shuts, she lunges for me trying to grab any piece of me she can.

Trying to untangle myself from her, she's clawing at my shirt, I can smell the alcohol on her breath and I realize that she's drunk. I haven't paid much attention to how much she's had but I know the group has been through three bottles of wine already and we haven't even eaten yet.

She's grinding obscenely against me and I'm careful not to hurt her as I figure out how to halt her progress.

"Nikki, *stop*."

"Jameson, I've wanted you for *seventeen* years. Let me show you I know you better than *Natalie*." Nikki hisses Nat's name just before she runs her tongue up my neck.

To hell with niceties, I shove her off of me, hard. She stumbles backward and lands on the bed. Immediately her hands fly to her clothes trying to tear them off.

I reach for her to still her hands right as the door opens.

"Jameson? Everything oka...ohmygod." Shit. It's Nat and it looks like I'm undressing Nikki...not trying to keep her clothes on her. "What the *fuck,* Jameson?" she whispers before closing the door and retreating down the hallway.

Nikki is still clawing at me and I smack her hand away. "Get your shit and get the fuck out of my apartment.

"Natalie, wait!" I yell as I rip the door open and make my way back to the dining room only to find that they aren't there. "Rach, where'd they go?"

"Home, dumbass. You decided a make-out session with

my best friend in the middle of your date was a good idea and you're shocked that your girlfriend left?"

All I see is red. I grab my sister by the shoulders. "Rachel, I wasn't making out with Nikki! I was trying to get her off of me! She's been coming on to me since you guys got here!"

Rachel eyes me suspiciously and then says the most hurtful thing she could. "I know how women react to you, Jamie, but this is *Niks* we're talking about and it sounds an awful lot like the *she*-groped-*me* story we just went through with Vanessa."

Chapter 39

Natalie

I can't *believe* I fell for a pretty face and that damn uniform *again*.

"God, I want to quit life right now."

Ty wraps his arm around me on the couch back at my apartment. "You had that rule for a reason, Nat."

At least I took off for Ty's birthday and don't work for the next three days. I need some distance. Jameson hasn't even tried to call since we left. Although, honestly, what's he going to say? *Sorry, I got confused about which one of you I was fucking?*

"Well, what do you want to see while you're in town?" I ask Tyler, needing a change in subject.

"Museums, a ball game, the pier, a jazz club, you know, the normal tourist shit." The grin he gives me makes me smile and I'm so glad he's here.

My phone dings before I turn out the light an hour later to go to bed. It's from an unknown number.

NO CALLER ID 10:19 PM

> I'm sorry my brother is such a shit-head. I really thought he was better than that. It was nice to meet you and I'm sorry it didn't work out. Maybe just give him some space.

I quickly deduce it's from Rachel and only briefly wonder how she got my number. Then I remember she works for the FBI. *Awesome.*

Give him some space? He was the one more hellbent on invading my space than I was on his, but whatever.

I don't text her back because I'm not even sure it would go through since there's no number that registers. I crawl into bed and try to focus on showing Tyler a good time for the two days he's here.

Jameson's text finally comes through right after I turn the light out.

JAMESON 9:47 PM

> Natalie, I swear that wasn't what it looked like. Please give me a chance to explain.

The severely unwanted thought flashes through my mind: *At least Luca broke up with me first.*

My first tear falls as my phone switches to Do Not Disturb until seven a.m. and I roll on to my side.

My phone rings at 8:05 the next morning. I have a headache from the wine the night before and it intensifies as the evening's events wash over me anew. I'm surprised to see

Stevie calling me so early but I'm relieved it isn't Jameson. I'm not ready to hear his excuses yet.

"Nat! My schedule got accepted already!"

Stevie must be able to tell that I'm extremely confused because I only get out, "Umm..." before he explains.

"Our bids for the London route, Nat! They were approved already. Well, I'm assuming yours was because we ran the domestic route together; it would make no sense to only take one of us. Check your email!"

Shit. Shit. Shit.

Sure enough. "Oh, yeah, I got it too."

"Nat, what's wrong? I thought you'd be thrilled! Three trips to London a week, bigger plane, we'd get First class cabin priority as the home base crew for the flight, *and* you'll be spending basically all week, every week with Jameson."

"Yeah, no, it sounds...I, um...can I call you later? My brother is in town and I promised to take him sightseeing for his birthday today."

"Tyler or Josh?"

"Tyler."

"Oo, I'll be down in a minute to wish the birthday boy happy birthday!" Before I can tell him that Tyler isn't even awake yet, Stephen hangs up.

I drag myself out of bed and see there are three texts and six missed calls from Jameson from the night before.

JAMESON 12:37 AM

Nat, please. Hear me out.

JAMESON 12:57 AM

I know you're pissed but I swear it wasn't what it looked like.

JAMESON 1:30 AM

This is a mess. Congratulations on the London route.

The last one stings a little but I have no desire to play these games so I text him back.

NATALIE 8:17 AM

Your sister told me to give you some space.

His response comes immediately.

JAMESON 8:17 AM

My sister is an idiot. When did you talk to her?

NATALIE 8:18 AM

She texted me last night around 10

JAMESON 8:19 AM

That wasn't my sister. She was in bed already and her phone is plugged in on the counter in the kitchen. It was Nikki, Nat.

NATALIE 8:22 AM

Stevie is here to wish Tyler a happy birthday. I've gotta go.

JAMESON 8:22 AM

Please, let me explain.

When I don't answer right away, Jameson tries to call me. I silence the call and text him back as I greet Stephen at the door.

NATALIE 8:25 AM

Later.

Chapter 10

Jameson

The girls are both still asleep, but to hell with this. My sister went to bed, fuming, right after hitting me below the belt with her last remark and Nikki was too drunk to reason with. They will both be paying for their sins now. I walk to the guest room, bang loudly with my fist, twice as a warning, before throwing the door open.

"Rise and shine. We need to talk." All I get are groans from both of them and Nikki tries to cover her face with a pillow. Not today, bitch. "*Now,*" I boom. I leave the door open so I can yell from the living room and drag them both out by the ankles if they aren't out here in the next two minutes.

Lucky for them, they shuffle into the living room a few minutes later.

My sister starts to speak but I hold up my hand to silence her. "You said plenty last night. It's my turn." Sensing my anger, my sister wisely shuts her mouth and Nikki won't make eye contact with me. She must know what's coming. I'm about to rat us both out to my sister. I will not go down with her sinking ship.

"First of all, both of you better be prepared to grovel at Natalie's feet if she doesn't call me and give me the chance to explain. Secondly, Nikki, you will tell my sister everything you've done since you arrived here a couple of days ago, because if you hope to stay a part of her life, your shit stops now."

Rachel looks at Nikki with a huge question mark on her face. "What the hell is going on?" she asks her best friend.

I see Nikki swallow hard, her eyes still trained on the floor as she wraps her arms around herself. "I might have hit on your brother."

Rachel shrugs her shoulders. "That's it? So what? Everyone hits on Jamie."

When Nikki looks at me and sees the hard set of my jawline and the pissed off look in my eyes, she sighs and keeps going. "Okay, okay...God, this is awkward."

"You should have thought about that before you did it," I snarl.

"I've sent your brother naked pictures over the last couple of days. I was trying to get him to..." she pauses, clearly uncomfortable, "remember something from the past."

The shock on Rachel's face is comforting. At least she didn't know.

"And?" I prompt her.

"Oh God, there's more?" Rachel looks horrified.

Nikki lets out another sigh. "And I was kind of rubbing his thigh with my foot under the table last night which is why he wanted to speak to me privately. In my defense, I'd had a lot to drink, but when he shut the door, I sort of tried to rip his clothes off. He shoved me away from him but I landed on the bed and Natalie walked in on Jameson trying to shut me down, only my top was halfway off. God, Rachel, I'm so sorry."

My sister sits stunned for a beat before replying, "Don't apologize to me, you bitch. Apologize to Jameson. And Natalie." I appreciate my sister finally taking my side, but it doesn't excuse her comment from last night.

Before I can call her out on that though, Nikki stands up, clearly angry that Rachel just called her a bitch.

"*I'm* a bitch? You've said it for years, Rachel, women don't handle it well when Jameson walks away."

"He didn't walk away from Natalie! You set him up!" Rachel yells and I feel like a full-on catfight is about to erupt in my living room.

"I'm not talking about *Natalie. I'm talking about me!*" Annnd here we go. Not how I would have liked for my sister to find out that I bagged her best friend all those years ago, but there's not much I can do to stop this train now.

"You guys were never together! How could he have walked away from you?" Rachel asks.

"You wouldn't understand. There isn't anyone else like him, and after he fucked me that night, I swear I was ruined for every man that came after. He's all I've wanted ever since." Nikki looks utterly defeated. I do feel sorry for her. I'm afraid she has built me up in her mind to be something that I'm actually not.

"Wait. You *fucked* my little brother and never told me? When the hell was this?" Rachel's voice has gone up an octave.

"When we went to visit him at the frat house when he moved back to the States for college."

"Nikki, that was *seventeen* years ago! You've been pining for my brother for *seventeen years?*"

"Yes. No. Maybe? Look, I know it's fucked up but when

you told me he was single again, and he had just gone through all this shit at work, I thought maybe this was my chance. I didn't expect to get here just in time to meet his new girlfriend."

"I literally don't know what to say." Rachel looks at me with a stunned expression on her face.

"Oh, there's more. Nikki, care to tell my sister how you pretended to be her and sent Natalie a text telling her to give me space?"

Rachel whips her head around to Nikki. "I think you need to pack." Nikki opens her mouth to say something but closes it just as quickly because honestly, what can she say? Instead, she stands and heads back to the guest room without a word.

Rachel's eyes soften as she looks at me. "Jamie, I'm so sorry. But also, what the *hell?* You fucked my best friend and didn't think I should know?"

"Rach, I was nineteen and drunk. I fucked *everything.*"

She laughs and I see some of the tension leave her shoulders as she reaches over to hug me. I hate to ruin the moment, but I still need to address her comment from last night. After I'm satisfied that her apology is sincere, she taps a few things on her phone screen, then turns to me. "I booked Nikki's ticket. I'll go let her know she's flying home earlier than planned, then let's go win your girlfriend back."

Chapter 11

Natalie

I feel bad because I'm so fucking distracted. I'm supposed to be Ty's moral support for the breakup he just went through, but instead he's witnessing the fallout from my own.

Is that what Jameson and I are?

Broken up?

Stevie's quick visit was fun and had me laughing - no small feat right now - but he has an afternoon flight that will take him out of town on an overnight. The new international route starts Thursday so he picked up a couple of extra routes to run with Sherri before then.

"Let's get tickets to the game," I suggest after our good-byes to Stephen. The White Sox are in the playoffs but there are still a few nose bleed seats left. Besides, it's more about the hot dogs, beer, and atmosphere than actually seeing the game.

Well, for me anyway.

"Sounds great." I can tell Ty is trying to assess my actual desire to be out and about in light of last night's chaos but I remember that I never wanted to be one of those women whose life was dictated by her man...or her former men... and I've spent too long in that camp already.

"I'm fine, Ty. Really." In truth, I'm not fine. I'm barely standing. But I try to reassure him as best I can.

I change into leggings, boots, and a long sweater and throw my ponytail under a ballcap. I loop my arm through Tyler's as we head down the steps of my building when I hear a familiar voice.

"Nat? What a coincidence." Luca eyes Tyler suspiciously. The two have never met.

I look at Tyler and opt for a plea only he will understand. "S'il vous plaît ne mentionnez rien à propos d'hier soir. C'est Luca." *Please don't mention anything about last night. This is Luca.*

He nods his understanding. And his eyes darken.

"I forgot you speak French," Luca says, still eyeing my brother. "Moving on from Hunter already?" He obviously doesn't know about last night, or how close to home his words hit.

"Luca, this is Tyler, my brother, and we're late, so if you'll excuse us." Tyler and I start to head toward the rail station when Luca calls out behind us.

"Natalie, wait."

"Luca, I have nothing to say to you. You made it clear how much our relationship meant to you. I've moved on."

At that exact moment, Jameson's Land Cruiser comes to a screeching halt at the curb.

You have got to be kidding me.

He practically bounces the curb and runs over Luca's shoes. Jameson is out of the SUV in two seconds flat. Tyler nods for me to go back into the apartment. "Je vais m'en débarrasser. Va m'attendre à l'intéieur." *I'll get rid of them. Go wait for me inside.*

How fucking cute. My brother, my ex-boyfriend, and my...well, I don't exactly know what Jameson is right now, are all squaring off on the sidewalk. Jameson the clear winner by mass alone.

Jameson responds to Tyler in perfect French causing my brother to pause. "Je ne pars pas avant d'avoir parlé à Natalie. C'est un malentendu." *I'm not leaving until I speak to Natalie. It's a misunderstanding.*

Tyler turns back to look at me. Rachel gets out of the car, a pleading look on her face, while I try to make up my mind.

In this second, I want to be that badass vixen who tells them all to go to hell and takes my brother to the baseball game like we'd planned, but he and I both know if I don't have this conversation now, I'm going to be so distracted I won't be any fun to be around anyway.

Let's just get this over with.

As if reading my thoughts, Ty looks at me and gives a slight nod. *Go ahead.*

I look at Jameson - which, honestly, is a bad idea if you're trying to hold on to any resolve - and tell him, "You have five minutes and then Ty and I are going to celebrate his birthday."

When Jameson and Rachel start to follow me up the stairs, I turn, motioning for Ty to follow. I don't want to have to repeat the story, so he might as well hear the explanation himself.

Luca, being the petulant child that he is, starts to protest. "So, everyone gets five minutes but me? Natalie --"

He doesn't get past my name before Jameson flies down

the steps and stops an inch from his face. "No." I can hear the angry tremors in his voice from here. "You don't get five minutes. You had eighteen months and then you blew it. Or rather, Lauren blew you, but either way, it's over, Luca. Leave my girlfriend alone."

Luca's next move is his dumbest one yet. He uses two hands to shove Jameson backwards so that he can create enough space to throw a punch. Jameson sees it coming a mile away and catches Luca's fist mid-air, movie style. Instead of letting it go, he rears back and throws a solid punch right in Luca's stomach.

Luca doubles over and my instincts go into overdrive. Sure, I've wanted to do that to Luca a time or two, but the reality of it is so much worse.

"Jesus, Jameson!" His arm is like a tree trunk. Luca's doubled over on the sidewalk and passerby are probably whipping out their phones. This is too much. All of it. I don't want guys fighting over me. I don't want explanations about why he was ripping some girls' clothes off in the middle of a dinner date with me. I don't want this kind of drama...and yet, I know I have to fly to fucking *London* on Thursday with Jameson.

This is why I don't date pilots.

Frustrated at the fact that I'm so overwhelmed, I'm about to cry, I tell them all to get the hell off my sidewalk.

Ty puts his arm around me and starts to shuffle me toward the rail station. It's no longer just about the game, but creating space and distance from this bullshit. He leans in and whispers, "You're like fucking Helen of Troy, inspiring wars back there. Let's get you drunk."

"Ty, this is the worst birthday ever. I'm so sorry."

He laughs, and it brightens my mood a hair. "Clearly

you forgot that year Mom took us all to the beach for the weekend...where everyone got food poisoning but I had it the least severe so I had to take care of the rest of you. I spent *that* birthday cleaning up puke and terrified I was going to have to call a cab to drive everyone to the hospital because I didn't have my license yet."

I'm doing some combination of laughing and crying right now. "Oh my God, I totally forgot about that," I admit. "Okay, so it's not the worst, but definitely top three."

"Na, not even that. The bright side is that your drama really puts mine into perspective. Melissa didn't want to be with me anymore for whatever reason. She moved away. And now I don't have to see her ever again. Unlike you." He gives me a sheepish smile. "You could always relocate to Miami?" he suggests, nudging my shoulder with his body.

Once we arrive at the ball field, Tyler makes it his mission to get me as drunk as he can, as fast as possible. I loathe the taste of beer so he's been force-feeding me vodka and ginger ale for the last hour and right now I feel much better.

I'm singing all the songs - I'm not sure if they're the *right* songs, but I'm singing. I've made friends with the frat guys to my right, and I don't think I've flashed anyone yet, so overall it's a win. I can barely even remember good 'ole Jimmie's name.

The game is a blast. Three hot dogs later, the bread must have soaked up a large portion of my alcohol and Ty has switched me to water. This is why he's my favorite sibling. The game flies by and before I know it, the crowd is filing out of the ballpark and Ty and I regroup. It's only two-thirty so we decide to try a few more tourist attractions.

As we move throughout the Field Museum, Ty starts to get fidgety and distracted. "Do you want to go?" I ask.

"No, this place is cool."

"Then why have you been looking at the floor instead of the exhibits for the last twenty minutes?"

He stops walking and starts messing with his fingers like he's never seen them before. Why do people do that when they're nervous? Like somehow those cuticles are going to make whatever shitty thing you have to say any better. I don't like the look on his face. "Ty, what's wrong?" Automatically, I'm assuming the worst: one of our parents is sick. Or *he's* sick and that's why he wanted to spend his birthday out here.

"I've really struggled with whether or not to tell you this but since this day is already in the shitter and your relationship is on the fence...I have a really awkward confession."

My relationship? "Out with it, Ty, this doesn't sound good."

"That's because it isn't. Look, just know that the universe is cruel and honestly, there's no way I could have known that Jameson Hunter was going to enter your life."

I'm momentarily stunned. "What about Jameson?"

Ty looks me right in the eye as he says, "I was the one who provided the character witness statement that got him fired."

"You *what?*" I shriek and the sound of my high-pitched voice echoes off the walls of the nearly empty room. I clap a hand over my mouth as my own echo comes back to me. I can't believe this. "I thought you said you didn't know him!"

"I don't. Not really. I know Vanessa. I guess Jameson and I must have crossed paths when I was in Charlotte but if we did, I don't remember. Or at least, we both crossed paths with Vanessa." Tyler is playing with his right earlobe, which he does when he's stressed. He blows a breath and continues, "I'm sorry to say I got taken in by a beautiful face." Hell, it's easy to do. It happened to me with Luca so I'd be the hypocritical pot calling the kettle black if I come across as harsh and unforgiving. "Vanessa came to me shortly after Melissa left and I was in a bad place. She told me this story of being harassed and I'll admit, her details didn't totally add up, but when I signed the statement, I didn't think about Jameson at all, just that I was doing something to help Vanessa. She seemed pretty shaken up at the time, but after hearing Jameson's sister talk at dinner last night, and seeing how Jameson was with you - right up until he fucked it up, of course - I started to realize maybe Vanessa was lying and that Jameson was telling the truth when he walked me through the details. But then you came storming out of his room, pale as a ghost saying we needed to leave, so I don't know what to believe anymore."

This is unreal. My hands are trembling and I have to sit before my knees give out.

Tyler continues talking to eat up the silence. I can tell he's nervous about my reaction because he's repeating himself, just with different words like that will somehow make it better or easier to process. "When you told me your boyfriend's name, I almost shit myself. I've wanted to confess ever since. At first, I felt really bad but after the shit he's putting you through, I'm thinking maybe Vanessa wasn't lying and I did the right thing anyway?" He ends his statement with a question. He's looking to me to grant forgiveness and tell him his stupid desire to please a woman didn't totally fuck the life of an innocent man.

Despite everything, I *know* Jameson didn't sexually harass Vanessa. I know in the depths of my soul that he would never force himself on a woman. Hell, look at him. He doesn't have to. They go fucking nuts just to be around him. "Tyler," I grind his name out through my teeth,

"Jameson would *never* do that to a woman. I may be mad as hell over this shit with Nikki, but if he was undressing her, it's because she *wanted* him too and that makes him a shitty person, but it doesn't make him a rapist, an assailant, or a pervert."

I can't believe I'm sticking up for him. While I'm processing all of this, Rachel's words come slamming into my head. *I've watched what happens when a woman gets attached to Jamie and can't handle it when he's ready to walk away.*

Something about this statement is nagging at me and I can't tell if it's because I can now relate to that statement or if it's something else.

I check in with Stevie and give him the brief text version of what's been going on. Knowing that the next route I fly will be the Thursday trip to London brings a knot of tension back to my stomach. At least Stevie can help serve as a barrier. I briefly imagine Stevie trying to keep Jameson away from me. The image in my mind shows Jameson lifting Stevie by grasping his shoulders and moving him out of the way like a toy solider and a laugh escapes my lips.

"What's funny?" Ty asks.

"My life, Ty. My life is fucking hilarious."

Ty drapes an arm around my shoulders and kisses the side of my head. "Welcome to the club." It feels like it did when we were little. The world burning down around us, but Ty and I always had each other's backs.

"Happy birthday," I deadpan. I have so much anger rolling through me as I try to process everything. I'm so pissed at Ty for lying for Vanessa but I can understand his shitty headspace and thinking that maybe he was helping her in some way. I'm also pissed at Jameson for throwing punches and whatever he was doing with Nikki. I'm pissed at Luca for showing back up in my life just as I was trying to start a new relationship, but most of all, I'm mad at myself for breaking my own rule and landing myself in all this drama.

Chapter 42

Jameson

It's been two days since I punched Luca on the sidewalk. Natalie isn't returning my calls or texts. I'm pretty sure her brother has left town and Rach and Nikki are both gone as well. I'm not sure if Nat's still pissed over Nikki or the fact that I punched Luca, but if she won't give me a chance to explain then I guess there isn't much else to do. The first run of the new route is today. I've been holding my breath, waiting for a phone call from Natalie that hasn't come yet.

More than once, I've asked myself what in the hell I was thinking. I feel like a hormone-driven teenager who can't control his cock or his fists.

There are several reasons I don't date coworkers and this thing with Natalie has damn near reminded me of them all. Yet, as I get dressed for work this morning, I can't help but think about her. I'm almost giddy to see her today which is fucking ridiculous because I'm a grown-ass man who isn't even sure the woman I'm pining over ever wants to see me ever again.

I pin my wings on my uniform and head to the parking garage under my building.

My phone dings in the elevator, causing my heart to race. *Knock it off, Jameson.*

STEPHEN 6:44 AM

She won't admit it, but she's excited to see you. Don't fuck this up, Hunter. I'm rooting for you. I don't think you're a cheater but you'd better have one hell of an explanation.

JAMESON 6:50 AM

Thanks for the heads up. Think you could help me by convincing her to give me a minute to explain sometime on this flight?

STEPHEN 6:51 AM

Absolutely.

But only because I like your sweatpants.

JAMESON 6:51AM

Noted. Thanks, Stevie.

STEPHEN 6:52 AM

You can thank me over dinner...while wearing said sweatpants.

JAMESON 6:52 AM

Deal.

I don't even care that I'm basically flirting with Stephen and whoring myself out. Right now, he's my best chance at getting her back.

I'm at the airport early. Nervous about seeing Natalie and excited about flying international again. We're on a Boeing 787-9 Dreamliner. It's a big bird and requires eight flight attendants. With Stephen, Natalie, and two others selected - I haven't heard who they are yet - being the home base crew for the flight, they will be the senior attendants which means they choose their cabin.

Unable to pace in the lounge any longer, I make my way to the gate. I'd like to have a minute or two on board before everyone shows up.

The gate attendant eyes me appreciatively as I swipe my badge to the jet bridge. Making my way toward the cockpit, I hear voices. Looks like I'm not first after all.

Natalie's back is to me but she stops talking when Stephen's eyebrows shoot up upon seeing me. I see Stephen gently touch her forearm and whisper, "Hear him out, Nat," before heading through the door that leads to the first-class cabin. On a plane this size, it's actually pretty easy to find privacy when only ten people are on board. I hear others moving around the aircraft but I'm unconcerned with their presence. If they interrupt, we'll just switch languages.

"Natalie," I start and I see her eyes widen and her lips part slightly when she turns to face me. I take this as a good sign. I step closer to her, causing her to have to look up. I grab her hand and lead her into the cockpit. If I close the door, I'm breaking more rules but seeing her right now after two days, her skin flushed just from holding my hand, and her breathing as shallow and rapid as mine, I don't give a fuck about those rules and I push the door shut, only satisfied when it clicks. "It wasn't what it looked like, and trust me, I know what it looked like. Nikki and I have a history. It was brief and I regret it, but it happened nonetheless. However, I was completely unaware that she never moved on." I try to explain that Nikki thought it was open season on me which is why she agreed to come to Chicago in the first place. "She was coming on to me and I was trying to tell her to stop it. I didn't want to do it in front of everyone because she's my sister's best friend but when she and I were alone, she lost it. She was in the middle of trying to take her top off and I was trying to make her keep it on when you walked in, I swear." I'm trying to read Natalie's face. I've never had to beg a woman before, for anything. I can think of fifty other things I'd rather beg for than forgiveness, but here we are.

"A history?" She narrows her eyes. Of course this is the part she'd latch on to.

I rub the back of my neck. "Yeah. We, uh, slept together at a frat party one time. *One* time. Seventeen years ago. I was drunk as hell and don't even remember anything other than it happened. My sister never knew until a couple days ago, which was another reason I didn't want to call Nikki out at the dinner table. Although, now I wish I would have." I can't handle the distance anymore so I. take a chance and reach for her. She lets me pull her to me, but she still seems hesitant. Wary.

She puts her hands on my shoulders to prevent me from pulling her any closer.

"Nat --" I start but she holds up a hand.

Shit. Her eyes are watering with unshed tears and we're running out of time.

"I'm really sorry," she says, catching me off guard. Fuck, this sounds like a break up speech. I let an exhale out and look away. She uses her hand to bring my face back to hers. "I'm sorry I lost it before giving you a chance to explain." Now she won't meet my gaze. I can tell there is something else she wants to say.

"Nat, what's wrong?"

"I don't know how to tell you this. Especially now that I don't want to burn your apartment down." She gives a small, humorless laugh. She's staring at my shoes when she whispers, "But I feel like I need to if we're going to give this a real shot."

I cock an eyebrow at her. What's changed? She's now apologizing to *me?* "Nat, what's going on?"

Finally, she comes right out with it. "Ty was the reason you got fired from your last carrier."

There's no way I heard that right. I'd never even met him before a couple of days ago.

She can read the confusion in my face as she launches into the story about how Ty didn't know me...he knew Vanessa and the version of the story she spun. Tyler and Vanessa worked together for a period of time before he relocated to Miami. It's scary how distracted some people can get over a defined chest and pretty face. Vocal about his break up, Vanessa turned to him, knowing he was vulnerable. She poured on the sob story, enlisting Tyler's help to retaliate against me. Supposedly, he thought I'd get a slap on the wrist or have to pay a fine and he would land Vanessa. Well, he was wrong there...on both accounts

My initial reaction is that I'm pissed. What an immature move, that cost me fucking *everything*. But ironically, it also landed me in his sister's path, so my anger cools shockingly fast.

"Natalie, look at me." When she does, her first tear falls and it's my undoing. I tell her I'm going to kiss her even as I lean in. She meets me halfway and I swear I hear fireworks. Or maybe it's just the blood pounding in my ears. She's murmuring apologies against my lips as her hands fly to the buttons of my shirt.

The door of the cockpit opens and I half expect Luca to walk in. Natalie jumps away from me in surprise as a first officer I don't know boards. He's younger than me, but looks close to my age. Thirty-three maybe?

His eyes land on Natalie first. She's righting her blouse from where I had it bunched in my hands. "Wow, full-service flight, huh?" The insinuation boils my blood in my veins as he openly gawks at Natalie. "I'll have what he's having." He points a thumb in my direction as he goes settled in to his seat. If this guy was just trying to clear the air after walking in on us, something like "Sorry to interrupt" would have been more appropriate.

"This is my girlfriend, you asshole." The remark is out before I can stop myself. Natalie's right, we're all a bunch of dicks. No wonder she wanted to stay away from pilots.

"Jameson," she smiles at me and pauses, "I need to get back to work." I know what she's asking. It's the same thing I want to know.

"Sommes-nous bons?" *Are we good,* I ask.

"Oui, mais maintenant je veux te baiser et nous devons voler pendant huit heures." *Yes, but now I want to fuck you and we have to fly for eight hours.*

A growl escapes my throat as I feel my cock twitch at her words. "Natalie," I say in warning.

"Jameson," she replies sweetly. The first officer has briefly busied himself with his own pre-flight duties as Natalie leans in. I think she is going to kiss me but instead she runs her tongue up the side of my neck. "Safe flight, Captain."

I catch her wrist as she turns to go, my voice harsh when it comes out, "Nous finirons cela quand nous atterrirons." *We'll finish this when we land.*

Chapter 43

Natalie

I 'm on Cloud Nine after making up with Jameson and getting all of our confessions out in the open. Perhaps I shouldn't be so trusting of his explanation but I am. I now know why his sister's words from dinner were bugging me after Ty's confession. Hearing Jameson's explanation made the pieces fit perfectly. He even told me that Nikki was aggressive and he didn't want to be left alone with her. It's just hard to believe the lengths some people will go to get what they want.

I can't stop the smile that is spread wide across my face as I work today. Stevie and I settle in for the longer journey. My first working a transatlantic route. There are eight total flight attendants: two in business class, four for the main cabin, and two in the background working to refill carts and manage patron requests. There are a couple of needy passengers but no one is out of line or rude which feels like the biggest win. Stevie ends up with six phone numbers and plans for the night.

Our crew is overnighting in London before the return

trip tomorrow, and since I've never been here, I'm pretty excited.

Jameson touches down in London and a rush of heat heads straight between my thighs. We land so lightly it's as if he used magic and none of the sleeping passengers stir a bit.

It takes an hour and fifteen minutes to deplane an aircraft this big and get the carts restocked for the next crew. Four of us are overnighting, four are heading back as passengers.

I barely have time to grab my bag before Jameson comes out of the cockpit. God, how does he look even more beautiful after an eight-hour flight? I hear the whispers around us so I know I'm not the only one who feels that way. Stevie loops his arm through mine as we watch Jameson run a hand through his hair as he signs a final sheet and hands it back to the first officer.

When he sees me, he looks hungry. Actually, he looks like a starving man who just laid eyes on his first meal in days. Stephen detangles himself from me. "Based on the look on that man's face, I'd better let you go," he says with a wink. "I'll see you tomorrow." He starts to head toward the jet bridge.

"Stevie." I catch his wrist and he stops to look back at me over his shoulder. "Text me when you get back to your room tonight. I don't care what time it is. I don't want to have to call Interpol because one of your lovers got out of control."

"Yes, Mom." He gives me a kiss on the cheek and turns to Jameson before exiting the plane. "Take care of her."

Jameson grabs my hand and pulls me out of the plane. "You heard the man. Let's go," he growls in my ear.

Jameson has a huge stride that causes me to practically

run to keep up with him. As we exit the airport, he flags down a taxi and I can't help but notice it's the cleanest, nicest-smelling taxi I've ever been in. And the driver is so cheerful. I already love everything about London. Jameson gives him the name of a hotel I don't recognize.

"I thought the airline put us in the Hyatt at the airport?"

"The airline did. *I* put us in a hotel near Windsor Castle because you've never seen London." He looks at me, his eyes darkening by the second as his pupils dilate to erase the color of his irises. "I wanted to show you around London, but I'm not sure we're going to have any time for that."

I look at my watch. "It's only 6:58p.m."

"Exactly."

Oh.

I try to take in the sights from the window as we pass by but my attention keeps drifting back to Jameson in the seat next to me. His tie is off and shoved in his bag, along with his hat. He's undone the top two buttons on his shirt and his jacket is draped across his lap. I see the muscles of his thighs clenching and unclenching like he has a year's worth of pent-up energy after being cooped in the cockpit for eight hours.

I place my hand on his thigh and slowly drag my fingers upwards, smiling to myself when he catches my hand. "Are you trying to raise my blood pressure dangerously high?" he whispers. Seeing a man like Jameson Hunter come undone at my touch is the most powerful feeling I've ever had. His reaction to me makes me bold and brave and ridiculously happy.

"Quite the opposite," I whisper back.

The tension in his jaw is visible as we check in at the hotel. The lady takes her sweet time explaining the attractions that are close by, the features of the hotel, and the number for the concierge in case we would like dinner reservations. I silently giggle at the vein popping out on Jameson's neck as he tries to be polite. Finally, she hands us our keys and Jameson takes off at a sprint for the elevators.

As soon as the doors close, his hands are on me. In my hair, on my ass, cupping my face, cupping my breast. In our room, he tears at the pieces of my uniform with urgency as I fight for control to tear him free of his first.

Having successfully gotten him out of his jacket and shirt, he goes for the clasp on my pants and drops to his knees, pressing kisses to the inside of my thighs and it hits me that I've been at work, on a plane, for the last eight hours. I feel disgusting.

"Jameson." He doesn't stop. "*Jameson.*" I try again and he finally looks up at me with lust clouding his irises like cataracts. "Let me grab a quick shower."

"Nat, I can't wait." That's evident in the raging hard-on he is sporting at the moment.

"Then come with me. I just wan to rinse off."

Jameson pulls my pants off the rest of the way then hooks his thumbs in my panties and pushes them down my legs agonizingly slowly. When I'm rolling my hips in antici-pation, he hops to his feet and unbuttons my blouse, tossing it on the floor, my bra following behind. I finish my earlier task and get rid of the rest of his uniform as well, satisfied only when it's in a heap on the floor.

Jameson pulls me into the walk-in shower and spins me so I'm facing the tile shower wall. Pressing lightly on my upper back, I know he wants me to lean forward. I oblige. The cold tile in stark contrast to the heat of the water and the man standing behind me has me arching my back, aching to feel him inside me.

Jameson is torturing me with his fingertips as they run down my back, over my ass, and down my thighs, feather light in their exploration.

I groan, "*Now* you want to take it slow?"

He chuckles behind me. "Nat, you tortured me with your silence for two days, so yeah, I plan to make you a little uncomfortable."

So much for not being able to wait while I took a shower.

Deciding I can live with a little revenge, I reach behind me to pull him closer but he catches my hand and puts them both over my head. "Don't move," he breathes in my ear. I feel him pat the inside of my right thigh, indicating he wants me to spread my feet farther apart. Pulling back on my hips, he rubs me back and forth over his erection making my knees weak. When his hand reaches around the front of me, I start to beg shamelessly.

"Jameson, please."

"Please what?" His soapy hands are lathering my skin, giving me a minute before his assault starts again. I bring my hands off the wall and try to face him but he pulls me back against him, one hand securing me in place around my waist, the other around my throat. "Please *what*, Natalie?"

"Fuck me."

He takes his time lathering his hands with soap and then rubs me down before doing the same to himself before he shuts off the water, turns me to face him and scoops me up by my ass. He deposits me on the bed, not even bothering to towel off, and pushes my knees wide as he buries his face between my thighs. My hands twist in the sheets as I get tunnel vision and feel myself slipping over the edge.

"Good girl," Jameson growls and the orgasm rips from me. "You have thirty seconds and then I want you to do it again," he demands. Apparently by *thirty* he really meant *eight,* and before I can catch my breath, he's hiking my leg up to guide himself in slowly. "*Fuck.*" As he sinks into me the whole world disappears. Nothing matters except the man next to me.

"I'll make up for it in round two, but this won't take long, baby."

His words make me spiral and it's either my cries or my nails in his back that send him plummeting with me.

Time is a funny thing. I feel like I've known Jameson *years* instead of a couple months. When he shifts me so I'm on top of him looking down, I know it's a sight I'll never get tired of. He moves his hips and I feel him getting hard again. Already. The grin he gives me is wicked in the most wonderful way and I feel more connected to him than I've ever felt to anyone.

As he thrusts his hips up into me, I realize I've completely fallen for Jameson Hunter and I'm pretty sure he can tell by the look on my face right now.

The bed has a fabric headboard sturdy enough for me to grip for leverage as I ride Jameson to within an inch of our lives. His monosyllabic grunts give me all the encouragement I need as I roll my hips violently against him.

Knowing me better than I know myself, when I don't come after a few minutes, he pulls my hands off the headboard. "Place your hands on my thighs and lean back." I do as he says while he uses his hands to spread my knees farther apart. I'm in a saddle position with my legs tucked under me, completely open to his hungry gaze. He places his thumb on my clit and it has me plummeting over the edge within sixty seconds.

He flashes me a shit eating grin that clearly says *told you.* I'm not arguing.

After a brief moment to allow my body to recover from its hypersensitivity, Jameson whispers, "Get on all fours."

I slowly roll over and push up onto my hands and knees. I have serious concerns about Jameson's ability to fit this way. I'm like Pavlov's dog to the rip of the foil now and I'm instantly wet again. I feel Jameson guide himself to my entrance as he places a hand on my back, wanting my chest on the bed. He starts slow like usual, giving me time to accommodate his size. I feel him pause his entry every couple of seconds. "Jameson, I'm okay," I tell him reassuringly. It's a stretch but he isn't hurting me.

"I'm glad, but it's not for your benefit that I'm stopping."

Oh.

"I had hoped after already coming once, I'd last longer in this position, but you hug me so tightly, I'm not sure I'm going to make it past a thrust or two."

He doesn't.

Round three is less hurried and we spend the rest of the night covering all the bases from fucking to making love and then start over.

Chapter 44

Jameson

The first run of the route was great. No delays, good weather, competent crew. I'm looking forward to the stability of running this route on the regular. Sure, the distance is farther and the hours in flight are longer, but I'd rather be earning money in the air than sitting on the ground for multiple layovers.

The jet lag is a bit of a bitch though.

Thankfully Natalie and I are finally on the same page and aren't ready to be apart so I drop Stephen off at his apartment and wait at the curb while Nat grabs some stuff to come to my place.

"I get the feeling I'm going to be seeing you a lot less," I hear Stephen tell Natalie as they step onto the sidewalk.

"Stevie, you're my best friend. Even if I'm not in the same building as much, we now have unlimited transatlantic hours to catch up on everything. Plus, we both have Thursdays off, so breakfast is my treat."

I watch as they link arms and head into the building. Seeing him care for her so much makes me want to do something nice for him. I make a mental note to ask Nat what he might like.

Fifteen minutes later, we're pulling into the underground garage of my apartment building.

As we get out of the car, an officer approaches us.

"Jameson Hunter?" he asks.

"Yes, sir." I respond, my heart rate ticking up. I assume someone broke in to my apartment or maybe Nikki was hell-bent on revenge and spray painted the building or something.

Instead, he comes over to me and hands me an envelope. "You've been served. Have a good night."

"What the fuck?"

The officer doesn't stick around to answer any questions; he's already done his job. I tear open the envelope and blow out a breath. I knew this was probably coming at some point but it's still a shock to see.

Natalie tries to read the letter over my shoulder, so I just hand it to her to make it easier. "Luca filed a report for assault."

"That *asshole!*" Natalie cries. It's the second time she's been outraged on my behalf. My mind flashes back to her pacing in my living room when I told her the whole story about Vanessa.

Not again.

"Jameson, I am so sorry. He shoved you first! And threw the first punch!"

I appreciate that Natalie is processing the events of that afternoon in rapid fire, trying to find proof of my innocence but unfortunately, "I escalated the situation by throwing a punch that connected. Technically, he didn't strike me because I caught his fist. I should have stopped there." She looks deep in thought and I feel a little nauseated but there isn't anything I can do about it now. Right now, I just want to take her upstairs and get her to bed. I'll probably have to disclose this to the airline at some point but I'll worry about that tomorrow...after I hire an attorney. If Luca didn't go to HR, then maybe I won't lose my job. The incident didn't happen while I was on the clock or while I was in uniform so technically this is just a civil matter...of total bullshit.

I grab Nat's hand and pull her toward the elevator. "Come on, let's go to bed."

"Jameson, it's three-thirty in the afternoon."

"I didn't say we were going to *sleep.*"

"You just got hit with *another* lawsuit that you don't deserve and you want to have sex?"

Her tone of incredulity makes me huff out a deep laugh. "Well technically, the first one wasn't a lawsuit. Vanessa went to our HR and demanded the worst, but she never pressed charges in a civil suit so it isn't on my record. Good 'ole Luca seems to have gone the other route. I haven't heard from HR, although I'm sure that he knows I'll have to disclose the suit myself. And yes, I want to have sex because I forget all the bullshit when I'm inside you." I can't help but smile when I hear her intake of breath at the bluntness of my statement.

She leans into me and grabs my hands with hers and walks backwards as she leads me to the elevator. Once we're tucked inside, she wraps her arms around my neck and presses herself flat against me. "We'll get through this," she whispers and God help me, I believe her.

By the time we reach my floor, my white shirt is completely unbuttoned. It's only three-thirty in the after-noon but it feels like ten at night. Stumbling into my condo, I hit a button to draw the blackout curtains closed. Encased in darkness, in a familiar space that is my own, it's time to relieve some tension and show this woman how desperate I've become for her touch. Last night already feels like a lifetime ago. It was slow and gentle. This afternoon will be anything but.

It seems like Natalie is on the same page when she connects her phone to my built-in Bluetooth speaker and the dirtiest song I've ever heard comes piping into every room in the condo. She spends the next hour and a half making me feel like the luckiest guy on the planet despite the amount of shit creeping into my life.

We fall into bed, sated and spent and sleep like the dead for ten hours, adjusting to the time difference.

When I wake up early the following morning, dread fills my stomach as I immediately think about the call I have to make to human resources. I can't believe that Luca's hurt pride would propel him to take one punch this far. Then again, maybe it has nothing to do with the punch, and everything to do with keeping me away from Natalie.

I try to slip out of bed without disturbing her, but as soon as I move to swing a leg over the edge, she tightens her grip around my waist and doubles her efforts to crawl on top of me. She isn't awake but she huffs out short breaths of air through her nose like she is pouting about that fact that I'm trying to leave her alone in bed. I allow myself to be pulled back under the sheets with her. Unable to stop myself, I kiss the top of her head. Despite the amount of utter bullshit thrown at me over the last several months, I feel more at peace now, with her by my side than I ever did before.

I'm able to lay still for another hour but finally, I can't keep my mind from racing which makes my limbs jittery. Not able to put it off any longer, I gently slide out of bed, grab my sweatpants and slip a t-shirt over my head as I start doing research on attorneys who can help me fight this.

The good news is that I learned that civil suits usually end up with monetary payments, unlike criminal suits, which can end with jail time. The problem is that I still have to notify human resources, who will most likely notify the FAA. I swear to everything holy, if I lose my wings over this shit...

Needing to move, I leave a note for Nat, grab a towel and my tennis shoes and hit the gym on the second floor of my building.

Chapter 45

Natalie

Waking up sore and smelling like Jameson is how I want to wake up every day for the rest of my life. I stretch like a cat - and purr like one too - as I throw on one of Jameson's t-shirts and pad down the hallway in search of the coffee.

My eyes land on Jamie's note and all the drama of the last week comes rushing back in. I can't believe Luca is *suing* Jameson. A small part of me knows this is Luca's attempt to punish me for not taking him back, but why is Jameson always on the shit-end of the stick?

Curling my legs up under me on the couch, I set my coffee down on the end table and grab my phone which had been charging there all night. I gear up to help Jameson fight and win this battle against Luca. Exuding a calm and focus I was unaware I possessed, I dial Tyler's number.

I catch him up to speed about the events of the last three days and ask if he'd be willing to help Jameson *keep* his job this time instead of causing him to lose it. Tyler agrees wholeheartedly, glad for the chance to right his wrong.

We talk through a plan for thirty minutes: hire attorney,

write down order of events, ask for any camera footage from the building, witness statements, etc...

By the time we get off the phone I'm feeling a little lighter. However, it's clear when Jameson comes in the door that he's not feeling the same way. His eyes are rimmed in red. Not like he's been crying, just like he didn't sleep at all and stress is permeating his system. He's sweaty and looks like he just went hard on himself for a long while.

His gray t-shirt is dark from sweat stains and clings to him like a second skin. Muscles are standing at attention from the increase in blood coursing through his veins - which are also popping out.

I'm still in awe that this machine of a man, with his knowledge, skills, appearance, and protective nature wants to be with me. Unaware of my own actions, I untuck my legs and set my elbows on my knees with a hand over my mouth.

I see his mouth curve up into a half-smile.

"Nat? You're staring again."

His words snap me back to reality but I don't stop openly gawking. Shaking my head in disbelief, I tell him, "If you could see my boyfriend, you'd understand why."

He reaches over his head and pulls his gray t-shirt off and tosses it at me playfully. "How would you feel about helping him reach his back in the shower?"

God, his lines. They're everywhere. I can't get off the couch fast enough. Just as I crash into him, my hands roaming over his chest and playing at the waistband of his shorts, unsure of where to start and what to touch first, the shrill tone of Kenny Loggins' *Highway to the Danger Zone* fills the air.

"Shit. Hold that thought, I've gotta take this," Jameson says as he pulls his phone out of his armband. I unwillingly detach myself from him and watch as he paces up and down the hallway to his room.

A few short "Mmm hmm's" and "Yes, I understands" later, he bursts out loudly with "I absolutely do *not* want to settle. That would be to admit that I'm the only one in the wrong and I won't let that asshole have the satisfaction of spending my money."

I hear the very female voice on the other end of the line - because Jameson put his phone on speakerphone and set it on the counter - reply calmly, "I understand, Mr. Hunter. I'm just reviewing your options and letting you know which one would make him go away the fastest."

Jameson lets out a frustrated breath.

Twenty minutes later, Jameson's retelling me everything that his attorney just went over with him. It's complicated and stressful but ultimately Jameson punched Luca so that's bad, but if there's footage that shows that Luca's arm was making forward progress to connect with Jameson when Jameson caught his fist, then it most likely will get thrown out. No serious injury, no time missed from work. Two punches: one that connected, one that didn't. Tit for tat.

At least we can hope. I don't even think Jamie is aware of the circles he's tracing on my thigh as he talks. It seems to calm him though, so even though he's throwing me into overdrive, I let him continue to trail his fingers over my thigh as it peeks out from the bottom of his shirt.

When he's done sharing his information, I stand and pull him up with me. "Come on, let's grab that shower and get something to eat." Unless something changes, we fly back to London tomorrow.

In the shower, I tell him about my conversation with Ty and that I already emailed the superintendent of my building to see if the lobby cameras caught any of the incident. I told Jamie he should ask Rachel to write down the order of events like Ty and I did just to confirm. When I finally stop talking, he seems a little more calm knowing the ball is rolling and we've done all we can do for right now. I make a mental note to grab the name and number of his attorney so I can forward any information that Ty and the others pass along to me.

I don't intentionally mean to make it sound like I think this is all my fault. I don't. These guys are grown ass men and they're responsible for their own actions, but I'm undeniably the reason Luca is coming after Jameson and I feel the need to apologize. "Jameson, I'm so sorry to add this drama to your life."

He lets a humorless laugh escape. "It's not you, Nat. My life just seems to have inescapable drama these days. It'll calm down at some point."

There is zero conviction in his voice as he utters the words.

Chapter 46

Jameson

The route home from London two days later is long and tedious but we hit storms about halfway over the Atlantic so I had something to keep me awake. Natalie and Stevie even had Sherri along for this trip and they were giddy the whole route. Although Natalie and I are distracted, I'm glad we're on the same side of the argument this time, and we're finding our groove.

The jet lag hurt a little less when we got back this time. There are a couple of options for the return flight as long as we get mandatory rest off the clock so we're playing around with what we like the best, opting for the red eye back as it was the first return flight we could work after our rest period.

The email comes at two o'clock the morning the day we return to the States. The Federal Aviation Administration - FAA - has grounded me until the suit is over and a hearing is conducted to look at my file considering this is the third strike against me in such a short period of time. Dread fills my stomach at what this could mean for my future.

I touch base with my attorney and I can barely process

the words she's speaking before she moves on to more words. The part that I catch is that I need to come into the office to meet with her, sign some papers, and discuss some options before proceeding any further. Unfortunately, she wants to "check on a couple of things" first so I just have to wait for her call.

The last forty-eight hours have been hell. The waiting, killing Nat and I, both. We've gone over every scenario we can think of and only one of every twelve has a decent ending. Nothing like life-altering stress to know if you're compatible with another person, and Natalie has been incredible. Supportive but not clingy. Honest and real without giving false hope. And *very* good at distracting me with sex despite the fact that I'm pretty sure the stress in my system may have me on the path to an aneurism. She's made me laugh a couple of times and never once did I crave space from her.

My attorney has called a couple of times to clarify a few things but wanted to give time for the "dust to settle" before calling us in - whatever that means.

Finally, she called this afternoon to have us come into the office. When we arrive, we're led to a small waiting area and given coffee. Nat's knee bounces with nerves, giving me something to focus on so I don't drown in my own sea of nervousness.

It feels like forever before someone leads us to a private office, but the clock indicates it's only been six minutes.

When my attorney enters the room, she abruptly stops

as her eyes land on me. Her eyebrows shoot up in surprise and she sways a little where she stands. It's her first time seeing me in person. She recovers quickly but not quickly enough and I feel Natalie bristle beside me.

"Captain Hunter?" she asks.

I nod and point to Natalie. "And this is my girlfriend, Natalie. It's her ex-boyfriend who's bringing the suit against me."

"Amanda Balterra, nice to meet you both in person." She seems to have gotten herself under control as she gets back in her element. "I must say, you have some very loyal friends Captain Hunter."

"Please, call me Jameson." I pause, processing her words. "My friends?" I ask, confused by her statement.

A smile spreads across her face as she explains. "As it turns out, the report I had to file with the FAA alerting them to the case, and our plan of action, names Luca as the instigator of the incident based on video footage provided by Natalie's building manager. Not only does the video show that Luca made contact with you first, but that he made contact in an attempt to strike you. The footage was also accompanied by two letters; one from Stephen Dagenheart and one Tyler Redding, explaining your true character and the nature of what transpired in the video. I believe Mr. Redding's letter also contained a confession of unintentional defamation regarding a sexual harassment suit you were involved in. The FAA has decided that it no longer needs to conduct a review of your file." She pauses for effect but when I don't respond, she continues to explain. "Your punch was considered self-defense and it forced the FAA to ground Luca Barbieri pending your next move."

"My next move?" I know I must sound slow, repeating everything she says.

She actually laughs this time. "Yes, Jameson. You now have the option to counter-sue for assault as well as a few other things like emotional damages for being dragged through this mess."

I don't even need time to think this through. "I don't want any of that. I want to be left the hell alone. I want to fly planes and take my girlfriend out to dinner."

"Very well. I won't file any paperwork for the counter-suit. If you sign these, you're free to go. Barbieri has no choice but to drop his case unless he wants to pay an attorney for a case he'll never win. Plus, now that he's grounded, at least until I inform everyone there will be no action taken on your part, I'm sure whatever revenge plot he hatched doesn't look quite so promising anymore."

"So, it's over? Just like that? I can fly again?"

"You're back on the schedule effective tomorrow. As far as this being over, it's officially over once we have Luca's signature, but if his attorney is worth anything, he'll make sure Mr. Barbieri signs as soon as possible."

I can't believe it. I sit, completely stunned, as I hear Natalie exclaim next to me, "That's wonderful news! Thank you so much!" Her voice breaks me out of my reverie and I address my attorney.

"Yes, thank you, Ms. Balterra. I greatly appreciate your time and efficiency." I reach my hand forward to shake hers. She lets go after one firm pump. I appreciate her boundaries and awareness.

I'm still processing as we leave the office and it isn't until Nat and I are grabbing pizza at Gino's and sipping a beer, that I start to feel the tension leave my shoulders.

"I'm finally excited to fly again!" she says with a smile on her face a mile wide.

"Me too," I say, shocked to find that I mean it. As the stress ebbs away, it creates space for other emotions to fill in the gap. "That was really nice of your brother to help me out."

Natalie laughs. "You mean it was nice of him to tell the truth after telling a lie that cost you your job?"

I can't hide my smirk. "Yeah, that."

"God, I'm stuffed." She pushes back from the table, her eyelids heavy, the stress of the day leaving us both drained.

"Come on, baby, let's go home."

Chapter 17

Natalie

We're on our way to the airport at the ass-crack of dawn. Stevie is in the backseat listening to me retell the ending of the tumultuous saga that has plagued our lives for the last week. It feels like so much longer. After everything we've been through, it feels like Jameson and I have been in each other's lives forever when in fact the timeline is much shorter.

Stevie is a great listener. He gasps and *ohmygods* in all the right places. His sincerity reminds me why I love him so much when he says, "I'm glad it all worked out. Nat, you deserve the best and I think you've finally found him."

All's quiet when we park and hitch a ride on the employee bus. My eyes scan the crowd for Luca but I don't see him. Most likely he's tucked tail and is purposely avoiding our gate seeing as it's the same every time. Fine by me.

First class is a little rowdy today but Stevie and I are ready for them. We have fun bouncing around taking requests, turning off lights, passing out headphones, and finally catching up once breakfast has been served and cleaned up. We're both really enjoying the long flights. More time to get settled. Overall, less time on our feet. We enjoy working when Jameson is at the helm, especially since he always calls to let us know when the radar shows rain and storms. His landings continue to be orgasm-inducing and Stevie and I cackle during take-off while we discuss every innuendo we can think of involving the words: thrust, power, force, lift, speed...you get the idea.

The phone rings quietly about four hours into the eight-hour flight.

"Hello?"

"I'm coming out, can you have Stephen block the aisle? Retrouvez-moi dans les quartiers des pilotes." *Meet me in the pilots' quarters.*

This flight has three pilots. Because Jameson has the most senior rank, he can call when he wants a break. They rotate in thirty-minute stints in the pilots' quarters. The access is a small locked door that looks like a closet and is next to the flight attendants' station. I ask Stevie to watch the cockpit and let him know to text me if he needs me.

"I promise to only text if this bitch catches on fire," he says as he winks. "Go live out every fantasy I've ever had."

I climb the stairs already primed for Jameson's touch. The space is cramped and there are a lot of parts to our uniforms so it isn't glamorous, but that's part of the fun. When Jameson's lips touch my skin, I'm afraid I'm the one that might set fire to this plane. With the roar of the engines that are keeping this thing in the sky, there really isn't a need to be quiet so we moan our climaxes together, thirty-eight thousand feet in the air.

"You know, I'm pretty sure you have a higher thrust ratio than this plane." I can't help myself. The puns are too good to pass up.

Jameson playfully rolls his eyes. "Is this where I make a comment about your landing strip?"

My fits of laughter bring tears to my eyes. "That's so bad."

"They're *all* bad." He's right. But they're so bad that they're hilarious.

As I right my uniform and straighten Jameson's wings on his jacket, I can't hide my goofy smile - not that I'm trying to. Despite my plan to stay away from pilots, this life is the one I love. It means the world to me that the man I love enjoys this fast-paced, hectic, chaos-driven lifestyle too.

"Every time you announce for us to prepare the cabin for landing, I'm going to lose it now," I confess, still giggling, thinking about female shave patterns.

"Take-off, turbulence, landing, I feel like we've already been through it all," Jameson says growing serious.

I reach up and place my hand on his cheek. "It's been turbulent alright, but I'll fly with you through anything."

He tucks a strand of hair behind my ear. "I'm so glad I decided to date a co-worker."

"I'm so glad I didn't give up on pilots and that you made me *break my rules*."

Chapter 48

EPILOGUE

Jameson Two weeks later

Natalie opens the door to the condo and looks exhausted. "How bad was it?" I ask.

She kicks her heels off at the door and groans as she bends forward to rub her feet.

"Just one of those days where nothing goes right. I'm glad I'm home. It smells good in here."

"Gino's."

Her tired smile makes my heart thump in my chest. Standing from the couch, I meet her in the kitchen and pull her face to mine. "I'm glad you're home."

"Me too. And I'm glad you had the foresight to order..." she trails off when she lifts the lid of the pizza box. "Why is there Italian sausage on this pizza?"

I know she hates Italian sausage. She wrinkles her nose at the beer on the counter. "And a twenty-four pack of IPA?" I stay quiet as she looks up at the T.V. and swallows hard. "America's Got Talent? Oh my God! You got dinner for Stevie? What the hell?" she cries, making me chuckle.

"Relax, baby. Your mushroom pizza is waiting for you

next to your bath and there's a bottle of wine already chilled for you."

She arches a brow at me, waiting to explain further.

Running a hand through my hair, I grimace. "I promised Stephen dinner if he helped me get you alone so I could explain the situation with Nikki on that first flight to London."

She looks down at my outfit.

"You might want to change pants and add a shirt. You know those sweatpants make Stevie feral. I can guarantee your bare chest isn't going to help either."

"Yeah...that's...uh...part of the deal."

At this, she bursts into laughter. "You whored yourself out for five minutes with me?"

"Yeah, I'm not proud of it, but it was worth it."

"Aw, baby, that's the sweetest thing anyone's ever done for me," she says, still laughing as she pulls my face down to kiss me.

Suddenly, there's a knock at the door.

"Oh, I want to see his reaction to this."

She dances to the door and opens it with a flourish. Stevie enters our apartment wearing the biggest shit-eating-grin the world has ever seen. Until he turns the corner and sees me standing here, leaning against the counter, arms crossed over my bare chest.

His smile quickly fades and I see the man gulp.

"Not so smug now, huh, Davenport?" I tease. "Didn't think I'd follow through on my promise?"

It takes him a second to find his voice. "I'll admit, I'd figured it was made in jest, out of desperation."

I push away from the counter and reach to grab him and I plates. I feel his gaze on me the entire time.

"Oh, I was desperate alright. But a deal is a deal."

"Are those real?" he asks, pointing to my pecs, making Natalie giggle delightedly. She's eating this shit up.

"I can confirm they are, in fact, real."

"Here." I thrust a plate of pizza at him and nod at the T.V. "We're watching your favorite."

Stephen makes the sign of the cross. "Forgive me, Father, for I have sinned."

"Stephen, no one in here is a priest," I remind him.

Natalie's still laughing. "And you aren't Catholic, Dummy."

His eyes flare over my torso and across my sweatpants again. "The thoughts in my head warranted acknowledgment and forgiveness. Jameson, can I lick this tomato sauce off of your abs?" he asks, grinning.

"Abso-fucking-lutely not."

"What do I have to do to win that deal?" He asks, grabbing a beer and heading toward the living room.

I don't know why I'm even still entertaining this conversation as I give him an answer. "That's like pulling Nat out of a burning building kind of shit right there."

Without missing a beat, he looks over the back of the couch. "Natalie, dear, where do you keep the matches?"

Cackling, Natalie heads into our room to unwind. When she softly closes the door, I pull my t-shirt out from behind a pillow and slip it over my head.

"Thanks for helping me cheer her up. As soon as you guys landed, she said it'd been a pretty rough flight. Figured I could kill two birds with one stone: keep my end of the deal with you and brighten her night. I was glad to see her smile. You were pretty convincing."

"Who said I was acting?" He winks as he settles back into the couch, pizza in his lap, making me laugh. It feels good to make that sound again.

. . .

Ready For Your Next Series?

Dive into the world of music and fame with rockstars of Beautiful Deceit. Continue reading for Chapter One of Invisible Burdens!

Chapter One

NOAH

"This is the worst idea I've ever heard."

Okay, maybe that's a little dramatic, but I don't love change, and adding dancers will be a *big* change, not just for us but for our tour and our entire genre of music. Without being able to gauge how our fans will react, I'm hesitant. It's definitely outside the box, and although this is what Matt, our balding tour manager, is known for, it isn't a move I would've picked.

I lean forward, planting my elbows on my knees, and pinch the bridge of my nose. Like somehow, more pressure *there* will alleviate the pressure building in my chest.

There's always pressure in my chest these days.

If it hadn't been going on for the last two years, I'd think I was having a heart attack . . . every day.

Fucking Nicole.

Our rise to fame skyrocketed almost overnight when our last album dropped. As we gained attention, I lost time to devote to my girlfriend and realized I was no longer in a place where I could handle that kind of commitment.

When I broke things off with her, she retaliated by

leaking private, unflattering pictures of me, knowing how much I value my privacy.

I lean back in the uncomfortable chair and move my hand from my face to rub the burning spot on my chest. "It's always been just the four of us on stage," I argue with Matt. "We have a chemistry that works, but if you start adding people, we risk fucking that up and now is definitely *not* the time to fuck that up."

Matt's large mahogany desk sits to my left against a set of floor-to-ceiling windows, while Matt and I face each other in leather wingback chairs around a spotless glass coffee table.

"Noah, why did you hire me?" he asks in that smug tone he knows I hate as he steeples his fingers and looks down his nose at me.

I'm tempted to make rude hand gestures, but since Matt's the best concert tour director in the business, I keep my tattooed hands firmly wrapped around the coffee cup in my lap.

Even his legs are smug as he crosses one Armani clad thigh over the other, bobbing his foot impatiently and continuing to stare at me from behind his frameless, designer glasses with one brow arched. His artistic vision is second to none even if his wardrobe choices are usually atrocious.

His thinning gray hair is a testament to either poor genetics or the stress of his job. Coupled with his ruddy complexion and expanding waistline, I'd say Matt's lifestyle does not consist of hummus, vegetables, an alcohol-free mentality, or regular exercise.

I glare at Matt, angry heat creeping up my neck as I hold my unimpressed stare, refusing to give him the answer he's looking for. I'd hired him because he's fucking brilliant and sells out tours. But he already knows this and I'll be damned if he gets me to stroke his gigantic ego.

He's unfazed by my rudeness as he starts speaking again over the quiet whir of the air conditioning fan. I'm glad for the light breeze coming out of the vent because this meeting has me feeling a little clammy and panicked.

I hate the idea he's pitching, and I already know I've lost the argument. Somehow, the more famous we become, the less control we have over our image and if that bleeds into a loss of control over our music, I'll lose my fucking mind.

"You aren't just some boys making music in your mom's garage anymore, Kinkaid," he says, calling me by my last name.

I want to argue that we haven't been those "boys" in a while, but I hold my tongue because he's right.

I can't even pump gas without inciting chaos these days.

When I stay quiet, he continues dishing out what sounds like a slimy, well-rehearsed sales pitch.

"You're selling out venues multiple nights in a row. There's a *demand* for you that you've never had before. Similarly, your fans are no longer just broke college kids trying to get drunk at a cheap metalcore concert. They want a *show*. They're people willing to pay $120 a seat. They want to be *entertained*, Noah. It's your music that draws them there, but it's our *production* that's going to leave them wanting more."

I know he's right . . . again.

Doesn't mean I like it. Or that I'm ready to hand over all the control and decision making to him.

A sigh of defeat escapes my lips.

"Do we get to pick them at least?"

Matt laughs a hearty, belly laugh causing me to throw

my hands in the air, almost dumping my coffee everywhere, and roll my eyes.

Still laughing he asks, "What do you know about dancers, Noah? And I don't mean *pole* dancers. Do you know what to ask? What qualifications they need? What the actual vision is?"

No.

No.

And *hell no*, seeing as it wasn't my vision in the first place. In fact, I think it's a gigantic waste of money.

He continues, much to my chagrin.

"Do you even know what a pirouette is? No. You do not. If I let you pick the back-up dancers, they'll all be pin-up dolls with questionable dance experience. I'm not taking exotic dancers on this tour. I need *artists*. If we're lucky, you will all find them ugly with the personalities of dry-erase markers and none of you will even be tempted to look twice at them." He grins like the Cheshire cat before continuing, "But I've got a plan in case Betty Ballerina has a good sense of humor and a rack to match. I'll let you know when I've made my choices and when you're needed. Now get out, I have work to do." He uncrosses his legs, stands, and strolls to the chair behind his desk.

Looks like the guys and I are getting back up dancers whether we want them or not. We'll be the first metalcore band to share a stage with them, and it's either going to be groundbreaking or we're about to be the laughing stock of the music world just as we really start to enter it.

I resent that Matt's opinion of us is basically reduced to horny dogs with our dicks hanging out as if we can't control ourselves, but I bite my tongue and keep my mouth shut.

We may be red-blooded males, but our band is our life, not to mention our livelihood, and I'm feeling all the pressure as its founder and front man to make sure we don't squander our recent success.

Pushing out of the leather chair my ass feels glued to, I throw my parting shot over my shoulder and hope he hears me loud and clear. "I'm not getting on that stage with sequins and anything resembling Taylor Swift's pop culture."

His response is immediate, and he doesn't even bother to look up from his screen as he gives it.

"Her first twenty-two shows this year grossed over $300 million. Not only would you get on that stage with her, you'd lick the sole of Taylor's sequined, thigh-high boot if I told you to."

I grit my teeth and storm out the door, tossing my coffee cup in the trash and smiling a little when coffee splashes on his wall.

It's never been about the money for us, and we aren't going to change that now. Staying true to who we are is imperative or we'll just become another cog in the machine. This newly acquired fame is adding pressure I should have seen coming, yet somehow didn't. I think perhaps it's because I never dreamed our names would be painted all over the world with fans trying to get their hands on tickets to shows almost a year in advance.

Now that our fanbase has exploded and the demand is high, there's an expectation to turn everything I touch into gold, and I'm afraid of what the pressure will do when it's time to write new music.

Thankfully, Apex Records, our record label, has given us ten months before we need to start laying down new tracks. Our contract with them isn't great because when we signed three years ago, we were young and eager and pretty much took whatever the owner offered, but that's a problem for a different day.

I rub a hand back and forth over my sternum for the second time in twenty minutes to quell the discomfort rising behind it as I step into the elevator.

While the metal box hurtles me toward the ground floor, there are horrible images running through my head. Bad light shows and girls in glitter shaking their asses on the stage around us not meshing with the vibe of who we are at all.

I have a feeling we're going to hate this, but worse, I fear what will happen if the fans actually like it and we let ourselves be swallowed up by the masses, losing ourselves in the process.

Another thought crashes into me. We're not exactly peaceful up on that stage. All it will take is for Sloan to get rowdy one time and the neck of his guitar is going to collide with some poor girl's head, making a mess.

People will be talking about the *production* alright.

I sigh, pulling my phone out of the pocket of my jeans to send a text to the group as I head out of the building.

NOAH
We're getting dancers.

BRETT
groan how many?

NOAH
4

SLOAN
Sweet. One for each of us.

RYAN
Dibs on any redhead.

NOAH

Ryan, you're supposed to be on my side.

RYAN

Shockingly, Brett's got that covered.

That *is* shocking. Despite my offense at Matt's earlier statement, Brett is known for his affinity for women, and I was surprised when he protested the addition of the dancers as much as I did.

BRETT

Our stage is no place for pussy . . . that's the reward for after the show.

Hmm . . . maybe we aren't much better than horny dogs.

This is where it usually devolves into an hour of pointless conversation even though the guys are most likely all sitting in the same room since we've lived together for the last five years.

We grew up together and got stupid lucky. Our parents agreed to help support us financially our first year of making music *if* we all completed college. The guys and I have natural talents we were fortunate enough to have our parents recognize, even if Brett's parents took some convincing.

It was a no-brainer.

We went to school for business, music production, and graphic design and are grateful our parents made us get those degrees in case the fickle opinions of the masses change and we have to stop making music – or at least get additional jobs to support ourselves while we continue to make music.

College wasn't for Sloan, but his parents got on board after he agreed to four years in the military. I often wonder what his deployment was like, but he doesn't bring it up. Even living with him and sharing almost every waking moment with him, I can't tell if Sloan's ever-present sense of humor means he's really that carefree or if he uses it to deflect something darker from shining through. There never seems to be a good time to ask.

I silence the chat and let them talk it out.

When I round the corner of the building, I'm met head on with a group of five girls, dressed all in black, who shriek my name and start flashing their phones in my direction.

Not being able to walk down the street without being recognized is still new to me. So new in fact, I often forget I can't do it anymore. Wanting the girls to stay quiet and not attract any more attention, I hold my hands up in mock surrender and duck back around the corner, motioning for them to come to me.

"Tell you what, I'll take selfies with all of you if you promise not to scream." I feel like I'm negotiating with terrorists as the girls immediately go silent, giving in to my demands as they surround me on all sides.

If they're true fans, they'll know the rules, but just in case, I add, "Hands to yourselves, please."

I don't like being groped by people I don't know. Hell, I don't really like being touched by people I *do* know, either. The guys are different because they're basically an exten-sion of myself but when Nicole leaked every picture she had of me with no shirt on, and even a few riskier than that,

I felt overly exposed. Not to mention, wary of trusting people.

Now, people assume I never take my shirt off because I'm still the same pudgy guy I was two years ago in those photos.

I'm happy to let them assume.

I never actually cared what I looked like in the pictures, it was the fact that I had no control over the rest of the world seeing me half-naked and asleep. The other one was of me sitting on a toilet. I actually have pants on because I was nauseated from some food poisoning and was between bouts of puking, but you can't tell and it looks like . . . well, it looks bad.

Two extremely vulnerable moments in my life made available to everyone in the world all because of a shitty break up I honestly tried to handle with maturity and respect.

Will fans post pictures from this tour?

Absolutely.

But at least I know it's coming. I'll be in my element, and I've given some semblance of consent by getting on that stage.

I stoop my six-foot-two self down to fit in the girls' camera frames and wait until I hear several clicks before straightening back up.

Selfies done and autographs given, I head to the parking deck where my driver is waiting and abandon any hope I had of getting another cup of coffee.

Probably better to hit the gym anyway. Something has to relieve the pressure in my chest, or I won't be around to enjoy a decades long career even if the fanbase is present to support it.

Other Books By Jillian D. Wray

NOTHING LASTS FOREVER
Romantic Suspense
(This series must be read in order)
Submit
Defy
Reign

BEAUTIFUL DECEIT
Rockstar Romance Series
(This series does not have to be read in order but will give
the best reading experience that way)
Invisible Burdens - The Lead Singer
Bearing the Burden - The Drummer
Beast of Burden - The Bassist
Unburdened - The Guitarist

Acknowledgments

Writing a book is extremely hard to do alone. I am grateful for everyone who has helped me along the way including the freelance beta readers, formatters, and editors I was fortunate to find on Fiverr. I absolutely love this cover and couldn't be more thankful for the designers at Deranged Doctor Design for having the perfect vision for this it. I'm grateful to my family who puts up with countless hours of my time in the writing cave to do what I love. And of course I'm thankful for the readers who take a chance on any of my stories.

About the Author

Jillian lives in North Carolina with her incredibly supportive husband and three awesome stepkids. After over ten years in the healthcare industry, it was time to pursue a new passion. An avid reader her whole life, she sat down one night and let the words begin to flow. Four hours and ten thousand words later, a love of writing was discovered. She writes spicy, bingeable reads that encourage self-discovery and come with all the angst and excitement of a new relationship. When she isn't reading or writing, you can either find her in her vegetable garden, at CrossFit™, or on a plane headed toward her next adventure.

Let's connect! I'm most active on Instagram!
    Instagram: @jillian_wray_author
    Facebook: Wray's Romance Readers